SMILE OF THE WOLF

TIM LEACH

HEAD OF ZEUS

First published in the UK in 2018 by Head of Zeus Ltd
This paperback edition first published in 2019 by Head of Zeus Ltd

Copyright © Tim Leach, 2018

The moral right of Tim Leach to be identified as the author
of this work has been asserted in accordance with the
Copyright, Designs and Patents Act of 1988.

All rights reserved. No part of this publication may be
reproduced, stored in a retrieval system, or transmitted in any form
or by any means, electronic, mechanical, photocopying, recording,
or otherwise, without the prior permission of both the copyright
owner and the above publisher of this book.

This is a work of fiction. All characters, organizations,
and events portrayed in this novel are either products of
the author's imagination or are used fictitiously.

9 7 5 3 1 2 4 6 8

A catalogue record for this book is available from
the British Library.

ISBN (PB): 9781788544122
ISBN (E): 9781788544092

Typeset by Adrian McLaughlin

Printed and bound in Great Britain by
CPI Group (UK) Ltd, Croydon CR0 4YY

Head of Zeus Ltd
First Floor East
5–8 Hardwick Street
London EC1R 4RG

WWW.HEADOFZEUS.COM

For Caroline

1

The feud began in winter, when a dead man rose from the earth.

In the distant lands where men worship the White Christ, I have heard that a ghost is not such a dangerous thing. They are creatures of no substance, who may wail and howl but cannot hurt a man. But in my country, the people are warriors even in death. Our ghosts are not shadow and air, but walking flesh. They wield their weapons with as much strength as they did in life, and more bravely, for they have nothing left to fear. And so, when we heard that Hrapp Osmundsson had crawled from his grave and begun to wander his lands at night, no man in the Salmon River Valley would leave his house after dark without a good blade at his side and a shield on his arm.

In life, Hrapp had been the terror of his neighbours, ever covetous for their lands, their women, their blood. When the winter fever came on him and he knew he was soon to die, he commanded his wife to bury him upright beneath the doorway of his house, so that he could watch over his lands even in death.

Soon enough, the stories spread throughout the dale. Thord

the Sly had gone to check on his sheep at night and been set upon by a dead man carrying an axe. Erik Haroldsson, a braver man, had grappled with the creature when it came for him, but was sent running for his life with the heavy tread of the ghost behind him.

No man sought to buy the farm from Hrapp's widow. Indeed, there was talk amongst the neighbours of selling their own lands and moving on elsewhere, though there were few farmlands so prized in all of Iceland as those in the Salmon River Valley.

For all that was spoken of the ghost, I thought it mere winter talk at first, one of those foolish tales spun to pass the long cold months of near-permanent night, when men do little but huddle round their fires and drink mead, sing songs, tell stories and wait for the sun to return. I am a collector of such tales, yet I tell only the ones I know to be true – or half-true at least. This ghost story held little interest for me.

But then one night I heard Olaf the Peacock speak of it when I visited his farm to trade milk for ale; he was an honourable man, a respected chieftain of the people, and he would never tell a lie. He said that he had seen the bruises on Erik's arms, and gone in search of the ghost himself. He had found it wandering Hrapp's fields, bearing Hrapp's old axe. Olaf cast a spear at it and the ghost had fled from him.

I wish he had not told me that. For it was then that I believed, and I began to tell the story myself.

I am Kjaran. Kjaran the Landless is what many call me, though some of the sharper-tongued call me Kjaran the Luckless, for they think it the worst of fates to be a man without land.

It is true, I am no man of property or wealth. My father

was a slave – gifted his freedom but nothing else, and so he had little to leave his children. But my voice is sweet and my memory is good, and I have always traded stories for food and songs for shelter. I am not one of the truly great skalds of this country, such as Kormákr Ögmundarson or Hallfred the Troublesome Poet. But I was not afraid to stand beside a friend in a feud when the odds were against him, and I never overstayed my welcome or chased after another man's wife (rare qualities in a poet, I know), and so I earned myself a good name amongst the people of this island. Twenty-four winters had I passed, the year the feud began.

I had spent that winter with the man they later called Gunnar the Killer, though he was merely Gunnar Karlsson when I met him, a farmer with a little land and a good-sized herd. I had spent the summer there, hunting for seals along the coast and helping to tend his sheep, for a humble skald earns favour with the sweat of his hands as much as the strength of his voice. But in winter it was the stories that I traded for shelter and food. And when I told Gunnar the story of the ghost, one late winter night, he said this:

'So. The ghost fears a spear?'

He did not speak in mockery or in doubt. He merely thought out loud, picking out the detail that, to him, seemed most important. That the ghost feared iron, and a man brave enough to face it.

He said nothing more for a time. We sat beside the embers of the cooking fire, his wife asleep at his feet, one of his children sleeping at mine. I had been his winter guest for many months and we had passed countless nights in this way. The taste of those nights is icy water and salted fish, the sound is the burning of the fire and the whistling of the wind, the smell is smoke and sweat and ash and earth. Now it was almost spring.

The time of storytelling was almost over – soon it would be the time to act.

Perhaps this thought was on Gunnar's mind, too. For it was then, after the long silence, that he said: 'I will hunt this ghost.'

I should not have been surprised. He had been a Viking in his youth, one of those restless men who took their due from the lands of the Saxons, the Scots, the Irish. But he had tired of the bloodshed, so he sailed his ship to these lands, broke it to pieces for timber, and built a house with that wood. He was a farmer, his ship forever stilled in the timbers of the roof above us, beached and capsized and never to sail again, his warring days long behind him. Yet killing is like any other art: when it is learned, it cannot be unlearned. Once learned, it will always long to be practised.

'You believe the story that Erik has told you?' he said. 'I have never thought him a trusty man.'

'No. But Olaf the Peacock would not lie to me.'

He nodded. 'Will you come with me?'

'Why not? At the very least, it will make a good story for next winter. Maybe even a song.'

He grinned at me. 'That it will.'

Many men had gone hunting for ghosts in the past and had never caught them, for the dead only prey upon the unwary and flee the brave. But there was little enough to do on the farm. It would be a good excuse to go walking together in the night, for ale never tastes so good nor a fire feels so warm as after a winter's walk. We would prove ourselves brave men who did not fear the dead, and I would make a song of it. There would be nothing more to it than that.

In the end, I did get my song. It was a good one, too, but not worth the price I paid for it. But I did get my song.

4

The loneliness of an Icelandic night – how would I speak of it to one who was not of our people?

There is no place that is so lifeless, so isolated, as our island in the depths of a winter's night. The scattered turf-walled houses all but disappear into the ground, looking more like hills or grave barrows than homes for the living. There is no movement in the fields. The herds are dead, butchered and salted for the winter, the few survivors huddled in the darkness of the barns. Out in the night, one can almost feel the land longing to return to desolation. The dead have more business here than the living.

We had set out in that half-light of late winter, a two-hour dawn that becomes a two-hour sunset with the sun barely above the horizon. For it is as the old song says: 'He must rise early, who would take another's life.' We had been merry as we trudged through the snow, heavy cloaks on our backs and weapons in our hands, singing together to keep the cold away. Yet the short day was almost spent by the time we reached Hrapp's lands, the wind snapping and biting at us like an unseen spirit, and we circled his fields in silence. We no longer felt in the mood for song.

Soon Hrapp's longhouse lurked before us in the half-light. The turf walls ragged after a winter spent untended, but still there was smoke rising from the chimney. Hrapp's wife Vigdis lived alone now on the farmstead. Alone, save perhaps for a slave, a servant, or the company of the ghost.

'Perhaps she still cooks him supper at night,' Gunnar said, looking at the smoke.

'You think the ghost can be hungry?'

'Let us find out.'

I began to laugh, but the sound caught and died in my throat. For it was then that I saw it. A quarter mile distant, a dead man walking through the snow.

His back was to us as he moved with a heavy, steady tread, seemingly ignorant of the cold. There was no mistaking him for anything else. He was no farmer chasing after a wandering flock, no lover sneaking back from a midnight tryst in the next valley. He wore a helm on his head, a shield on his arm, and an axe – Hrapp's old axe – in his hand. He was wandering his old lands, seeking men to kill.

'Do you see him?' Gunnar said.

I did not reply at first. I did not want to believe.

He spoke again, barely louder than a whisper. 'Am I mad? Do you see him?'

'Yes,' I said. 'I see him. What should we do?'

Gunnar did not reply with words. He beat his blade against his shield – a hollow, echoing sound, like a knocking on a tomb. The ghost turned towards us then, though we could not see his face in the darkness, and Gunnar gave the battle cry.

We did not run, the way you may have heard the old stories say. A warrior does not waste his strength, does not commit to questionable footing in the dark. We stalked forward, always keeping our left foot ahead, our shields presented, moving together as a shield-wall of two.

A howl split the night, the scream of the dead man answering our battle cry. A sound like nothing else I had ever heard, but we did not falter. Then the ghost took a few steps back – no doubt seeking a better footing, though it looked for all the world as though he were preparing to run.

We were close now, close enough to see the pale eyes glittering through the eyelets of his helm, to see the breath frosting upon the air, for it seemed that ghosts still breathed as we do.

The dead man offered a warrior's salute, and Gunnar, grunting in surprise, returned it in kind. Seeing such a sign between them – a challenge offered and accepted – I let Gunnar go forward alone. Even a ghost deserved to be fought honourably.

They gave no further sound as they closed the distance, for men fight like dogs do: all screaming and howling at play, silence when they fight for their lives. There was only the sound of deep, steady breathing, of boots crunching against snow. Then the sound of iron into wood.

The ghost fought with reckless fury, and Gunnar was forced back at first, kicking up little puffs of snow from the ground as he retreated. A quickening of fear stole through me to see him so hard-pressed.

But I was a fool to worry. They will still be telling stories of Gunnar a hundred years from now, for my friend was a patient warrior who knew his trade all too well. He did not fight the man, he fought the shield, catching the blows that came to him on the metal boss, answering them with strikes to the wood. Always to the same side, the left side, a woodsman chopping at his mark. I could hear the shield cracking and groaning, and then, under a great back-handed strike from Gunnar's sword, the shield fell in half.

Now it was Gunnar's time. He circled to his right with every step, towards the broken shield, driving the dead man's guard wider. The ghost fought as best he could, but it is exhausting fighting with half a shield, every movement doubled. I could hear the sobs he gave with each blow struck back, could see his movements slowing.

Then it came, the killing moment – Gunnar feinted another step to the right and the ghost's shield went with him. But my friend danced to the left instead, levelled the sword and thrust forward, into the break in the guard.

'Wait!' the ghost said and my heart went still at the sound of his voice, a voice that I knew. But it was too late. The sword was already through him before he had finished speaking the word, the snow darkening at his feet.

And it was then, in the distance, that we heard a woman begin to scream.

SETTLEMENT

2

The voice seemed to come from all around us in the dark, as though every woman who had seen her kin slain were screaming down upon us. It took me a moment to see her – another figure in the dark, running at us from Hrapp's longhouse.

The light of the moon caught her face as she drew close; it was Vigdis, the wife of Hrapp, who was screaming. I saw another thing under that light, that it was no ghost on the ground before us. It was a living man who lay there, gasping wetly for air, drowning in blood on dry land.

He wore Hrapp's tunic and his face was daubed white with curdled milk, but there was no mistaking who he was now that battle fever had left us. A neighbour of ours: Erik Haraldsson, one of the first to tell the stories of the dead man walking.

'Erik,' I said.

The dying man lifted his head at the name. He tried to speak and bubbles of blood burst upon his lips, black under the light of the moon.

I did not even see her move, she was so quick. In a moment Vigdis had leapt at Gunnar and held his right hand with both of hers, trying to wrestle the blade from him. And when he tried to pry her away with his free hand, she sank her teeth into the flesh of his hand, right between the thumb and forefinger.

He bellowed in pain and struck her. She twisted away, nose pouring blood and legs shaking, but still as full of fight as any young warrior. Her eyes strayed to the axe on the ground, and perhaps she would have taken it up and fought like a shield maiden from the old stories if she had faced one of us rather than two. As it was she watched us silently, teeth bared and eyes black.

I knelt beside Erik. I showed him the knife; he wept and clawed at the red snow with his hands. Then he nodded. He watched the knife come, but at the last moment he closed his eyes and turned his head away. He could not bear to watch.

The blood steamed against the snow; the sound was like river water when you break the ice in spring. And though I thought she would fight and struggle and kick and howl, Vigdis gave up all fighting the moment the knife bit deep. She stood still and soundless and watched the man die.

I rubbed my hands clean with snow, stood and faced her.

'What is your part in all this?' I said.

'It is cold out here,' she said. 'Come with me. I will tell you all.'

'We must bury him and mark the grave. We must tell his family what has happened.'

She looked up at the stars, judging the colour of the sky: the time we had left until the sun rose upon the killing.

'It is cold,' she said again. 'That can wait.'

She turned from us then and picked her way carefully through the snow, back towards the squat house in the distance. And, like the fools we were, we followed her.

★

They are as dark as tombs, the houses of the Icelanders. In other lands some light may bleed through a thatched roof; the occasional gap in the walls is permitted to let in a little light. But our homes are without windows, walled over with earth. They seal out the winter cold, and sun and moon and stars are sealed out as well. There is only the light of the cooking fire to see by, and that is little more than embers at the end of winter.

Vigdis gave us bread and that watered-down, end-of-winter ale that I had grown to hate. She moved around the narrow building and I could see that she was a handsome woman, slender and flaxen-haired. More beautiful than in daylight, as I was to learn later, for in daylight one could see her eyes – thief's eyes, my people call them. But in that half-light of the fire, I began to understand why she was a woman that men might fight and kill for.

We sat together in that homely barrow and did not speak for a time. Had some lost wanderer come in, we might have looked like any other household. Family and friends, host and guests. Not the killers that we were.

At last, Gunnar spoke. He had been hard at thought in the near darkness, yet still he said: 'I do not understand.'

'Your friend does,' she said, looking at me. 'Don't you?'

'Yes, I do,' I said, as I stretched out my hands over the embers of the fire. 'Who would hold land that the dead walked upon? Who would have a ghost for a neighbour?'

'You are clever,' she said. 'That was what we thought.'

'A trick. A trick to win land from other men.' I took another sip of ale. 'Was he your lover before Hrapp died?'

'Erik?'

'Yes.'

'No, he was not.'

'But afterwards, Erik came to you.'

'Yes. I was lonely. He was kind to me.'

'And was it your plan?'

She shook her head. 'It was Erik. I was afraid to refuse him.'

'I do not believe it,' Gunnar said. 'It was a womanly trick. Erik would not think of it.'

'Believe what you want,' she said.

Gunnar stood and raised his hand as if to strike her again. She did not start or flinch, merely stared back, unafraid, ready to take the blow. There was still dried blood on her lips and chin from where he had struck her before. Knowing the kind of man Hrapp had been, perhaps she knew what it was to be beaten and feared it no longer.

'Gunnar,' I said, a note of warning in my voice.

There was a hiss as Gunnar spat into the fire. 'Enough of this. What need is there to speak? We have witnesses to the killing and can say that it was a fair fight. We will go to his family tomorrow, pay the blood-price and end this matter.'

I said: 'Why should you pay for killing a dishonourable man?'

'He has brothers, uncles, friends. I will pay them. Pay them well. That will be an end to it.'

'No.' The word cut through the darkness, but it was not I who spoke it. Vigdis waited until we both turned to her, before she bowed her head and spoke again. 'Think of the shame of it.'

'Why should we care for your shame?' Gunnar said.

'Not mine. Erik's,' she replied, and that was the thought that gave us pause.

Our lives are short on the cold earth and we all long to leave something behind. A little gold for our sons and daughters – but more than that, an honourable memory: to be spoken of as a good man. And here was Erik, playing at being a dead man, a coward's trick to cheat his neighbours of their land.

'What would you have us do, then?' I asked.

'Nothing,' she said.

I saw Gunnar shudder. He whom none could call coward, and I saw the touch of fear on him. For a man may kill, and so long as he speaks of it openly, so long as he pays the blood-price to the family, it will do him no dishonour. Yet to kill and to conceal the killing – our laws knew no greater crime than that.

I thought on that, it is true. And I thought of how little Gunnar had to call his own, the price he would have to pay for the man he had killed. He had laboured for many years to have something he might leave for his sons. A little land, a decent herd, a few ounces of gold, a good sword. No king's treasure, but something a father might be proud of. Now it would be taken from him.

I thought of how rarely a feud had been settled with silver, for all that the laws decreed. How the dead man's brothers would come for us, if we allowed the killing to be known.

Gunnar looked on me then. In his eyes, I saw him asking me to decide.

We did not dare risk the light of a torch, for fear of who might see it. And so we dug through the snow and broke open the icy ground in darkness, a miserable act of labour that took the rest of the night. It is always harder work to bury a man than it is to kill him.

When we had covered the unmarked grave, Vigdis came to us with a skin of water. 'Thank you,' she said, and kissed our hands, our murderers' hands.

'You shall speak of this to no man?' she said, and we swore that we would not. She clasped our hands in turn, as though we were merchants concluding our trade. When she took Gunnar's hand, I saw him pull her close, whisper a question to her. But I did not hear the words, nor did I hear her answer.

We walked in silence for a time, and I thought of the man we had killed. I had sung in his little farm two autumns before, but had not sought to winter with him. He was a quick man with a jest, kind as well, but it was a wifeless and childless home he had and so he was always touched with sadness. I remembered one night, when we had drunk too much too quickly, I heard him weeping when he thought I was sleeping. He was lonely, I think, and I have always feared the lonely.

'No good will come of this,' Gunnar said.

'Perhaps,' I answered. And though we tried to speak again many times in that long walk back, we found no more to say than this.

Wait. Something is not right.

The fire grows low and we must not let it die. It is dark outside and I know you must be weary. We should let the fire burn to embers, we should lie down and sleep. But we shall not. There is much more I have to tell you this night. I will not give this story to you a piece at a time, like a starving old woman eking out the supplies from her petty pantry. We shall feast tonight on this story. I shall tell it all to you.

So – throw the good brush upon the fire. No, no, not that from that pile, use the best wood we have, there is no need to save it. Why? I shall tell you that, soon enough. But not now.

That is better. I see you clearly now. A good thing, to see that face of yours in this light. A sadness, too, of course. For once I spoke and sang in the longhouses of great chieftains, a hundred souls in a silent room, listening to my words alone. I never sang to a king's court, not as those truly great poets do, but I did have some honour granted to my voice. Now it is you alone that I sing for.

The fire burns brighter. And now I will tell you another story. Let me tell you of how our people first came to this island.

Ah, yes – roll your eyes if you will. You shall tell me that you have heard this story many times before. This is true. But you will listen once more. For this is a story that cannot be told too many times. No other story matters, if this one is forgotten.

There was an empty land before them, a tyrant at their heels
– that was the way the first men came to this island. That is the
way all new countries are settled.

When they gathered on the shores of the old country, what
they could not load on to the long ships they burned. They
would leave nothing for the king who drove them from Norway,
the man they called Harald Fairhair. They kissed the soil and
the sand, and wept for the homes they would never see again.
They cast away, that great fleet of exiles, out across the dark
sea to a place known to them only by rumour and myth.

Not all lived to see the new land. Storms and drift ice tore
ships open, sending many to feed the fell spirits that hunt in
the black water. Others wandered lost in the storms, washing
ashore in hostile countries where they received a welcome of
iron, a home in shallow earth. But the survivors pressed on,
sailing past the coast of Scotland, past the islands of Orkney
and Faroe. At last, they reached their new home. Your family,
and mine.

It was a great island in the midst of the cold sea, a place of
green shores with an icy heart. An unpeopled country, its name
hard and unforgiving, but that was what drew the settlers. It
was their protection, to live in a land that no others wanted.
A place that seemed uninhabitable. But with a little skill, and
fortune from the gods, they knew there was a living to be made
here. Not much of one, it was true. They would never be rich
or powerful men – just a nation of farmers scratching at near-
barren soil, fighting to keep their herds alive through the long
dark. They told themselves they did not want wealth or power.
Perhaps some of them even believed it.

As they drew close to shore, the captain of each ship lifted a
long, narrow object from the deck. They did so carefully, as if
they held a child in their arms, unwrapping the sealskin blanket

to reveal the treasure within. No gold or weaponry, but a simple piece of wood. Part of a door or a roof or a column from a high seat, some fragment of the home that they had left behind. And for some it was a coffin they unwrapped, one of their kin who had begun the voyage, but had not lived to see its end.

Each man threw his memento out into the wild waves and watched them go. Some of the pieces of wood went straight to shore, others followed the eddies into closed coves and fjords, others still were caught in currents and wandered to some distant part of the coast. Where each of those staves went, a ship followed. Where they washed ashore, there a family settled and made a new home from the wood of the old.

They came to build a country without kings and cities. A place where every man was equal, every man had land. A place with no rulers save for honour and the law.

And, for a time at least, it was true.

3

In the long winter, even the wealthiest of Icelanders curses the day that their ancestors came to this land. They forget the dream of the people, that dream of a world without kings, and know only that they live in a dark, lonesome place. But when the sun begins to ride higher in the sky and the snow begins to quicken and thaw, it is an easy land to love. The dream grows strong once more, for we are a stubborn people.

Men and women emerge from their homes like bears from their winter caves, the sunlight feeling as sharp on the eye as a blade against the skin. They break the ice from the rivers, begin the first sowing of the crops, free their herds to wander to the high mountain pastures, go to trade for supplies and visit distant friends. And as they travel the stories travel with them.

There had been no more sightings of the ghost of Hrapp. Rumour spread that it was Olaf who had killed the ghost, since he was the last to have seen and fought with it. He denied it, honourable man that he was, but they mistook his honesty for modesty, and so the story spread.

As for Erik, there were stories of him, too. Some thought he had fallen through the ice in a river, others claimed he had gone in search of lost sheep and wandered, lost himself, until the cold murdered him. There were many who said that the winter madness had taken him as it takes so many, that he had cast himself from a cliff or gone to lie down in the snow and waited to die. They had seen him lonely, as I had, and knew it was a hard thing for a man to make it through the winter alone. I waited to see if any would make the connection between the two stories, between Erik and the ghost. But no man did. It takes a woman to think in that way.

A pile of blunt weapons beside me and the whetstone at my feet – that is what the first day of spring means to me. For soon we would be hunting again, and so whilst Gunnar tended the herd I took the weapons of the house to the sharpening stone.

I was working on my weapon of choice, my spear, and enjoying the feel of the sun on my face, when I heard the door of the longhouse swing open. I listened; would it be the whispering footfalls of Freydis, Gunnar's daughter? The stamping tread of Kari, the boy who wished to be thought of as a man, and who mimicked the heavy steps of his elders, though he did not have their weight? The children liked to play with me, fascinated by my red hair, convinced it was some trick or illusion. When the day's chores were done I would lumber around on all fours chasing them through the house, or tell them the stories my father told me – the old Irish stories of the Red Branch and the Fianna – whilst Gunnar watched and grinned and shook his head, and told me I had missed my vocation as a nursemaid. Perhaps they had come to bother me early.

It was not the children who stepped out. It was the strong tread of Dalla, Gunnar's wife, and I saw her lean around the edge of the turf wall and look upon me.

She could have been a rare beauty, black haired and pale

skinned, were it not for her warrior's nose, broken and reset long ago, so that it was almost flat against her face – a parting gift from her father, or so Gunnar told me. In truth her shattered nose suited her, for she was a hard woman, well suited to these lands. Without a word she dipped a horn cup into the pail of milk she carried and offered it to me.

'My thanks,' I said as I drank it down, still warm and thick.

'Hard work,' she said.

'It is. Harder to sharpen a spear than to use it, easier to kill a beast than to skin it…' I trailed off. There was an ending to that proverb that I did not wish to speak.

'Easier to kill a man than to bury him,' she said, finishing the saying.

The night we came back from hunting the ghost we had found her awake, for it was in the early hours of the dawn when we returned, stumbling with exhaustion and covered in the filth of battle and burial. Her hard eyes asked the question and perhaps words would have followed. But Gunnar had reached out and taken her by the hands. He closed his eyes, and I thought for a moment that he would shame himself with weeping. But when he opened his eyes again, they were clear. He kissed her on the forehead and said: 'Please, do not ask me. All is well. But do not ask.'

She had looked at the bite on his hand, the blunted edge of his sword, the marks on his shield. She read a story in our eyes, the eyes of men exhausted with killing, and it seemed as though she did not wish the story to be spoken. She let us go to sleep, rolled up in furs upon the floor, and when we woke she asked no questions. From the way she acted, we could pretend we had dreamed it all: a nightmare of blood and snow and an ill-struck pact.

I looked down and tested the edge of the spear against my

thumb. Sharp enough. I took the next blade from the pile and said: 'I am glad to see the end of winter.'

'As am I. But I suppose you will be leaving us soon.'

'I shall,' I said. For soon it would be the Day of Movement, when a wanderer such as I would have to find a new place to call my home.

She put down the pail and sat upon the ground, her back against the house. 'I wish that you would not go,' she said.

I smiled at her and sang her an old quatrain:

One must go on, and not stay a guest
Forever in one place:
A loved one is loathed if he lingers too long
In another man's hall.

Then I said: 'It is ill luck to winter twice in one place. One winter makes a man a guest, two makes him a thief. I have never seen it go well.'

She did not answer. Instead she looked down on the weapons at my feet, at one in particular at the top of the pile. Gunnar's sword, a blade of Ulfberht steel worth more than his farm, its edge still hacked and blunted from winter. I lifted it, and I began to sharpen it against the stone, as carefully as I would have tuned a rare harp.

'Why would you want me to stay?' I said.

Her eyes were on the edge of the sword. 'I am afraid.'

'There is nothing to be afraid of.'

'Truly?'

'Truly.'

She nodded slowly. 'I shall hold you to those words,' she said, and there was a hardness to her voice – the kind you hear in the words of a chieftain or the captain of a warband. For that longhouse was her domain: the key to the stores hung around her waist, not Gunnar's. She would not have me in her home if she did not will it, no matter what Gunnar might say.

'Your husband has done nothing to bring shame to you,' I said. 'He is an honourable man.'

'As are you.'

I shook my head. 'No. Honour is a luxury for the wealthy, the brave. I am neither of those things. I cannot afford it. I settle for cunning and loyalty. But Gunnar is an honourable man.'

And as if my words had summoned him, I saw him crest the rise of the hill, bearing a trussed sheep beneath his arm, the stray he had gone in search of. Even at a distance I could see the smile on his face as he waved to us, and I waved back to him and took up a brace of spears from the ground. Once again, it was time for us to hunt.

'Why were you speaking with my wife?'

A dangerous question that Gunnar asked me, as we walked towards the sea. Many have answered it poorly and paid for it with their lives. But Gunnar asked it with a smile on his lips, and so I answered him in kind.

'The business of love, of course. It is a difficult thing to conduct a love affair in winter. This spring season suits me better.' I levelled a finger at him, and sang:

For when a husband shepherds sheep
Even a wolf may woo his wife.

He roared then, but there was laughter in it, and in a moment we were wrestling on the ground, laughing and cursing each other in turn, fighting for the lock of the head or trap of an arm that would end the contest. I could not have stood against him with a blade for more than a moment, but there in the grapple his tall and rangy swordsman's build worked against him and we were evenly matched. Perhaps I could even have beaten him if I had truly been trying, but after a time I was careful to offer him a left arm that he could easily put into a lock. We might have been friends, but it would not do to show up one's host.

When we rose from the ground, brushing the dirt from our clothes, he handed me the spear I had cast down when we fell and clapped me on the back.

'We should find you a wife,' he said. 'That might stop you from chasing after mine.'

'A man of no property does not hope for such a thing. Nor does a wanderer want it.'

'There is a time when you will grow tired of moving on, Kjaran.'

'I doubt it.'

'Where will you go to this time? To Olaf's house?'

'The Peacock? Perhaps. I have never much liked a chieftain's home. Too many people.'

He chewed on the corner of his moustache, his habit when thinking of what to say. I saw it often, for he was not much a man with words. 'I would like you to stay.'

'*One must go on and not stay a guest—*'

'Yes,' he said, 'I know that song. You have sung it often enough. But I wish that it was not so.'

As he said those words we reached the top of a hillock and what I heard struck me into silence. For the first time in many months, I could hear the sound of the sea.

We are a people that came from the sea. We have given it up now, broken our ships for timber, set aside the life of the

Viking for that of the farmer, chosen peace. And yet it still calls to us, fills us with that longing to wander upon it, to listen to it speak. It is a great prophet, is the sea: one need only sit upon the shore for a time to know that the answers to all mysteries are contained within the chanting of the waves. But we have lived apart from the sea for so long that we no longer speak its language. And so we look upon it like deafened men towards a singer, trying to understand what has been lost to us.

We come to hunt upon its shore, for any man may claim what falls upon the common ground of the coast. Driftwood from distant lands, whole trees washed white from their long journey, invaluable in a land where the tall trees grow no more. Seals, lost and sick, who come to the shore to die. Wood and meat; with a little luck, a man may earn a fortune in both from the leavings of the waves.

The drift ice had barely cleared and there would be little offered up by the god of the sea. We were out more to enjoy our freedom than in any hope of finding such a bounty. To walk on grass and not snow, to feel a fragile heat from the sun on our backs and to listen to the sea once more – this was all that we had expected.

Then, a turning of the coast, a cove unseen. There before us, a great black shape so large and so strange that at first I could not name it, sprawled upon the sand and unmoving in the tide so great was its weight. Only the stink of rot – distant, but still sharp in the air – gave me understanding. A whale, washed ashore. Long dead and partly rotted, but still a farmer's fortune in oil and meat and skin.

Yet no sooner had I seen it than I saw something else beyond: three black dots in the distance, hurrying forward. Some rival party of hunters on the common land, and they too had seen the whale. And then the wind was battering against

26

my ears and the shingle crackling beneath my boots as Gunnar and I began to run.

It was a race, for the coast was land that no man laid claim to except by the oldest right of all: by being there first. Gunnar outpaced me and ran ahead, casting aside his sack as he ran but keeping hold of his hunting spear, for to get to the whale empty-handed would mean nothing: dead as it was, we could only claim it by placing the first mark upon it.

Our chase was a lost cause. The other party was closer than we to begin with, and they had a fast runner with them, a shorter man who ran ahead of his companions. We would not come second by much, but I saw no way that we would make up the ground. Still, we ran as hard as we could, for what else was there? To do anything less would be shameful.

Something changed in the way Gunnar ran. I thought at first he had stumbled or hurt his foot, for he ran side-face, leading with his left foot for a couple of steps. Then I saw his body arc and twist and heard a great shout as he let the spear fly.

I stopped still and watched it go, the point twisting lazily through the air. I heard a cry from the other party, saw their leading man throw his spear in imitation, but though he was a strong runner his arm was weak and his weapon fell well short. A smack of iron into flesh echoed out across the beach; Gunnar's spear found its mark.

A cry of victory, and Gunnar and I were walking then, grinning like children who have won a race in the fields. We would offer that other party some portion of the whale as tribute to their efforts, for I had seen feuds start over such things before. Honour would be served and each of us would go home with a prize.

But when we reached the whale and looked upon the other men, I saw the smile fall away from Gunnar's face. The three who came towards us – I could not name them, yet it seemed that I knew some aspects of them all too well. The hooked shape of the nose of one man, the hard edge of the jaw of another, the coarse black hair that crept over the knuckles of the third – all were familiar to me, as though one man that I knew had been split amongst these three that I did not.

The knowledge came to me then and I knew why Gunnar did not smile.

'A fine throw,' said Snorri, the small quick man who had almost beaten us to the carcass.

Gunnar licked his dry lips. 'Thank you.'

'Your skald should compose a song for it.' This from Hakon, the eldest. 'The Saga of the Rotting Whale.' They laughed. We did not. The largest man – I remembered his name as Björn – noted our silence, and his great black brows came together in a frown.

Snorri, Björn and Hakon. The sons of Harold the Serpent-tongue. Brothers of the man we had killed.

I had heard that they had spent the winter travelling from one man's house to another, searching for news of their brother. They had never come to Gunnar's farmstead, for we were too far from Erik's farm to fall under suspicion. But they had questioned many others in the first month that their brother went missing, leaving only an empty house behind. There had been no feud, no man who stood to gain from his death, no one who could give them any clue as to what had befallen Erik. They were left only with that unknowing, that hollow in the mind when a loss cannot be answered for.

'I am sorry to hear of your brother,' Gunnar said.

'What do you know of it?' asked Hakon.

'Only what all men know.'

Björn spoke. 'They seem to know nothing at all,' he said.

'Perhaps it was an outlaw that killed him.'

'Why would you say that?'

'It seems the most likely thing.'

'It is not our place to guess, Gunnar,' I said. I looked to Hakon. 'If I hear anything more than rumour, I will tell it to you.'

'I thank you, Kjaran.' He clapped me on the shoulder. 'It is good to talk with you once more. It would be even better to hear you sing again. My wife still speaks of your last visit; you must come to us soon. Gunnar cannot keep you to himself for two winters now, can he? Perhaps you will winter with my family this year?'

'Perhaps I will. I would like that.'

'You are always welcome in my home.' He slapped the flank of the whale and its flesh rippled at his touch. 'A rich prize. What will you do with it?'

Gunnar said nothing. The brothers looked to one another. Then Björn spoke, a blunt demand: 'What portion of the whale will you give us?'

'Björn,' Snorri said, a warning in his voice. He turned back to us and smiled. 'But I am sure that so honourable a man as Gunnar will not begrudge us some share of the prize. We did sight it first, after all.'

Still Gunnar did not speak – his face blank, his eyes unseeing, like a seer in a trance. I saw the brothers grow restless, shifting halfway into fighters' stances, their hands twitching towards their weapons.

'Gunnar,' I said, hoping that my voice might shake him from his silence. And at last he did speak – the worst words he could have said.

'Take it all.'

Björn recoiled as if struck.

'You insult us,' said Björn. 'I will not be in your debt. You think us beggars?'

'You won it fairly,' Hakon said. 'I will not take your prize from you. Come, gift us a tenth, a third if you feel so generous. There is no need for this.'

But Gunnar stood there, staring at the ground and shaking his head, mouthing *no* over and over again, and he would say no more.

'Give our share to the gods,' I said. 'That is what Gunnar means.'

'I did not think you both such pious men,' Hakon said.

'This bounty is a gift from Ægir,' I replied. 'We need his favour more than we need the meat. Take what you will from it and burn the rest for the god.' And with that I put my hand on Gunnar's back and led him away as if he were an exhausted child. As we walked down the beach I heard Björn muttering something, and I quickened my step to outpace the words. If we heard the insult, we would have to fight them.

'I did not think the shame would be so much. How do you lie so easily?'

We were far from the beach when he spoke to me. Far from the beach and far from home, sitting beside the shore of the river, trying to find the words that would make sense of it all.

I washed my face in the water, feeling the sharpness of the cold against my eyes.

'Because I have to,' I said. 'There is no breaking from it now. We must fight for this lie as if it were our king. It keeps us safe.'

'I will not fight for a king. Or for a lie. I fight for my family. I fight for you.'

'Then lie for us.'

'I cannot.'

I said nothing more and I let the silence come.

It should not be so difficult a thing, to keep a secret in a country like ours. It is a lonely life where one's family is one's world, where months can pass before a man spoke to one who was not his wife or child. The farmsteads as scattered as the stars in the sky, distinct and separate. An Icelander with a secret has no priest pleading for his soul or king threatening his body, and yet still he feels the longing to confess.

As we walked back towards the farm, Gunnar moved slowly, weighted with his secret. I thought on the coming summer, when I would leave him and his family behind, to move on and find a new home for the winter. Once I had told myself that I lived as a wanderer because I had to, that a slave's son had no hope of becoming a landed man. Then for many years I had thought of it as a blessing, to wander the land free and unshackled. And now I wondered if it was the coward's longing: to stay moving, one step ahead of the feuds that come as inevitably as the winter ice.

'Home,' Gunnar said, as we came in sight of the farm once again, a quiet relief in his voice. To return to the dark, like a beast returning to its caves and tunnels. I suppose it is an easier thing to be a murderer in the darkness than to try and stand as one in the light of day.

Gunnar patted the figurehead that hung above his door, the carved dragon's head that had once been part of his ship, and I touched it too, for I was in need of a little luck. We must both have felt some premonition to have acted so, for when we went inside, we could see an unfamiliar shadow in the darkness. I saw the two small shapes of Gunnar's children, the flat-nosed profile of Dalla, and one other whom I did not recognise at first. Yet it took only a moment to know who it was, for as the months had passed I had seen that silhouette many times in my memories, and in my dreams.

It was Vigdis, the wife of the ghost.

4

'Welcome to my home,' Gunnar said, after a moment's silence.

'It is the first day of spring,' Vigdis said. 'A good day to visit neighbours.'

'That it is,' my friend replied. He sat down and passed me bread. I took my place beside him; I did not take my eyes from Vigdis.

'It is good to have the company of a woman again,' Dalla said. 'Too many men in this house.' At this her daughter protested and pawed at her. Dalla laughed. 'And you of course, my love.'

Unappeased, her daughter tottered across the room to Vigdis, sat between the guest's knees and pouted at her mother. Vigdis's hands circled Freydis's neck, wandered back and fell to braiding the child's hair.

'Your home is well, I hope?' Dalla said.

'As well as can be expected. Olaf Hoskuldsson shall send me servants soon, to help me tend the house.'

Gunnar's mouth tightened at the name of our chieftain.

'A generous man,' Dalla said. 'It must be lonely, out on the farm with no company.'

'It is not always so lonely,' Vigdis replied, and she looked towards Gunnar.

He met her gaze and made no reply. A silence came, like that particular quiet before a duel. Dalla watched them both – the guest and her husband – and I saw the guessing begin in her mind. Who? What? When? I was glad she did not look at me. I do not know if I could have met her gaze.

The children began to fuss. They always feel discord most keenly, like those birds who will swarm in the sky hours before an earthquake, shaken from their roosts by tremors too soft for us to feel. I took Kari on my lap, gripped his hands and tried to get him to wrestle with me. He was a strong boy, and he loved to fight. But not this time. No matter what I did to urge him, he would only twist his head away and look towards his mother.

Gunnar dipped his cup into the barrel of water once more.

'Well. Have you thought on my proposal?' he said.

'I have,' she said.

'And what do you think to it?'

'I say no.'

'I see.' His mouth twisted as if he had bitten into rotten meat. 'Then we have nothing further to discuss.'

'What proposal is this?' Dalla said. Gunnar did not reply and she spoke again, asking the question of me.

'I know nothing of this,' I said.

Vigdis tilted her head, like a mother speaking to a lazy child.

'Dalla, your husband thought to marry me to his friend.'

'Speak no more,' Gunnar said. 'It is finished.'

'You thought to give me to him, the way you would give him a horse to ride or a knife to gut fish with. You think I would marry a man without a piece of silver to his name?'

'I do not think you will have any better offers. To come and live in your ghost's home.'

'And yet the ghost no longer walks.'

'Gunnar,' I said. 'You should not have done this. You should have spoken to me. This is not what I want.'

He cast the cup of water upon the ground. 'I am sorry that you are content to live as a beggar, trading your songs for scraps of food. It is shameful. And you,' he said, pointing at Vigdis, 'You can go now. You have caused trouble enough.'

'Our business is not finished.'

'No?'

'No. I do not wish to marry your friend.' She stroked the hair of the child who sat beneath her feet. Then she said: 'I wish to marry you, Gunnar.'

On my lap, Kari went still. He no longer twisted to face his mother or fought against my grip. He sat utterly still for a moment, and then he leaned forward and put his arms around me, and he buried his face into my shoulder.

Gunnar spoke. 'What did you say?'

'That is why I have come here. To tell you to divorce your wife and to marry me.'

'You are mad,' Dalla said, her voice soft.

'I bear you no malice, Dalla. But I will not marry a beggar. And your husband is bound to me in ways that he has not told you.'

'Out,' he said.

'Will you test this, Gunnar? Shall I tell her?'

The whispering of the embers, the low and flickering light. Dalla's mouth tight with anger, and Vigdis at the centre of it all, her hands clasped neatly in her lap, her dead eyes unblinking as she looked upon us.

'Take the children out of here, Dalla,' I said.

'No. I will not go. I will have no more secrets.'

Gunnar leaned forward and in the light of the fire I could

see the hate in his eyes as he spoke to Vigdis. 'Say what you want. Do as you please. But I will not leave my wife for you. For you are a whore. Or a witch. Or both.'

'As you wish.' Vigdis stood and smoothed down her dress. 'But I will not tell your secrets for you. That you will have to do yourself.' The light flooded in for an instant as she opened the door, harsh and pitiless. Then she was gone, and the darkness returned once more.

I looked up and even in the dim light I could see the timbers of the roof, pitted with salt and warped by water from their previous life as part of a longship's hull. Gunnar always liked to stare at that ceiling, to remember the man he had once been: a great warrior of the sea. But it always made me uneasy, looking up at that upturned skeleton of a ship. The only man who saw a ship from below was a drowning man.

It fell to me to break the silence. 'Kari, Freydis. Come with me.'

Kari shook his head. 'I want to stay.'

'Go with him,' Dalla said. 'Go with Kjaran.'

Kari went to speak again. A look from Gunnar silenced him. I wonder if he had ever seen that look in his father's eyes before. The eyes of a killer.

I took each of the children by the hand and led them out of that place, out towards light and water and air. I did not move as fast as I should, for before we had left that place we all heard something we should not.

Behind me, I could hear Dalla talking, calm and insistent, though too softly for me to hear the words. And I could hear Gunnar weeping.

As soon as we were in the open air Kari shook himself loose

from my grip and strode away from me. He snatched up a stick the size of a sword from the wood pile, and on any other day I would have struck it from his hand. Wood is a precious thing on the island and not a toy to be played with. That day I let him keep it.

He swatted the stick through the air, but it was no random play of an angry child. He held it in a swordsman's grip the way his father had taught him, and every movement he made had the echo of a lethal purpose. The backhanded cut that will split a head from ear to eye; the quick sideways thrust that passes behind a shield; the low, reaping strike that flays a man's knee. Only ten summers old, but he knew them all.

I let him lead the way, wandering behind him and guiding his sister's steps, for she was content to move in a red-eyed silence, sucking silently on her thumb. We went beyond the boundaries of the farm, striking west, following the fjord. I wondered if he would go all the way to the sea if I let him, to fight the waves like Cúchulainn of the old stories.

Freydis looked anxiously over her shoulder, back towards the farm, shrunk to the size of a hand behind us.

'That's far enough, Kari,' I said, but he ignored me. I let go of Freydis's hand and ran after him. 'Enough. Stop. It is not safe.' And he turned on the spot and swung at me with the stick.

No doubt a better fighter would have dodged the blow, a slip of the shoulder to let the weapon go past. But I have never been a quick or skilful man with a blade. A certain brutal directness, a willingness to endure pain – these are what I bring to the fight. And so I did not try to dodge that strike, but instead lifted my forearm to meet it, skin and bone as my only shield.

The pain was so sharp that it stole my sight for a moment,

and with the sound of snapping wood in the air I thought at first he had broken my arm. But the pain was useful, it gave me anger. Before he could draw back and strike again, I had his arm in both of mine, twisting his wrist until he shrieked and the stick fell from his hand. I hit him twice about the face, picked him up by the throat and threw him to the ground.

He lay quite still, the breath struck from him, croaking for air. I looked to Freydis to see what she would do: run or fight or cry. But she did none of those things, merely watched to see what would happen next. It must have been quite a thing, to see her brother treated like a man.

'You shall have to save that trick for when you are older,' I said, 'or you have a sword in your hand. Until then, you do as I say.'

I offered him my hand, he took it, and I pulled him up to his feet. His knees bowed and his back bent as he continued to struggle for air, but he refused to go to the ground again.

'Sit down. There is no shame in it.'

When he could breathe well, he said: 'Did I hurt you?' There was no apology in his voice. I would have been disappointed if there had been. I tried to shake some feeling back into the arm he had struck, for it was still half-numb.

'Yes, you did. It was well struck. Another year on you and you might have broken my arm.'

He smiled and turned his gaze to his sister, who hovered uncertainly behind me. He beckoned her towards him and took her hand, like he was one of the warrior poets from the old stories who win a woman in a duel. She sat down beside him and put her head on his shoulder.

Cross-legged before them, a poet come to entertain that court of children, I said: 'Do you want a song? A *drapa* or a *flokk*?'

'No.'

'A story, then. Of gods and heroes.'

'No!' He looked on me like I was a fool, and perhaps I was, for I knew then what he wanted to hear. What else would a child want to hear at a time like that?

'Do not worry about what you heard today,' I said. 'All things will be well.'

'What about her?' Freydis said softly.

'Stay away from Vigdis. She is a liar and a thief.'

'I do not think she was lying today,' Kari said.

I cursed the cunning of children.

'Will our father leave us?' Freydis said. 'To go with her?'

'Of course not. Do you know how well he speaks of you all? His family is all he speaks of to me. You are everything to him.'

'But she will cause trouble for us?' the boy asked.

'Nothing that your father cannot contend with.'

The children were quiet for a time. Then Kari said: 'Once you told me the story of Wulf, who tried to rescue the woman he loved from Eadwacer. And he tried to get his friends to help him and they would not. He had to fight alone in the end. They killed him.'

'Will you stay with us?' Freydis asked. 'I am afraid.'

I did not reply at first, and Kari repeated his sister's question: 'Will you stay?'

'I do not know if I can,' I said.

They looked beyond me then and I turned my head to follow their gaze. Gunnar and Dalla, walking towards us, she in front of him and neither of them speaking. I sat cross-legged on the ground amidst the children, as if I were an overgrown infant myself.

When they came to us, they did not speak. I looked upon Dalla, to gain some sense of what she knew, what she thought.

'I wish you had not lied to me, Kjaran,' she said. 'That I had nothing to fear.'

'I thought it true when I spoke it.'

She nodded to me, but what that gesture meant I could not say. I have seen warriors give that nod to worthy opponents, fathers make such a gesture to sons they never wish to see again.

She reached out for her children. They went to her and she turned back towards the farm without another word.

'So,' I said, looking towards my friend. 'That was your plan?'

He nodded.

'It wasn't a very good plan,' I said.

He almost laughed – his mouth open, his lips twitching to a smile – but the sound would not come. 'I am not so clever as you,' he said. 'Or that bitch Vigdis.' He fell silent and began to pick at his fingernails; blood or dirt lay under them, I could not tell which. 'I should never have come to this place,' he said, after a moment. 'I understand the sword and the sea. And my wife. Some of the time, at least. But I am a simple man. This seems to be an island of schemers. Women goading men to do their bidding. Men bullying and tricking each other for land. Chieftains growing fat and rich from all the squabbling.'

'I have cunning enough for us both, Gunnar, and you're a match for two men with a blade in your hand. We have nothing to fear together.'

'I do not know what trouble this woman will bring down.'

'I am not one to back down from a fight.'

'I would not see you harmed over this.'

'That is for me to decide, is it not?' I got to my feet and struck the dirt from my shirt. 'Did you speak to Dalla?'

'I told her everything.'

'What…' I said no more than that. The look he gave stopped me.

'And what do we do now?' he asked.

'We can do nothing but wait.'

'That is your plan? It seems little better than mine.'

'A woman cannot bring a charge against us. She cannot act as a witness. She has no power under the law. She can spread nothing but empty rumours.'

'And what of the brothers? Men have killed for rumours before.'

'They have. We must hope that they won't.' I hesitated, and then I said: 'Will you answer me something, Gunnar?'

He set his jaw and said, 'Ask.'

'You wanted me to marry her. So that I would stay and be your neighbour.'

'That is so.'

'Why did you want me to stay so much?'

He did not speak for a time. He looked out across the open land, the scattered farms in the distance, the black rock of the mountains and the deep green of the valley.

'I think I will be lonely if you go,' he said at last. 'I never met a man I liked so well as you.' And, as if he had spoken some terrible, shameful thing, he leapt to his feet and strode away. I watched him go, and I did not speak to call him back.

I looked up towards the sun and knew that I did not have much time. The days are so short that early in the year. I took my bearings from the hills and the water and I struck out across the valley, away from Gunnar's farm.

5

The home of a chieftain is not like any other. It is not a place of darkness and quiet, but of noise and heat and light. Everywhere one looks, servants tread on dogs, warriors boast and wrestle with one another, children scurry in packs. I have always hated such places, yet it was to there that I went – taking the long path around the home of Vigdis, for Hjardarholt, the home of my chieftain, lay just beyond those borders, and I would not set foot upon those lands again.

The sun hung low by the time that Hjardarholt loomed before me. The turf walls of Gunnar's longhouse might be thought a curve in the land or a little hill, but there was no mistaking this place for what it was. Bigger than a longship, smoke pouring from a pair of chimneys at all hours of the day and night. We have no castles or great halls on our island, but Hjardarholt was as great a longhouse as any Icelander might hope to see.

A *thingman*, Ketil Hakonsson, sat at the entrance – a merry sentry, who offered me a skin of mead as I came forward.

'Kjaran! I am glad of your company. Olaf shall be too, no doubt.'

'The Peacock is within?'

'That he is. We have not had a skald in the hall for a long time. You will stay, I hope?'

'Perhaps.'

It was not a moment after I entered the longhouse that I felt the embrace of my host. Such was always the way of the man they called Olaf the Peacock: every traveller greeted to his home as a long-lost friend. But then, a man of his wealth and stature could well afford the generosity.

'You should not be travelling so late,' he said as he guided me to my place at the table. 'You must have been walking in the dark for hours. Ghosts, trolls, who knows what else might be plaguing the hills.'

'It is good to see you again, Olaf.'

'What brings you here? More than my good company, I suspect. But we shall come to that in time. Come along and make yourself comfortable. Perhaps you'll give us a song, if you are not too tired.'

'Anything to please the Peacock.'

He laughed at the sounding of his nickname. He had earned it from the bronze torc at his neck, the well-wrought rings on his fingers and the gold bands upon his arms, as well as the rich red clothes that he wore, for he was not afraid to show the wealth he had won in his adventures abroad. Quite a sight to look upon, and there were some who whispered womanly rumours about him. But though there was always gold on his arms and a smile on his lips, there was iron in his eyes, a steady sword hand and a strong arm to back it. There were many who had underestimated the Peacock. Some had paid a price in honour and silver when they had tried to cross him. Some had paid with their lives.

'So,' Olaf said once we were seated, 'Gunnar has finally let you go, has he? I thought he was going to hoard you to himself for many summers to come.'

'A traveller like myself must put in a good summer's work to earn his winter home.'

'You would not stay with Gunnar for another winter?'

'No. It would be ill luck.'

'Well, there is a place for you here, if you want it. Though I hear Hakon Haroldsson may come courting you. He is building a strong household.'

'A rival for yours?'

'Hardly. Though you would break my heart if you chose his hospitality over mine.'

'Ah, Olaf, but that is the way of the skalds, ever leaving their chieftains unsatisfied. They make for such good songs, do a chieftain's tears.'

He smiled. 'Ah, had you been born a slave, my life would have been simpler. To buy and sell the poets as I please and not have to win their favour! It would be an easier world.'

'I am sure that it would.'

He picked up a piece of bread, tore it in half and handed the bigger piece to me. 'When I saw you come in, I hoped that Gunnar would be with you.'

'He is busy with his farm.'

'He often seems so. It makes a chieftain nervous, to see so little of a man. Especially one such as Gunnar.'

'He means you no disrespect.'

'Do not mistake me, I am not a petty king in search of tribute. It is his right to stay away if he wishes. But he is something of a mystery. Men do not like mysteries. There are some who would call him aloof.'

Before I could make a reply, one of the warriors in the

hall called on Olaf, asking him to settle some drunken wager or another. He held up his hands in apology to me and stood from the table, a little unsteady on his feet. I watched him speak and wondered if he was quite so drunk as he seemed.

I put down my cup and from the corner of my eye I saw it filled once again. The servant did not go once her task was done, and when I looked upon her in enquiry, she stared back quite openly. A handsome woman; I thought her seventeen or so, with flaxen hair and eyes that seemed to change colour as I looked at them.

'Do we know one another?' I said.

'I have heard you sing. Last winter, when you came here to trade.'

'Ah, I am sorry for hurting your ears. I was unused to playing for such company.'

'No need to be modest. It was quite good, you know.'

'Only quite good?'

She laughed. 'You belittle yourself and expect to be hailed a master?'

'The poet's game. We insult ourselves in hope of praise. An honest response is the last thing we wish for.'

'I'll remember that, and lie better in future.'

A man's voice called to her from across the room. I watched her go and felt Olaf's hand on my shoulder.

'I see you have met Sigrid. A princess amongst servants, or so you would think from how she acts.'

'She's not afraid to speak her mind, is she?'

'I do not know how she gets away with it, speaking as bluntly as she does. She does not offend you, I hope.'

'Quite the opposite. Beauty forgives many things.'

'Ah, I think now I see why you have left Gunnar for this

45

place. No woman but his wife to look at, and he's a dangerous man to trifle with.'

'I do come with another purpose.'

'Other than to drink my wine and ogle my servants?'

'Other than that.'

His voice lowered a little. 'Is it a matter to be spoken of alone?'

'I need not be exact.'

'Tell me here, then.' He raised an eyebrow. 'Inexactly, if you must.'

I glanced around the hall, the bands of warriors drinking and laughing together. All the life and power of a great chieftain's home surrounded us. It was a hard thing to think of danger there. 'Would you back Gunnar,' I said, 'if it came to a feud?'

'That would depend upon the feud.'

'A careful answer.'

'I am a careful man.'

'There is no feud. Not yet. But there are those who envy him. Who would spread lies about him. Gunnar will fight them, if he has to. I want to know if you will let him fight alone.'

He fixed me with a testing look and for a moment all levity was gone from him.

'I simply ask that you be ready,' I continued, 'if trouble comes.'

'It does not surprise me that trouble would seek him out. He is the kind of man who inspires envy.'

'I suppose that he is.'

'Not in gold or wealth, mind you.' Olaf smiled to himself and looked down, rolling the lees around the bottom of his cup. 'He is the kind of man all Icelanders wish that they were.' He drained what remained and placed the cup down carefully. 'I will stand by your friend, if it comes to that.'

'Thank you, Olaf.'

'But it comes at a price. Not of gold, but of loyalty.'

'He will be a loyal *thingman* to you.'

'Not his loyalty. Yours. You must do something for me.'

'I am not sure what it is that you mean.'

He did not speak for a long time, his fingers dancing through the candle flame in front of him. 'Do you believe there are visions from the gods, Kjaran?'

'Of course.'

'Then believe me: when I think of you and Gunnar together, I see death. Of one or the other, and many more besides. You are ill luck, as a pair. You must stay away from him.'

I thought on that for a long time, Olaf's unblinking eyes upon me.

'If that is what it takes. I will come to you after the Althing.'

'Good, good,' he said, almost absently, as though he wished to forget what he had asked. 'You may stay here as long as you wish. Even winter here if you like.'

I looked around the home that he had built, that proud chieftain's household. I met the eyes of the serving girl across the hall, those strange and shifting eyes, like some witch's trick. And I knew that I would not stay long.

It was deep into the night when I returned to Gunnar's home. The fire down to scattered embers, yet even in the dim light I could see the white of open eyes looking back at me.

'Where have you been?' Gunnar whispered.

'I should not tell you that.'

A little gasp, then – almost a sound of pain. 'I would have thought that you wanted no more secrets.' A pause in the darkness. 'Will you stay? Will you stay another year?'

'I shall stay until the Althing.'

'So that is where you have been. Finding another hole to crawl into.'

'Gunnar—'

'Enough. Enough of your words. You have said all you need to.'

The white eyes closed and did not open. I waited for a time, to see if he would wake and speak once more. But he did not.

6

Each time before, I had always travelled to the Althing with a delicious anticipation, a warmth in the chest that is more than a little like love. That year, riding a borrowed horse, I felt nothing at all. No joy or dread, just an absent hollow in my heart.

Gunnar rode beside me, though for all the days we travelled we scarce spoke a word to one another. It had been so since that conversation by the fire.

We had passed the month as strangers; I working the fields with Gunnar's hired help, whilst he hunted or fished or tended the herd. As the sun came down, I would see Gunnar returning home with a net of fish, racing his son back to the house and losing on purpose, Dalla standing halfway out of the doorway, holding a hand palm up to judge the weight of the rain.

I counted down the days, until it was the height of summer. Then, wordless, Gunnar beckoned me to the stables and picked out a horse for me. We mounted and began the journey to the west. He knew that I was to leave his company at the Althing, though he did not know to where, to whom. And he did not ask.

I kept the silence in the days after, as we went through the mountain passes, across the black plains, towards the heart of the country. He made no sign of reconciliation towards me, nor did he try to drive me away or break company with me. He seemed to be waiting for something from me, and so I sang at the fire at night, even as he lay with his back to me. Perhaps, somewhere in one of the old songs, there were the words that would speak to him, but I could not seem to find them. And there was no more time left.

The sound of the Althing was in the air; first as a whisper, then as a voice, and then as a roar. For you hear it before you see it: the low hum of thousands of voices chattering together, as strange a sound in Iceland as silence in a city. Children who have not heard it before mistake it for the sound of the sea or the growl of some terrible monster. They clutch at their parents, weeping in fear, and are mocked with laughter.

As we rode across the black cliffs, the plain opened out beneath us. Cut deep into the valley, looking as if it were carved out by the shovelling hand of a god, and flanked by the great lake Thingvallavatn, bottomless and still. And everywhere that we looked upon that plain, there were people.

There are no cities on our island. No townships or great settlements of any kind. It is an island of families, a single village scattered across the landscape. A man may have a farm deep within the folds of a valley and, looking out, he might see no other neighbour, feel as if he is the only settler in Iceland.

Where there is a city, the local bully becomes a tyrant, the tyrant becomes a king. The gang becomes a warband, becomes a conqueror's army. The people came to this island, exiles and dreamers and fools, because they had tired of such things. It was our isolation that kept us safe, or so we believed. We left nothing for a king to rule over.

Yet now we could see the thousands who gathered there, the great lake that was a cousin to the sea and a mirror to the sky. The Althing, the great gathering of the People. It is there that we trade and sing, see the friends we thought long lost to us. It is there that the law is spoken and decided. All things that a man could dream of lay there – we had only to find them and choose between them.

'What will you do here?'

The voice a strange one to me, so long had it been. I stared at Gunnar, so that I could be sure that it was he who spoke and not some trick of the mind. He waved a hand at me, impatient.

'I will go to the poets. There are songs I must learn. And I have a new song to sing. And you?'

'I go to buy a horse for my son. I promised him a black gelding,' he said, and he stirred his own mount forward.

Perhaps it was as simple as that – he owed me the courtesy of an escort, and honour had now been served. Yet just as I was ready to believe this, he turned in his saddle and spoke to me once more.

'I shall see you with the poets. I will hear this new song of yours.'

My horse was tethered with the great herd in a canyon, my axe bound to my belt with white cords, for none may go to the Althing with a ready weapon. Then I was among them, passing into that sea of people like a swimmer into water, clearing a path through the crowd with my hands against their backs. Instead of the breaking of the waves, my ears filled with the cries of old companions reunited, of daughters seeing their fathers once again. I smelt the salt of sweat and not the sea.

I went not towards the great booths of the chieftains, where beneath the high black cliffs the Thirty-Nine gathered to discuss the great deeds of the people, to confer on the will of the gods. Nor did I go to the great trading grounds, where men and women gathered to see the treasures brought from distant lands – intricate silver jewellery, richly dyed clothes, fine Swedish steel – that few could afford but all could look upon and long for. I did not go to the Oxara river, to look upon the little island where countless duels of honour had been fought, where men had died for an insult, a word, a single untoward look. I went instead to that raised piece of ground to the west. I went to where the poets sang.

I sometimes wonder how the people of other lands speak of the Northmen. The Saxons and Picts whom we have raided time and time again. Perhaps they respect us for being braver warriors than they, for showing them how to fight and how to die. More likely they think us monsters and murderers. But that is because they have never heard us sing.

We may love the sight of a well-forged weapon, the glitter of silver in a chest, fine-worked jewellery, deep-dyed scarlet cloth. But there is only one true art that matters to the Northmen and that is poetry.

For we may spend much of our lives huddled close in the dark, waiting for the sun to rise. Those who do not die of sickness or starvation or to the feud spend their restless lives toiling in the fields and raising sickly cattle. Even our gods know that they fight a hopeless battle, doomed to die at Ragnarök. Yet we know what beauty is, and it is the voice that sings in the night. For when the shield is shattered and the sword is blunted, when all friends have broken fellowship and lovers grown cold, we will not be alone. The poets shall keep us company.

These were my people and there were not many of us. Many

had gone abroad to find their homes in the courts of kings, for it is known that we Icelanders sing truer and sweeter than any other. There are few who could resist that call of glory, the court of kings – only those of us bound by poverty or feud or lack of skill remained behind.

I knew them all. Hallfred – but a boy at that time, but already we knew that he would be greater than any of us. Kormákr, his eyes mad with love and poetry, face marked with the scars of the many duels he had fought for love. A little way distant, I could see the towering figure of Egill Skallagrímsson – an old man now, but looking half a giant at least, still glowering with such ferocity that men half his age kept their distance from him. The greatest of all the warrior poets, who had won a stay of execution with a single poem, ended a feud with a song. And there were more there, others whom I shall not name.

They nodded at me then – I the least amongst them, but I had enough skill to earn my place. No great king would ever call me to his court. No man would sing of me a hundred years from now. Yet I had drunk of the mead of poetry as they had, that gift from the gods which few men may know. They looked on, and waited for me to sing.

A crowd gathered round; not so great as that around the chieftains or the traders, but large enough for my heart to quicken, to taste iron upon my tongue. But I would not look into the crowd in search of men and women I knew. My words were not for them.

I closed my eyes, and stilled my breath. I began to sing. I sang of a man who fought a ghost in the snow.

A careful song: I left no clue for the curious, no chance that they would know the meaning behind the words. Yet I sang of the battle in the snow, of a great warrior whom none would acknowledge. A proud man who needed no acclaim from his kin or chieftain. For this man, to be forgotten was the greatest of praise: he fought for himself alone.

If I had lost his friendship, then the words at least would remain. As some sing of the loves that they have lost, so I sang of my friend.

I see in your eyes that you wish to hear it. Of all the songs I have given you, perhaps you want this one more than any other. But you shall not have it. Soon, you will know why.

I saw them then. As I finished my song and the first words of praise broke over me, I looked amongst the crowd and I saw the two who I most hoped for.

Gunnar first, standing in the first row, his mouth slightly parted, his fighter's eyes unreadable as ever they were. And Sigrid – further back, almost lost amidst the others, I could not see her face.

The words of the other poets fell upon me – guarded praise, questions of origin, a few cutting words. I did not answer them, but went forward to the crowd. Yet Gunnar was already gone. A little nod of the head that could have meant anything, and he drifted away into one of the shifting currents of bodies that ran through that sea of people.

Sigrid remained, a little smile across her lips. Sharp she had been before, bearing a studied indifference as carefully as a swordsman holds his guard. Yet now, for a time at least, that coldness had gone from her.

I saw the way that her eyes danced over the crowd, how she half-started at the shouts and the cries like a wild horse before the breaking.

'You have never been to an Althing before, have you?'

She shook her head. 'My father would not let me.'

'And he permits you now?'

'He is dead. He…' She fell to silence and I took her hand.

'Come. Let me show you.'

On that first day, the new world was still being built. We walked past those chieftains and merchants and priests who always came to Althing, hard at work on the booths they occupied every year, re-erecting roofs that had been taken by storm, shoring up walls pierced by vagrants or outlaws. They were like men rebuilding a lost city from its ruins, a memory. Elsewhere, those too poor for a regular place were arguing amongst one another, vying for the best spot from whatever space was left. The crafty traders waited for an argument to begin, and snuck quietly into a place that was disputed. If you have ever watched seals on the islands dividing up the breeding grounds in a brawling, shrieking, sneaking battle of voice and flesh, you will know this sight, or close enough.

There are great happenings to witness at the Althing, places where our little world is being reshaped by the speeches of great men, their words falling upon the rest of us like a hammer upon hot iron. I could have taken her to see where the priests would be arguing about the coming of the new religion that some Icelanders were practising in secret, spread by the followers of the White Christ. Or where great chieftains would be speaking to their followers, or where travellers from distant lands would be sharing stories of the raids they had fought in, speaking to an audience of wistful, shipless Vikings. Perhaps that is where Gunnar would be now, lost in memories of the man he once was, nurturing an impossible dream of pulling the bones of his ship from his home and setting sail once more.

But I did not take her to these places.

Instead I took her to where Thord the Sly was selling his axes to men who did not know him, and told her how one could tell from the flecks on the blade that he had scrimped on his iron. They were brittle axe heads that would shatter on shield and skull and chopping block alike. I told her how, young and foolish, I had bought one of his axes as a youth and won back my silver in a challenge.

'I stood there with a shield in my hand,' I said, 'and told him that he could swing at me as much as he liked with one of his axes. If it broke before my shield did, he would pay me double its worth. If the shield broke first, I would pay him twice the price. And he did not swing once. Just smiled for the crowd, called me a fool who did not know good quality when I saw it, and gave me back my silver.'

'Why do any still buy from him, then?'

'He talks well. Men want to believe him.'

We went to a horse fight run by Old One Eye, and I told her how to pick out the winner, how more often than not it was the horse that looked a coward, that rolled its eyes and danced away from its owner, that would fight hardest when forced to it. Cowards fear death more than the brave, and it is cowards who are the most dangerous when trapped. I showed her the mares that were tied behind each stallion, there to make them fight harder.

'Oh,' she said. 'They kill for love, then?'

'Yes.'

'Do men ever kill for love?'

'Not often. Most men kill for honour, or in anger.'

'So only horses kill for love.'

'Only horses. And poets, sometimes.'

She laughed at me then. 'Come. Show me something else.'

I did not take her back to the poet's quarter, where greater skalds than I would be singing their most famous songs, trying to fix themselves in the fickle minds of those who stopped to listen. Instead, I took her to that little hollow by the lake where, every year, the same old man told the same sad story. He had been there at every Althing I visited. His story was not that of a great life spent raiding or feuding, but a long, quiet tale of loss and ill fortune. A wife who divorced him when his fortune turned, children lost to sickness and shipwreck, a farm run down to ruin. He paid no mind to whether any came to listen, which was rare enough. He was blind and expected nothing from his audience. The telling of the tale, it seemed, was enough for him.

I showed her only these parts of the gathering, the Althing I knew, and hoped that she might know me from it. A crooked seller of axes, a duel of horses, a man telling stories to the air. A passing world. It was as close a thing to a city as either of us would see in our lives.

At last, we came to the heart of the Althing. A simple field by the sheer rocks, where we do not come to listen to the words of gods or heroes, chieftains or singers. It is where we come to listen to the law.

We were early and there were not many others there. Only a scattering of men, all wandering restlessly. Each of them had grievances to put before the court, walking in circles and muttering to themselves, repeating the particulars of their suit over and over again. We were the only ones, it seemed, who came without a case to prepare. We sat upon the warm grass and waited.

'So,' I said, 'you have seen the Althing. I would know what you think of it.'

'It is wonderful. As wonderful as I hoped it would be.' She looked at me, as if seeing me again for the first time. 'But I think you are not so pleased by it.'

'I like it well enough. I like the silence better.'

'A poet of silence. You make many difficulties for yourself, I think.'

'Truer than you know,' I said, and I held her gaze until she looked away.

'Why did you come here, then?' she asked.

'To pay my duty to a friend.'

'And did you?'

'I did.' But I said no more than that.

I watched her for a time – her rough hands, a servant's hands, clasped together in her lap. The dance of blood beneath the skin of her neck, quickening and slowing at the rise and fall of her breath. Her lips, thin and always slightly parted, always ready with a quick word, it seemed. I wondered what it would be like to kiss those lips.

Perhaps she saw those thoughts marked upon my face. 'Olaf's tolerance goes only so far,' she said. 'I must go. But come and find me again. We should speak more.'

I could not help but laugh. 'Where does that boldness of yours come from, I wonder? Some famous ancestor?'

'No. Perhaps my courage is the same as yours.'

'You think I have courage?'

'I do.'

'And where does it come from?'

'From one who has little to lose.' She stood, and as if by accident, let the edge of her hand brush past my face. Cool skin, the edge of a nail biting for a moment against my cheek. Then she was away, disappearing into the crowd.

I called one last question after her. 'Can you sing, Sigrid?'

'Better than you.' And she was gone.

I lay back on the grass and watched the clouds dance across the sky, and gave myself to thoughts of the future. I thought of the feel of her skin against mine, what it would be like to share warmth in the darkness. The way, at night, that a woman's eyes shine like silver under candlelight. Then I thought of nothing at all.

Before long, I heard footsteps, soft through the grass. A shadow across the sun, and then a presence on the ground beside me. I knew who it was before I sat up, and we shared the silence together for a time.

Then Gunnar said: 'Forgive me.'

'There is nothing to forgive.'

He looked back towards where Sigrid had gone. 'A handsome girl. You shall marry her?'

'Perhaps.'

He nodded, almost to himself. He reached to his forearm, that place where the men of Iceland keep their wealth in rings of gold and silver and bronze. There are men like Olaf who have arms that glisten like dawn light on the water, with much more kept under lock and key in their homes. Others, like Gunnar, carry all the wealth they have in the world upon their arms. When they take a piece off, you know exactly what has been given, and what is left.

He pulled a silver arm-ring away and offered it to me, pinched between forefinger and thumb.

'It is too fine a gift,' I said.

'No, it is not fine enough. But I can spare no more. Come, take it. Do not dishonour me. You might buy some land with it.'

I eyed the arm-ring and I tried to keep the doubt from my face. But I did not succeed, for Gunnar laughed at me and said, 'Not much land, I grant you. But something.'

'I would not need much.' I looked around at the gathering crowd. The time of the Lawspeaking was drawing close. 'I never thought I might give up the wanderer's life. You were right, I suppose. To think that I should marry and settle.'

'No. I was wrong, wasn't I? At least in the woman I chose for you. Perhaps I do not have that gift.'

'You chose well enough for yourself.'

'Yes. I did.' And yet there was something strange in his voice as he spoke. Something a little like regret.

I wish we had spoken more then, of women, and the future. It would have made for a good memory. But we had no time left.

An expectant silence was spreading across the plain, even as it grew ever more crowded, as thousands gathered to bear witness. For many it was obligation, as they came to support a cousin or a brother or a friend involved in a dispute. It was rare for a man to come to the Althing without a connection to one case or another, bound as we all were by blood and duty. Those who had the privilege of remaining uninvolved in the shifting feuds still came to watch and listen. For we are a people who love the battle, who live to go to war. And now our wars are over, our raiding days long gone. All we have are the legal duels of endless court cases, and the sudden, secret violence of the feud.

We sat together in silence, and waited for the law to be spoken.

7

There is a rock on the cliffs above the plain. None know its history, why it should contain such a magic as it does for our people. Perhaps some judgement was settled there in the years of the first settlement. Marked with reddish stains, it might have served as a headsman's block. It is uneven, it would be difficult to make a clean cut upon it. Or perhaps at some stand-off between rival families, with swords drawn and blood about to flow upon the snow, some man leapt upon the stone and shouted out for peace. We do not know the true history of that stone, and it does not matter. Now it is the place where the law is spoken, in incantation, in prayer.

The word is the law, the law that we have all agreed upon. Other lands might inscribe their judgements and laws upon scrolls and tablets, but we do no such thing. Written words are lifeless things and my people have no use for them. Our law lives in word and memory. Our chieftains do not command us, they ask us. Our laws are not chains to bind us nor whips to beat us. We pay no tithes or taxes, raise no armies. There is only the law we agree together, and the honour that binds us to the law.

One must not think such an unwritten law to be a simple

thing. Every Althing, the Lawspeaker will stand and speak for an hour, and even then he will have spoken only one third of the laws that we follow. The Lawspeaker speaks thrice, at three Althings, and once he has spoken every one of our laws he is released from his charge and another appointed, as if the law were some curse that could be lifted only by being spoken in its entirety. We sat and watched as the Lawspeaker, Thorkell Thorsteinsson, took his place upon the stone above us and began to speak to us.

That day, of course, he spoke of murder.

Had we done our killing a year before, a year after, we would not have had to listen to such a thing. We would have sat through edicts on theft of cattle, the settling of land disputes, the rights of men on common coastal land, the conditions of divorce. But that year the Lawspeaker spoke of murder.

Not every killing is murder. What law would fully forbid bloodshed? Only the law of the coward. The duellist who cuts down his opponent in the *holmgang*, the warrior who answers a spoken insult with a retort of cold iron, these men are given scant punishment. They tell of their killing to the next person they see, for they have nothing to be ashamed of. They give their reasons to the court, a blood-price paid in silver to the relatives, and all wait to see if the feud will be buried or live on. But secret murder was another matter. To kill and not declare it was the act of the shameful man. And so Gunnar and I listened to the Lawspeaker speak of the crime we had committed.

I resisted the urge to look at Gunnar for as long as I could, for I feared what I might see there. But when at last I turned to him, I saw that he showed no sign of guilt or shame. Instead he wore the blank, almost bored expression that I had seen him wear as he fought for his life on the battlefield, a more terrible thing for a warrior to behold than a berserker biting his own shield. It was the expression of a man to whom killing required no anger, no great effort of strength or will. The face of a man to whom a killing meant nothing.

At last, the law was finished. A little sigh passed through the crowd, for it matters greatly to us, this law of ours. We are a shipwrecked, leaderless people, and this is a dream that we dream together – a fragile dream that keeps the peace.

After the Lawspeaker had finished, Olaf was the first to stand.

'I am Olaf Hoskuldsson,' he said, though there were few there that did not know his name. 'Some of you know me. Many more of you knew my father.' A murmuring of condolence from the crowd. 'There is little to be said. He was a good man and a great chieftain. He left a land at peace. I hope that my sons too may grow up in peace.' He lifted his head and surveyed the great plain, and an icy stillness fell upon my skin. 'To that end,' he said, 'I ask now. Is there any man in the Salmon River Valley who has a grievance unanswered? Let us settle it now, in the open. With words, not with blood.'

A silence, and then a stirring within the crowd as a great figure came forward. It was Björn Haroldsson. The brother of the man we had killed.

I saw Hakon Haroldsson reach a cautioning hand on to his brother's shoulder, seeking to draw him back within the crowd, to confer a moment longer. Björn shrugged him off. 'I would speak.'

'What troubles you?'

'I am Björn. Björn Haroldsson. Some of you may know me.' He paused for too long, and the crowd stirred restlessly. The particular hesitance of a man unaccustomed to feeling intimidated. He was quick tempered, tall enough to tower over any but a giant. No doubt he was used to cowing men to his will. But there, with the eyes of half a nation upon him, I think that he was afraid.

Gunnar leaned across to me. 'I do not think he will make much of a skald.'

'I had not thought of taking him as an apprentice.'

Olaf broke the silence. 'And what have you to say?'

'My brother Erik was lost in the winter.'

'I know of this already.'

'But others may not.'

'Speak, then.'

'He left one night at the end of winter. His servant says that she heard him leave in the night. That he often walked at night and would not say why. And that night he did not come back.'

He fell silent, and there was a restless stirring in the crowd. But Björn, like any skilless speaker, did not seem to notice the mood of his listeners. He stood blankly expectant, waiting for some other man to answer him.

Olaf was not ignorant of the crowd's contempt. 'That is all you have to say?' he said.

'Yes.'

'You have not seen a body? You have no witnesses to any wrongdoing? You have no case to put before us?'

'No, but I—'

'This is not place to guess. We have no time for this.'

Listening to it spoken that way, forgetting what I knew, I could see why Olaf would dismiss it. Men died in winter. Madness and sickness and the cold, they all took their harvest. Erik had no feud unsettled or debt unpaid that might bring a man to commit murder. The truth that I knew was one that no man would think of. Beside me, I saw Gunnar nodding to himself, willing Olaf on as he mocked the man who spoke.

The way a man may wordlessly encourage a horse or a dog as it fights, fearful that if he speaks he will do more harm than good. That a loyal beast may turn towards the voice of its master and see its throat emptied upon the ground.

'Does any man wish to speak of this?' Olaf said.

A moment of silence, of perfect silence. Then a cry behind us, a scream of horror.

I once saw a mother pulling her dead child from a river. The child had fallen through the ice a month before and been entombed there, a shadow beneath frozen water. The woman had gone there every day, to peer into the depths and look upon her child. One would have thought that her pain, her grief, would have been dulled by time, by seeing the dead day after day. And yet when at last the river thawed and she held the stiffened flesh in her arms it was as though her son had died a moment before. The scream she gave, that was the same scream that I heard at the Althing. The scream of one looking on the dead for the very first time.

It was taken up by others, and a wave of motion broke through the crowd, akin to the instant that a shield wall breaks and an army begins to run. I saw many hands reaching by instinct to weapons that were bound away, thinking only that some sudden attack could prompt such cries of terror.

The crowd parted and I saw it was a single figure coming forward. It was a woman, and I smelt her before I saw her, the hot smell of decay, the stench of a battlefield a month after the killing.

There was something in her hands. Something that had earned her passage through the crowd, that had set every man and woman who saw it to screaming. And though I knew this, could see it at the corner of my vision, it is not what I noticed first.

When the heroes in the old stories meet their deaths, in those last moments they see not the faces of the men who have come to kill them, but focus instead upon some inconsequential thing. The dew upon the grass, the reflection of sunlight on a blade, the whorl of wood in a broken shield, a raven that watches from above. I had always thought it to be one of those lies that poets are so fond of, but on the plain at the Althing I discovered it was so. The first thing I saw was not her face or what she had brought, but the heavy curve of her belly, that she was heavy with child.

Then it was that I saw the stinking thing swinging in her hands, the face that was familiar to me. I knew who she was and what it was that she carried.

It was Vigdis, bearing the head of the man we had killed.

FEUD

There is something that I have forgotten to say. There is something that I have always been afraid to speak of with you. But I must speak it now.

Do we have ale left? Only a little? Well, no matter. Take a drink of it yourself. Come now, drink deeply, you may do more than wet your lips. This is a special day for us both, is it not? And I must drink too, for I have told you many stories and sung many songs, but none so long as this one. And there is much more for me to tell.

There. That is better. Now I am ready. Now I may speak to you of revenge.

Do not think it something of no substance. You can hold it, feel it, touch it. It is handed down from father to son, from brother to brother, from a husband to a wife. For whilst a man may inherit many things from his kin – land, cattle, a silver arm-ring, a favourite shield, a good sword – he also inherits something much more valuable. He inherits the duty of revenge.

For when one has kin who lie unavenged in the ground, they do not lie quietly. The dead speak, and they only speak of vengeance. Sometimes they are soft, whispering in your ear as you make love to your wife. Or they may shriek at you at night, waking you from sleep. No, the dead are never silent.

Those who hear such voices, they all look the same. Head cocked a little to one side, leaning towards a voice that only they can hear, their eyes blank, staring into a future that only they can see. When you try to speak to them, they pay no *attention at first. You must fight to be heard, for there is a voice that you cannot hear, drowning out every word that you say.*

You may think it madness, until you have heard such a voice for yourself. Then you will do anything to make it stop.

But it will take years. Long winters spent waiting for brief summers, brief summers spent waiting for some opportunity for the killing. Years that are spent watching and waiting, the whispering voice speaking louder and louder and louder in your ears, until you wish for madness or deafness to come. It would do no good to be thus afflicted. If you were deaf, you would still hear the words in your mind and have no other sounds to drown them out. And the mad – the mad hear the dead more than any. They hear not one voice, but an endless cacophony of all the unavenged dead, each clamouring to be heard over his rival.

If you are lucky, the moment will come at last. Your quarry will venture into common lands alone, and some loose tongued shepherd will tell you so. And when last you give the killing blow to an enemy, after the war cries have fallen quiet and the last shield is broken, you stop and listen and you hear nothing. The chattering dead at last fall quiet. There is nothing sweeter than that silence. There is nothing more beautiful than revenge.

I see that you do not believe me. Perhaps you believe in another false god. In love or song. Friendship, perhaps, or honour, or the joy of battle.

It does not matter. You will learn the truth in time.

8

At first, there was nothing but sound. Women screaming, men shouting. The stamp of hundreds of feet against the earth; as some crowded forward to hear and see more, others ran from the plain to gather their kin as witnesses. My eyes were open, but could not seem to see. I could feel the crowd closing around me, their hands upon me. Someone had grabbed my arms, but I felt his grip go slack a moment later, struck by uncertainty, not knowing what it was that he should do.

I closed my eyes, an instinct I learned as a child to wake from terrors in the night. If I closed my eyes in the dream, when I opened them again it would be in the waking world and my nightmare would dissolve into the dark. When I opened my eyes this time, my vision returned to a thousand eyes looking upon me in silence.

We were in a closed circle. Had I a sword in hand, I could not have swung it without striking half a dozen men. At first it was only Gunnar and I, but the mob parted a little and others joined us. I saw them then, the three brothers. Hakon, Björn, Snorri. And then their lost brother was there too, eyeless and lipless, grey skin and white bone, swinging from the hands of Vigdis.

I do not know how I appeared to them at that moment. But I could see that Gunnar did not wear the face of a guilty man. He looked like a man betrayed.

It was Hakon who spoke first. 'Gunnar,' he said, 'what did you do?'

Gunnar did not speak. He did not take his eyes from Vigdis.

'Will you speak it now, Gunnar?' she said. 'Or are you still a coward as well as a murderer?'

A wordless cry from Gunnar, a roar like a great wave breaking against a cliff. Then he did find words: 'I gave him a warrior's death. And you would call me coward?'

'It is true, then?' Hakon asked.

A shudder passed through the crowd at those words. I looked on the faces of those who surrounded us, saw that killing coldness stealing into their eyes. We would die there, I thought, and I only wished that my weapon was not bound, so that I might take good company with me into the darkness. I looked at the men closest to me and tried to think which of them would come for me first. Of how I would put my thumb into his eye, tear his cheek open with my teeth, beat his throat closed with the palm of my hand. I might, if I was lucky, be able to kill one of them.

'Enough!'

A new voice speaking – Olaf the Peacock, fighting his way through the crowd with a dozen of his *thingmen*. They were around us in moments and, though they were but few against many, the crowd drew back.

'Speak no more, you fool!' he said to Gunnar, his face white with rage. He pointed to me. 'Even the poet here knows to hold his tongue.'

Björn spoke to Olaf then, shoving forward against the men who fought to hold him back. 'You will protect a murderer?'

'Will you kill a man on the plains of the law and live in shame of it? You will have your justice. But by the law, not here.' He looked to us. 'Come with me. Now.'

'I will not run from men like this!' Gunnar spat upon the ground. 'I will not run from this woman.'

I put my hands on Gunnar's shoulders. 'Come,' I said. 'We must go.' He shook his head, and so I spoke again. I spoke the words I knew that he would listen to. 'Revenge, Gunnar. Think of revenge. We cannot have it if we die here.'

He smiled at me, then – a monster's smile of teeth below dead eyes.

'Yes,' he said. 'Revenge. I will have it.' And he moved away, encircled by Olaf's men. But they did not stand too close. They knew him to be a cursed man.

There is comfort in darkness. Any Icelander knows that, or must learn it to survive the long winter without madness taking his mind. To sit still and be unseen, to almost live through sound and touch alone this can be a pleasure, if one is attuned to it. As we sat together in Olaf's hut on the plain, sun creeping through the reeds but much of the room still in shadow, I have never been so grateful for the darkness. We might be dead before the day was out, yet I felt calm. There, in that moment, there was only Olaf and Gunnar and I. The rest of the world, for a time at least, did not exist.

Olaf leaned towards us, hands clasped together in the way that I had heard that Christian men prayed. Gunnar was in one corner slumped against the wall, but it was in rest, not defeat. The warrior's habit of gathering strength at any opportunity, never knowing when he will be forced to fight.

Olaf broke the silence. 'Tell me what you have done.'

Gunnar looked at him with contempt and shook his head.

'This one seems determined to die in silence,' Olaf said to me. 'And you?'

'I will speak,' I replied. Gunnar raised a hand – imploring or in anger I could not tell. 'Gunnar, I must speak. If not for us, then for your family.' At these words, he fell back once more.

'Be quick,' Olaf said.

I told him the story, then. Of the ghost in the night, iron singing against iron. Of our bargain with Vigdis to keep our silence, spare the dead man's shame. Of the price she had asked from Gunnar and how she had been refused.

'I would believe it from no man but you,' Olaf said, once I had finished. He sat back, one hand toying with a silver arm-ring, turning it over and over again. I listened to the sounds coming from outside, for the crowd was gathering once more, though it seemed that they kept their distance, that their respect for the chieftain still held. It was only once or twice that I heard shouts from Olaf's men, driving away the packs of curious children who had come to see a murderer.

'This is what we will do,' Olaf said, waiting a moment to see if Gunnar would offer any response, any objection to his words. 'We speak to the brothers in private. We tell them what you have told me. They will know that their brother was dishonourable, playing a womanly trick. They will take a lesser settlement. They will not ask for your life.'

'You think they will believe us?' I asked.

'It is too strange a tale to be invented.'

Gunnar shook his head. 'No,' he said. 'We will say nothing. A woman cannot be a witness under the law.'

'You have spoken it!' Olaf said, rising to his feet, angry at last. 'Spoken your guilt in front of a thousand men.'

'As she intended,' I said.

'As she intended,' Olaf repeated. 'You were tricked by her. Now you will pay the price for it.'

Gunnar turned his face to the wall. He no longer wished to look on either of us. 'What must I pay?' he said.

'Give them your farm, Gunnar,' Olaf said. 'Your herd, too. And that sword you are so proud of. That may be enough. You may come to my home, be one of my *thingmen*.' He turned to me. 'I owe you your promise and I have kept my word. Though you should feel shame for your trick.'

'I do. And you have my gratitude.'

'There is much unsettled between us,' Olaf replied. 'I do not think well of your deception. I think that this will not end as you would wish it.'

'Your gift of prophecy again, Olaf?'

'One does not need the second sight to know how a man like you will meet his death.'

In his corner, Gunnar stirred at last. 'What promise is this?'

I hesitated, thinking that I might find the right words. But Olaf spoke before I could: 'You are a luckless man, but you are fortunate to have this one as your friend. He came to me begging for my favour. Begging that I would protect you in some unnamed feud. I see now why he came. Because you are too proud to beg.'

At this, Gunnar smiled. 'I will not give up my land,' he said. 'I will not be punished for killing a man in a fair fight.'

'It is that or they will make you an outlaw.'

'So be it.'

'You will not last a single winter,' Olaf said.

'I would rather live and die that single winter in my own home than beg your charity.'

'Die then, Gunnar. It means nothing to me. I offer my help and consider my debt paid.' Olaf turned from us then, his hands held up, and Gunnar smiled once more. That warrior's smile that confronts hopeless odds with a light heart. I knew then that he truly would die before accepting Olaf's help. I knew then what I had to do.

'Let me speak to you, Olaf,' I said.

'No man is stopping you,' Gunnar said.

'No. I must speak to Olaf alone.'

I thought I would have to fight hard for what I wanted, but Gunnar stood at once and looked on us both with scorn.

'More tricks,' he said. 'More words. They will do no good. But as you wish. I see you think me too foolish to understand. But I understand it. I know.' And he strode from the hut to face the howling crowd.

'There is nothing more I can do for you,' Olaf said. 'You will have to convince him to do as I say. Or both of you will die.'

'No,' I said. 'There is another way. This is what we will do.'

After we had spoken, I waited there alone. Olaf was gone amongst the people, working upon what we had agreed. Where Gunnar was, I could not say. Riding for home with a warband at his heels, sitting alone upon the grass, calling for vengeance with sword in hand – neither would have surprised me.

A shadow passed across the entrance. I thought it would be Olaf, come to tell if we had succeeded or failed. Or Gunnar, come back to demand an answer that I could not give him, or one of the brothers, seeking a settlement in blood. Yet when I looked up, it was the shape of a woman. I could not see her face, but I did not need to. I would have known her in any kind of darkness.

'Is it true?' Sigrid said, as she sat beside me. 'Is it true what the people say?'

'Enough of it is true.'

'Gunnar killed that man?'

'We both killed him.'

She leaned forward and her unbound hair spilled forward to cover her face. 'What will happen now?' she said.

'Olaf will offer a settlement to the brothers.'

'If they refuse it?'

'There shall be a trial. We shall both be made outlaws.'

She did not answer at first. Outlaws. The word hung in the air.

Since men were made to walk upon the earth, we have wondered what to do with the thief, the murderer, the blasphemer. I know there are many lands where the criminal is tortured, murdered in judgement. But what a cowardly thing it is to bind an unarmed man and lay a blade across his throat or hang him from a rope or burn him upon the pyre. It dishonours the executioner far more than the one who is killed, no matter what the crime may be.

My people do no such thing – there is no crime that I can think of that could earn such a shaming. The worst of men are simply put outside of the law. They are not men, they are meat. The outlaw can be killed by anyone, and no blood-price will be paid to his family, no revenge sought in the long feud. His life is worth nothing.

'You will die, then.' It was not a question.

'We do not have the silver to go abroad. Or the kin to protect us against the sentence.' For a rich man may flee his sentence. A powerful man may make a fortress of his home, gather his people to protect him. But we were neither.

'I have heard stories of outlaws who did survive,' I said.

'Those too poor or proud to flee, those who were most reckless and cunning, who tried to make a life in the mountains to the east, where nothing can live.'

'Do you believe those stories?'

'No. The outlaws always run, and they are always hunted and they always die. Yet they die on their feet, with a weapon in their hands.' I tried to smile. 'Never let it be said that we are a people lacking in mercy.'

I looked down at my hands, ran my thumbs across the palms to feel the marks, the scars. They were not marked with weapons, but with a farmer's tools. Who would have thought them a murderer's hands? Who would have thought that my poet's lips belonged to a killer?

She looked away then, stood and went to the door, one hand upon either side. How many different paths waited for her, out on that plain? How many better than the one that was left to her in the darkness, there with me?

And she returned out to the light, to the living.

I closed my eyes in the darkness and tried to sleep, like a warrior before a battle. I would need all of my strength soon enough.

9

'Murderer.'

It was Björn who spoke the word and I could not help but flinch at it. There was no such movement from Gunnar – a tremor, perhaps, like that of a man shrugging away a wound. But no more than that.

We were packed in close, there in Olaf's booth. Gunnar, the brothers, Olaf and myself. I could smell the sweat from the brothers, hear their breathing, our knees almost touching. It would take but the slightest of movements to put my hands around another man's throat, to reach for a stone on the ground and break open a skull. Only our respect for Olaf kept us from bloodshed.

The eldest brother Hakon looked to Olaf. 'Very well, Peacock. We are here, as you asked. Speak and we will listen.'

Olaf did not answer at first. He lifted up the strip of cloth that covered the entrance and for a moment the light flooded in. Outside, under the sun and open sky, the court waited for us. A circle of stones where all assembled to hear the crime, and the judges make their ruling. I imagined the crowd that would be out there, the fathers who would point at us and speak to their sons. 'Look at that man,' they would say, 'and remember his face. This is what a coward looks like.'

Olaf clapped his hands for silence and it was given to him. 'A man has been killed,' he said. 'A secret murder, not an honourable killing. The worst of crimes, and these men stand accused of it. And I have come to speak, to offer—'

'Why should we take your judgment in this case?' It was Björn who interrupted the chieftain. He pointed to us. 'They are your men. How can we trust you?'

'I do not impose a binding judgment,' Olaf said, as he held a hand up like a parrying blade. 'It is a settlement that I offer. You may take it or refuse it, as you wish, find some other chieftain to press your claim. But I think that you will be satisfied. I have spoken with these men. They have given me the truth.'

'Go on, then,' Hakon said, before his brother could offer any further dissent. 'Let us hear what it is you have to say.'

'They met with Erik in winter. They quarrelled and fought. And they did not report what it was they had done.' And Olaf turned and extended his hand towards me, and he said. 'Yet it was this man who gave the killing blow.'

There was near silence at this. The murmuring crowd outside, the moan of the wind against the walls, and nothing more than that to mark the unravelling of my life. Yet I felt the strange lightness of heart, so strong that I had to fight to keep a smile from my face. When the worst has come to pass, when your life has fallen to ruin and yet you still stand unharmed – what is there to do then but to smile or to laugh?

'This is true, is it not?' Olaf said.

'Yes, it is true,' I said.

Olaf paused, waiting for Gunnar to speak. But he gave no sign of dissent. His face was unmoved – that same empty mask he wore when he fought. His eyes were a different matter and

I did not trust what I saw there. But his silence would hold, for a time at least.

'What was Gunnar's part in this?' Olaf said.

'I made him swear as my friend not to speak of it.'

'Why would you do this?'

'I am a poor man. What compensation can I offer to pay the blood-price? I knew that I would answer with my life.'

'And what was the cause of this quarrel?

'An insult I will not speak of here.'

'Why not?'

'It would dishonor the man I have killed.' I met Hakon's gaze and held it. 'Yet I will tell the brothers, if they ask it. And they will understand why I acted as I did.'

Hakon asked the only question that mattered. 'Did he die well?'

'It was a fair fight. He fought well. He died without fear.'

'Is this true?' Olaf said, speaking now to Gunnar.

My friend hesitated and looked at me, weighing his choices. But we had planned for this. I had told Olaf that Gunnar would not lie, or if he did, that he would not do it well enough. He was only to be given questions that he could answer with the truth. And he did.

'Yes,' he said. 'It was a fair fight. One against one.'

'I have heard the reason why they fought,' Olaf said. 'And I swear, on my honour, that they speak truly. There was good cause to the fight and I only wish they had spoken of it at once. Yet a secret killing may hardly go unpunished. And this is the settlement I offer. Gunnar will pay a quarter of his herd and silver over to the Haroldsson brothers for his part in the crime. And Kjaran...' He waited then, and I did not know why. 'Kjaran,' he said, 'will be made an outlaw for three years. He will be given one month before the sentence. After that, the law will grant him no protection.' He looked back to the three brothers and spread his hands wide. 'Will you accept this? Or will we go before the Court?'

Blood and silver, and a good weight of each. The way that all debts are settled in Iceland.

'We accept,' Hakon said. 'It is a fair offer.'

I believed him as he spoke. That he was honest and true. And I knew it did not matter.

For Björn looked at me with a killer's eyes. He would never stop hunting me. Three years or not, within the law or outside of it. But that was a matter for another time.

First, he would have to catch me.

The brothers went, and it was Olaf, Gunnar and I who remained behind. Gunnar and I sat upon the ground, and Olaf stood over us like a father before foolish children, waiting for one of us to speak.

At last, Gunnar raised his head. 'Leave us, Olaf,' he said. 'We have nothing to say to you.'

'You order me out of my own property?'

'A request. I do not know what you want from me. Gratitude or shame, or some other thing. But you shall not have it.'

Olaf spat on the ground and spoke to me. 'My debt is paid. Do not ask me for another favour. Never speak to me of this again.'

He left and I felt a weariness descend such that I have never known, not even after battle or lovemaking. I expected that Gunnar would speak more – there were so many things that he could have asked, answers that I wished to give. But he said nothing and it fell to me to break the silence.

'Do you want to ask why?' I said.

'I think that I do not want to know. I think that it would shame me to know.'

'As you wish.'

'Where will you go?'

'Olaf knows a trading captain. Ragnar the Keel-farer. He sails in a month. Perhaps I will go to Ireland. I speak a little of their tongue. My father taught me.'

He nodded absently. 'I do not think that I could ever leave Iceland. I think I would die before I let that happen.'

'Three years is not so long a time.'

'You will come back, then?'

I thought of Björn, waiting for me with murder in his eyes. 'Yes,' I said. 'I will come back.'

Slowly, like a cut tree that falls of its own weight, Gunnar folded forward and put his head into his hands. I looked away and I tried not to listen or to see. I let my gaze drift to memory, my mind turn to song, and gave him the absence that he needed.

At last, he spoke again. 'Will you stay with me? Before you go?'

'Yes,' I said. 'I will.'

And with that, we both fell to silence. There was nothing more to say.

I did not think that I would see Sigrid again. As I walked about the Althing there were men who I had known for ten years, women who had played with me when I was a boy and laughed with me as a man, who stared past me as if I were a stranger to them. I was not an outlaw, not yet, but already they looked on me as they would look upon a dead man. Why should Sigrid be any different?

Yet I had not been long in my wandering on the plain – a purposeless, hopeless walk of farewell – before I saw her coming towards me. I turned aside, found a rock a little apart from the crowds to sit upon, its polished surface a testament to the hundreds of people who had sat upon it. Old men looking on their last Althing, young men brooding on feuds. And lovers, too.

She sat down and her eyes cut into me – unblinking, empty of tears. A fighting man's eyes. 'Why would you lie for him?' she said.

'You have heard the judgement, then?'

'Everyone has heard it.' She hesitated, her hands clasping and unclasping each other, as if she sought to break some invisible set of bonds. 'Why would you lie for him?'

'It was only half a lie. I put my blade to that man's throat.'

'But why do it?'

I looked to the ground. 'Gunnar has a wife. Children. Land.'

'You think his life is worth more than yours.'

'I know it is. In every way.'

'And what of me? Did you think of me?'

To that, I had no answer.

Her mouth twisted in grief, and she spoke again. 'You are a fool. Weighing your life in land and family and the herd. It is always men like you who die first. And you bards never sing those stories.'

'I do not understand.'

'Oh, you'll sing of those wealthy farmers, those mighty chieftains. The way they died bravely. But it always begins like this. Some poor slave or servant offered up as a sacrifice, sent to die on the command of their master. They are always the first to die. But they never sing songs of those men.'

'That was your father's fate, wasn't it? He died in his master's feud.'

At this, she flinched and could no longer meet my gaze. I had guessed well, it seemed.

'You are meat for these men,' she said, her voice cracking. 'To be cut and traded and destroyed. You owe them nothing. And now you will die for one of them.'

'They have to catch me first.' I waited for a moment, let her think on that. Then I took her hands in mine. 'I will go for three years and this feud will die. And I will come back.' I lifted my arm so that she might see the arm-ring I bore. 'This is all the silver I have in the world. It could be a beginning for us. Some land, a little herd. Nothing more than that. But perhaps it will be enough.'

She tilted her head, her eyes still as hard as beads of glass. 'You truly mean this, don't you?'

'Yes, I do. Will you wait for me?'

She did not speak for a long time.

'I will wait,' she said at last, in weariness and defeat. For it is a madness in the blood, that love with a morbid heart. It is no blessing. But it is unalterable.

The madness filled me too, and I do not know what we would have done, had we been given a moment longer, together there on the plains. But there was no time left. Footsteps were coming towards us, a figure running across the plain.

Ragnar the Keel-farer, a man I half-knew, the sea captain who would take me on my exile a month hence. I thought at first that he had come to discuss our journey, to name his price. But one look at his face and I knew it was some other matter that drew him to me.

He was too breathless to say more than a word, but that was all he needed.

'Gunnar,' he said, and pointed back the way he had come, back to the heart of the Althing.

Blood spilled at the Althing – that was my first thought of what must have come to pass. That Gunnar or Björn had broken the truce, taken weapons on to the field and that one had killed the other, a crime that might make the People forget their injunctions against execution, and murder the transgressor where he stood. I did not know which I would rather see, Gunnar dead on the ground, murdered by a blasphemer, or with a bloody blade in his hand, soon to die a shameful death.

Gunnar and Björn – I could see that they stood close, heads bowed forward like bulls before the charge. Soon there would be the screaming that goes beyond words, after which blood flows as inevitably as the autumn floods. But not yet – we were still at words. There was still hope that the quarrel could be put aside.

I went between them, caught Gunnar's head in my hands, placed my forehead against his.

'Speak to me,' I said. 'Tell me what has happened. The feud is settled, is it not?'

He smiled at me, his eyes alive with honour and madness. He levelled his finger over my shoulder and said: 'The horse.'

I looked upon it – a handsome black gelding that tossed its head and stared back at me, proud as a prince. The horse that Gunnar had come to buy, but I did not laugh. I had seen men killed for much less.

'It must be a black horse,' Gunnar said, 'for Kari. I promised him. And it was promised to me.'

I looked to the trader – a man I did not know, thin and hunched, shifting from foot to foot.

'A better offer was made,' he said. 'You cannot hold that against me. I sell at the best price, that is all.'

'Oh, I do not blame you,' Gunnar said. 'I blame him.'

Bjorn spoke slowly, seeming to weigh each word before he said it. 'I did not know you wanted this horse. It is not my fault you do not have the silver to match my offer.'

'I have the iron to match your iron. Will that be enough?'

'Gunnar, be silent,' I said, but he would not.

'Your family are all thieves,' he said, and at those words something between a sigh and a groan broke through the crowd. They knew what must follow.

I watched Björn's skin pale. He said: 'I will have an answer for that insult.'

'Wait,' I said. 'Gunnar, let him have the horse.'

'Let him die for it, if he wants it so much. I will have it for my son.'

I could see it in him, that hunger he had tried to forget when he came to Iceland, now returned to him as strong as ever it had been. The taste for blood that all the true warriors have. The longing that cannot be ended.

I stepped close again, whispered so that only he might hear me.

'Is this what you want, Gunnar? Truly?'

'They would murder you with the law, would they not? Why should I not do the same?'

'The feud can end with me. Gunnar—'

But he spoke past me, shouting towards the brothers. 'I say again, your family are cowards. And who will answer that?'

'You will be answered! Whoreson! Murderer!'

And then there were no more words. I fought to hold back Gunnar, and men I did not know restrained Björn.

I was a fool to believe that it might have gone other than this. For our people, who would rather see their stomachs opened and their guts steaming upon the snow than to see their honour shamed, a word and a blade are one and the same. If a man took a knife to you, you would not rest until you had seen him slain. Why should an insult be any different?

And so Gunnar looked from one brother to the next, that mad smile on his face, and he said. 'Which of you will fight me? Will it be you, Björn? I think it must be.'

'No,' Hakon said. 'You have insulted a family, not a man. I am the elder.' He looked at Gunnar for a moment, perhaps hoping for the impossible, that Gunnar might take back his challenge. Then he said: 'I am the one you will fight in the *holmgang*.'

10

In the height of summer the sun barely sets. It touches the horizon twice each day, like a man bowing before a king. Just as our winter is a time of near endless night, summer is permanent day.

So when I say that we left at dawn the next day, you must not think of it as some dark awakening, shadowy figures shaking one another awake and setting forth in dim light. We did not sleep, merely sat and stared at the sun until it gave a shy kiss to the edge of the world, the sky never anything less than impossibly bright. Then we gathered our weapons, a little food and water, and we walked to the river.

They waited for us there. Hakon, Björn, Snorri, Vigdis, and other kinsfolk whose names and fathers I did not know. Ragnar was there, Sigrid and Olaf and some of his men, and standing a little aside from the rest was that unlucky horse-trader, the black horse at his side. The prize for the winner, a mocking reminder of how petty this was.

We walked with the sun and the river at our right hands, the low valley wall at our left. Travelling as a single company, a strange courtesy persisted between us. I saw Gunnar unthinkingly offer a hand to Hakon to steady him when he tripped upon a jutting stone, and when the heat of the sun began to beat down upon us I found myself offering a waterskin to my neighbour, only to find that it was Vigdis who took it from me. Soon, two of us would be fighting for their lives – perhaps it was that knowledge that kept the peace. When one knows blood will be spilt soon, there is no need to seek out the fight, no need to hurry towards it. There is a feeling that is almost happiness. One who saw our company, ignorant of our quarrel, might have thought us a family travelling to a great feast, or a pious band making for one of the sacred places of the island, where the world of the gods and the hidden folk crosses over into our own. And in a way, we were doing both of these things. For men like us, where the dance of iron is the most treasured art, the *holmgang* is a festival. The island we were headed towards, that was holy too in its own way. There has been enough blood sacrificed upon it.

It could not truly be called an island. A little patch of sodden earth in the centre of the river, separated from the bank by a few yards of shallow water. That was enough of a break from the land, for the *holmgang* must be fought in a different world to our own.

There are many such places, where one may step out from Iceland and into the duellists' secret country. The lopsided outcrop in the sea beside Borg, stinking from the seals who lurk there. The turf island in the middle of Hitarvartan, where duellists have fought up to their knees in black mud. And I have heard tell that in the mountains to the east, there is an island in the middle of a lake that is so still and clear that it is as if four men are fighting, two above and two below the water. But this island, being so close to the Althing, has seen more battle than any other. When one stands upon it, one can see the worn ground, the splinters of iron and wood, from the duels that have been fought before. Decades of feuds, begun and settled in that place.

We gathered at the edge of the water and I spoke to Sigrid. 'No matter what happens,' I said, 'do and say nothing.'

'You are not the duellist.'

'Shield-men have been killed before. I do not know what they will do on that island.'

She nodded, and when she was quite certain that no man was watching, she put her fingers to her lips and those fingers to my hand. I let them linger for only a moment before I stepped away. I hope that she understood why.

The water was cold against my thighs as I waded in, and I held the weight of three shields up high above my head. The others were at my back, Hakon and Björn among them, and it would have been the work of a moment to cut my throat and cast me down into the water, to let me drown in blood and water alike. I would never have shown my back to them at any other time, but in that moment I knew that I was quite safe – even a man like Björn would respect the law of the duel.

On the island, each man to his task. Hakon and Gunnar each went to opposite corners, weapons in hand – Gunnar with that beautiful sword of his, Hakon with a plain, well-crafted axe, and each with a second weapon beside him if the first one failed. Hakon sat upon the ground, cross-legged and picking at the grass, even as Gunnar paced restlessly, making little cuts at the air as he moved.

It fell to the rest of us to prepare the ground. Snorri and Rolf, who had carried the oxhide with them, laid it upon the ground as though it were an inlaid cloak or spun from gold. They smoothed it down, leaving no fold that might taint the duel, and we staked it down and marked the borders. This was where they would fight, for it is not enough to duel on the scarce ground of the island, with no hope of retreat. Such a place must be reduced again, and it is only if a man is willing to step into a space that it is quartered, then quartered once more, that he has earned the right to fight in the *holmgang*.

Once, the duel could only be settled in death, but it is not so any more. If a man's foot strays even a finger-length from that hide, or if a single drop of blood falls upon it, the *holmgang* is ended. I have seen such duels concluded by the smallest of cuts: a splinter that flies from a breaking shield and cuts a man's face, a chip of iron from a sword giving a tiny wound between finger and thumb. I have heard tell of a *holmgang* that ended the moment it began, when a berserker's frenzy gave him a bleeding nose, and a spattering of drops stained the hide at his feet. I have seen the *holmgang* settled with a drop of a man's blood, and with all of it. Until the last shield is broken, one does not know what kind of a duel one will see.

I knelt to examine the three shields I was to carry, testing for some flaw in the wood that I would need to protect. I heard the footsteps behind me and expected it would be Gunnar. I had not been a shield-bearer before, and thought he might have some last words for me, for there are many tricks in the duel that one must be wise to, all the traps a shield-bearer must know.

Yet when I stood and turned, I found that it was Hakon. His axe was in his hand, but I felt no danger from him.

'You would rather be fighting me, I suppose?' I said.

'I do not wish to fight either of you.' He knelt beside me, chopped the axe into the earth and leaned upon it. 'If I did, it would be Gunnar. For it was not you that killed Erik, was it?'

I said nothing.

'I understand,' he said. 'It matters little to me, Kjaran. I know you are both honourable men, though how you let that witch trick you into this cowardice I do not know.' He looked towards the sky, as if he thought that he might find his answer there. 'I am ashamed of what Erik did. I am ashamed of what you both did.'

'As am I.'

'I have seen too many feuds in my life. Winters spent wishing that the spring will not come, and the killing summers that follow them. Waiting and killing, killing and waiting.' I saw the touch of silver at his temple, almost white under the bright sun. I wondered how many of his years he had spent in one feud or another.

'I have seen feuds myself. I never wish to see another.'

'If only it were up to us. Let us hope this duel is the end of it. Gunnar means to take some blood from me, that is all. He will give me a good scar to satisfy his honour. But I do not think he will kill me.' He gave the slightest trace of a smile. 'I hope not. I do not wish to die this day.'

'You might defeat him.'

'Defeat Gunnar? I do not think the gods are feeling so whimsical today. I cannot beat the man and I cannot beat that sword of his.' He must have seen something in my face, for after a moment he spoke again: 'But if I do, I will not kill him. I promise you that.'

'I thank you. Fight well, Hakon.'

'I will. There is no honour in this.'

'No. But there is nothing else to do.'

He nodded to me, took his axe from the ground and wiped the earth from it against his breeches. There was no need to wait any longer. There was nothing left to say, and so Hakon stepped on to the hide and said to Gunnar: 'Let us see if you are as good as they say.'

Gunnar came forward without a word and took up his stance. I was at his left, the sun sharp in my eyes until I raised my shield. Björn held the shield for his brother; he looked at me and said, 'A shameful thing, to have an outlaw carrying your shield.'

'He is no outlaw yet,' Gunnar replied. He looked at Vigdis – for she was there, silent and watchful at the edge of the hide. 'A shameful thing to have that woman here.'

'She is of our family now.'

'So I see. Be careful, Björn. She has buried two husbands already. If you could call Erik such a thing.'

Björn came forward snarling, all teeth and spit like a fighting dog, only to have Hakon once more restrain him. 'Enough, brother! I am the one who fights today.' He raised his axe and lowered it once more. He wiped his mouth with the back of his hand and spoke to Gunnar.

'Did you lie in the trial?'

'Lie about what?'

'Did he truly fight well?' Hakon said.

'What?'

'My brother. Did he fight well?'

Gunnar hesitated. 'Yes. He fought bravely. He died well.'

'I am glad. Come, let us begin.'

Gunnar rapped his sword against the shield I carried, Hakon did the same. And then the iron sang.

I saw only a moment of grey motion and then the wooden shield jumped and snapped at my face like a dog. A ringing close by, like a bell struck once, and then the shield shivered once more. That was all for those first few blows, for I had no time to think or to see, only to hear and to feel. The gasps Hakon made as he swung, Gunnar's soft exhalations, fighting in near silence. Leather biting into my hand, wood pressing into my arm. And pain.

It was only after five blows had struck my shield that I

began to see – yet still I saw only the weapons, not men who wielded them. The axe that rose and fell in the same way each time against my arm, a clumsy overhand blow more fit for chopping wood. The sword cutting in from a different angle each time, like a snake biting at a man. Hakon swung to break the shield, to force us to yield. Gunnar fought to pass the shield. He fought to kill.

We did not try to move. Footwork counts for nothing in the *holmgang*, the tricks of weight and balance rendered worthless. There is only strength and fate, and the courage to stand rooted to the spot, trading blow for blow.

Then the sun was in my eyes, sudden and blinding, as half of my shield snapped and broke away. The blows stopped falling, Hakon waiting as I picked the second of the three shields, shaking life back into his weary arm. His first shield, chipped and cracked, still stood guard. But already he was tired, gasping hard and leaning on his weapon. Gunnar was breathing easy, patient as a poet with half a hundred lines yet to sing. Soon, he would be singing in earnest. He smiled his murderer's smile and said: 'It is early to be so tired.'

'We shall see.'

There was the rapping of sword against shield, and then we began again.

But not for long. Hakon's shield broke in moments and Gunnar cut the air with his sword, impatient, as Björn took up the next shield. It seemed to slip from his fingers, falling back to the ground, and when he picked it up again and dropped it once more, I understood what he was doing.

'You are as slow as you are stupid,' Gunnar said.

'There is no need for that,' Hakon said to Björn, for he must have been ashamed of what his brother had done. He looked back on us, a ghost of a smile on his face. 'I am glad to see that you have decided to fight properly. I had thought your reputation unearned, the way you swung before.'

Gunnar nodded, as he might acknowledge a good play upon the chessboard, a good strike of the ball in a game upon the ice. The rapping of the shields and, once more, iron played against the wood.

But something had changed. Before, the blows had fallen on my shield hard enough to shake my teeth and numb my arm. Now it was as if a boy swung that axe, growing weaker with every strike.

A snapping of wood as Hakon's second shield broke, and there were no words this time. He simply stood, grey sweat pouring from his skin, his eyes dull with exhaustion. Gunnar was tiring too, but it was to compare the exhaustion of the wolf with that of the deer it is running down. Weak as the men were, it would take much time to break the next shield. Yet both already knew how it must end.

Hakon sobbed with effort as he swung, and he seemed to find some last remnant of strength. He knew he had no chance to win the duel. To lose by a single shield, that was all the ambition he had left, and I thought that I saw Gunnar, even in his cold rage, soften his blows a little. One cannot help but admire a hopeless bravery.

But though the man might have felt pity, that flawless sword of his did not. The last shield fell to pieces and Björn stood there, staring without comprehension at the broken wood that hung from his arm. Hakon took one last, hopeless swing at my shield, but it did nothing. Now was the time for him to take one step back to signal his retreat and end the fight, to buy back his life and honour in silver. But he did not. He lowered his axe and shifted out of his fighting stance, both legs side by side. He waited.

Gunnar checked the blow he was about to give.

'Step away,' Gunnar said. 'One foot from the hide will be enough. I will not strike a helpless man.'

'No,' Hakon said slowly, gulping for his breath like a drowning man, 'I will not yield. Take what you think is your due in blood. A drop, or all that I have.'

Gunnar did not strike. He understood what to do in the *holmgang* if a man ran or if he fought. He did not know what to do if he stood and spoke.

'Or if you will not,' Hakon said, 'perhaps there is another way.'

Björn whispered to his brother and I only heard one word of what he said: '…shameful…' And at this, Hakon lifted his chin proudly, shook his head, spoke again to Gunnar. 'There is no shame in this. Let us put our weapons down together. We will clasp our hands and swear a brotherhood. You have taken a brother from us. Let yourself replace him. And what need is there then, to make an outlaw of your friend?' He waited for a moment, the only sound the wind echoing across the plain. He shifted his axe to his left hand, offered an open right hand to Gunnar. Then he said: 'Would that not be beautiful?'

And there it was, something that few men live to see. The end of a feud, there so close and powerful that it feels like a living thing, rare as catching sight of some beast of legend. For so long will a feud seem as unalterable as fate, as inevitable as the rise and fall of the sun. And yet after months or years of blood and hate, the knots of the feud drawing ever tighter like the winding loop of a snare, a gift is offered; gold, a cup of mead, a promise. If the gift is taken, it is the end of the killing.

'I want no blood from you,' Gunnar said. He levelled the blade towards Vigdis. 'I would have fought her, if I could. But I cannot.' Slowly, his sword dipped towards the ground.

Vigdis looked on those brothers, Björn and Hakon, shield and sword. And she said a single word.

'Cowards.'

It was Björn who moved first. The broken shield cast to the ground, the knife in his hand. And Gunnar did not raise his sword – a warrior of so many battles, and for once he was caught defenceless, and I did not raise my shield in time. But I saw Hakon move, his axe falling to the ground, hands reaching up to delay his brother. And then, as if suddenly awoken, Gunnar struck.

There was an instant of movement, so fast that I saw nothing but the light of the sun on a blade. A red rain falling upon the ground.

I have never seen a faster move with a blade.

11

I have heard some bards describe the dead as if they are sleeping. Still, at peace, gone to the gods. Perhaps in older times that might have been true, for I have never seen it. Old men deformed by the plague, women killed in childbirth lying in a sea of blood, desiccated infants that weigh less than a loaf of bread, men torn open by axe and dagger – the dead I have seen have always seemed more like monsters than men.

Hakon was no different. His eyes rolled back in his head until only a sliver of black remained to discolour the white, mouth impossibly wide open and teeth bared in an endless scream. And a second mouth in his throat, the sharp white of bone within giving him a second set of teeth, his spine smiling through his neck.

I could taste his blood in my mouth, feel it dripping from my face. My feet were wet with it, my clothes hot with it.

Björn was on his knees before us, one hand against his brother's forehead, as though he were feeling for the heat of fever. As if this were a sickness that could be cured.

For a time he seemed to forget we were there. He simply knelt there, feeling his brother's skin turning cold beneath his hand, his lips moving soundlessly, his face like that of a man trying to answer a riddle.

'You meant to strike me, didn't you? he said at last. 'Not him.'

'Yes,' Gunnar replied. 'I swung at you.'

Björn let his head fall, his eyes returning to his brother. 'Will you kill me? I cannot live with this shame.'

Gunnar turned from him. 'Would the law let me kill him?' Gunnar said – matter-of-factly, as he might have asked about the pattern of the tides or the borders of a grazing ground. At first I thought he was speaking to me, but he looked beyond me, to where Olaf stood at the edge of the hide, his mouth slightly agape.

Olaf hesitated before he answered. 'Have you been wounded?' he said.

'No.'

'Then no,' Olaf said. 'Perhaps when he had a weapon in his hand, but now...'

'That is settled,' Gunnar said, not waiting for the chieftain to finish. 'I will not break the law for you, Björn.' He wiped the blood carefully from the sword. Then: 'We all learn to live in shame.'

'It is over,' Olaf said. 'Let all witness it. It is no crime to kill a man in the *holmgang*.'

'And what of him?' I said, speaking of Björn. 'He broke the code of the duel.'

'He has lost another brother. Do you not think that payment enough?'

'And her?' Gunnar said. 'What of Vigdis?'

'A woman's words mean nothing to the law. It is no crime to speak as she did.'

'The law has fed well today,' Gunnar said, his lips curled

with disgust. He at last stepped from the hide, the blood still wet upon him, and I saw all those there take a half-step back, as if he were some monster from the old times. I wondered if that was how the stories would speak of him in the centuries to come. If they would speak of him at all.

The others stepped back and parted before him, and he made his way to the edge of the island, sword still in his hand. Before he walked down to the river he turned back, levelled that blade at the swollen belly of Vigdis.

'I cannot kill you,' he said. 'But I pray that you have a son. Perhaps then I will settle my debt.'

'You are a murderer,' she said.

'No,' he said, by way of correction. 'I am a killer.'

And that is how he earned his name. That is how they shall always know him. Gunnar the Killer.

The others went south. Back to the plain at the heart of the Althing, bearing the body and the news as well. Only Gunnar and I lingered behind, in view of that island which had seen so much killing.

We washed the blood from ourselves as best we could, watching it redden the waters for a moment before it eddied downstream, but our efforts were of little use. For months afterward I would find some black fragment beneath my fingernails and wonder if it might be some dried drop of blood from that day; some dark smear upon my tunic, and wonder whether it came from the earth or from a man.

Gunnar and I did not speak for a long time. Stripped naked and scouring the blood from our bodies with sand, rubbing stones against our sodden clothing to work out the gore, dressing and lying on the stones in the sun and waiting for the heat to dry us out – all was done in silence. Only the sound of the wandering water, the occasional snort and whicker from the black horse that was the cause of that duel. Our bloody prize.

At last, Gunnar said: 'Once more I have killed the wrong man.'

He began to tremble and I thought at first he was shaking from the cold, for his clothes were still wet. When the shaking grew stronger, I thought it might be some sudden palsy, a curse from the gods for the blood he had spilt. It took me longer than it should to realise that he had begun to weep.

I held him then, as I might have held a child. It was a shameful thing he did, but I suppose that he had earned that sadness. I tried to forgive him his tears.

'You could have killed the right one,' I said. 'He asked you to.'

'Björn knew that I would not do it. But he wanted to be seen to ask.' He pushed me away and got to his feet. 'I wish I had not killed his brother. It was needless.'

'The duel was your doing.'

'I know. I wanted to kill him, at first. But when he spoke…' He looked at me and hesitated. 'Have you ever killed a man?'

'I killed Erik.'

He waved a hand at me. 'Before him.'

'No,' I said, and he looked at me in disbelief, as though I had told him that I had never lain with a woman. 'Who was the first man that you killed?' I asked.

'I cannot remember,' he said.

A killer for as long as he could remember, unable to recall a time before he had been a taker of life. I thought of him as he must have been when it had first happened: a boy who had lied about his age, tricking his way on to the longship of one captain or another. Shivering and vomiting on his first voyage to the west, shamed by the mocking laughter of the other men. In his first battle he would have been kept at the back behind those more skilled or experienced or eager for death, unable to see the fighting, only to hear it.

His first kill would have been finishing a wounded man: some Saxon warrior lying on the ground, wrapped up in his own entrails, whose last sight in the world was a pale-faced boy kneeling beside him, knife in hand. Or it might have been some helpless priest who fell at Gunnar's knees during the looting, begging for a mercy that could not come. Perhaps that was why he had forgotten the killing. Perhaps it had been a shameful thing.

'What shall we do now?' I said.

He turned to the west, where the endless sun guided a way across the land.

'Let us go home,' he said.

He insisted that I ride the horse. He would not listen to my protests; having killed for it, he almost seemed to fear to touch it.

No doubt it should have been a miserable journey, and no doubt both of us should have spent it looking on the ruins of our lives. I would soon be an outlaw, exiled from my home, perhaps forever. He was hopelessly caught in the feud; for the rest of his life, he would have to watch for those who would come seeking revenge.

Yet I remember days spent singing songs as we walked and rode, and whenever we saw a farm we would shy around it, stopping only to trade for bread and ale when we had to. It was one of the blessed summers, rainless and clear-skied, that seems like it cannot end.

I wish that it had not. When we came at last to the hill that overlooked Gunnar's farm, we knew that we were returning to the world of the feud.

'Do you think they know?' I asked him.

He stared down at the smoke that rose from the house.

'She will know,' he said. 'Perhaps she has not told the children. But soon they will know too.'

'Do you want to wait? We can stay here as long as you want.'

'No.' He shook his head. 'We will go now. There is nothing else to do.'

I had thought we would return to anger or to tears. Perhaps Gunnar had, too, for he trod as carefully to his own front door as a man approaching bandit country. But when he stepped through the door into that welcoming darkness, Dalla stood and clasped him by the shoulder, handed him a cup of water and spoke as though she were a chieftain giving orders.

'Sit and rest,' she said. 'Soon we shall have much to do. You shall need your rest.'

And so we sat without a word, and in spite of it all I saw a small smile playing over Gunnar's lips. We should not have been surprised. She was a woman of the feuds, a warrior's wife.

It was the children who had changed. No doubt their mother had tried to tell them of the feud, and no doubt they could not understand. They came forward at first, almost to the point of embracing us, and then they shied away from us, huddling in the shadows.

It is a painful thing, to see children run from you. I slipped from my bench and knelt upon the floor, held out my hand to Kari.

'I have a good story to tell you. Of duels and betrayals. Of exile and of vengeance. You have always liked such stories before. Why should this be any different?'

Uncertain, he looked to his father.

'There is trouble coming, my son,' said Gunnar.

'Will there be killing?

'I hope not. But it may come to that.' Gunnar lifted his chin, looked questioningly down at his boy. 'Will you fight beside us, if it comes to that?'

Kari smiled then and nodded.

'The cub has fangs,' Dalla said.

'Good. He shall need them.' Gunnar stood.

The boy turned to me. 'You will fight with us, Kjaran?'

'I cannot stay.'

Dalla, who had gone to tend the cooking fire, went still. She put her hand against the timber of that house, her fingers tracing along the whorls of the wood. I could see her eyes glittering in the darkness as she looked at me.

'Where is it that you go?'

'I am to be an outlaw. Ragnar shall take me from this island.'

She turned her head from me to Gunnar, and returned her eyes to me. 'You take a heavy burden, Kjaran. I shall not forget this.'

A moment of silence that I could not find the words to break. Then Gunnar clapped his hands.

'Come, Kari,' he said. 'I brought home a gift for you. All of you, come with me.'

Out in the light once more, and looking upon Gunnar's land I could almost forget the feud. How could any man come to a place like this and think of bloodshed? A simple farm, crops hard fought from stubborn soil. The only sounds that of running water, the occasional faint creak of a few trees against the wind.

Yet I had only to look further to see the feud with my own eyes. The fold of land that marked the borders of Vigdis's home. The distant coil of smoke that rose from the house of Björn. We were all so close together – nothing but a few miles apart. For when the valley is at peace, one may look through it and see every friend one has in the world. In the time of feud, a man must look on the home of the man who has killed his brother every day as he works his fields and tends his herds. Every day he is reminded of his shame, his dishonour. How can there be peace in such a land? What amount of silver, paid to settle a feud, can hope to buy away that shame?

The horse, new come to this place, only seemed to fix that image more truly. Tied to one of the outbuildings, tall and black and brilliant, the sun on its flanks. No beast of labour, but certainly not one of war. A treasure in flesh, a gift of love, and at the sight of it Kari forgot to pretend to be a man. He was a boy once more, reaching out shyly to take his father's hand in thanks, in love. Then his sister spoke.

'A red horse, a red horse!'

I felt the cold touch of a god upon my shoulder. 'The horse is black, child.'

'Have you lost your wits?' Gunnar snapped.

She stammered. 'It is red to me,' she said, not yet wise enough to lie.

We said nothing for a time.

'A trick of the light,' I said at last, when I saw that no other would break the silence.

'Yes,' Dalla said. 'A trick of the light.' But her voice was hollow and I could see the clouding of her eyes. Perhaps she knew what her daughter saw. Perhaps she saw it too. 'And what do we do now?' she said to Gunnar.

He did not take his eyes from the horse. 'We will hold a feast,' he said. 'For Winter Nights. To say farewell to our friend, and to see who will not be afraid to stand beside us.'

'There is much to consider.'

'Yes. But there is something else we must do first. Come with me, Kjaran.'

'Where are we going?'

He did not answer, he simply pointed up to the outcrops above us, back to the high ground. I knew then what he intended.

'Where will they come from, do you think?' I said, once we had both caught our breath.

Gunnar's eyes passed over the shape of the land, looking at it with his raider's eyes, searching for weaknesses. 'Not from the hills. They would be exposed as they approach, slowed in retreat.'

'It will be from the stream, then. The sound of the water will cover their approach. Low ground to conceal them.'

'You have a good eye. But they can do better. And keep their feet dry.' He extended an arm, mimicking the flow of the ground with the palm of his hand. 'It will be from the ground to the east of the river.'

I looked to where he gestured and I saw it then, as clear as a vision from the gods – the future, or the possibility of a future, at least. A band of armed men, moving in the darkness, no moon in the sky above them. Creeping along the undulating terrain to the east of the river, using the rolling ground to conceal themselves. Each with a hand on the shoulder of the man in front to guide the way, as if they were a band of blinded killers, hunting by sound and scent. They would come through the few trees and fall upon the house from the south. The striking of a spark, the lighting of a torch. And then fire. After the fire, the killing.

'And they can retreat along the riverbed,' I said. 'Afterwards.'

'That is right.' His lips twitched; proud of me, perhaps, for learning from him.

'When will they come?'

'Perhaps they will come scouting soon. But it is too soon for the killing. It will take them time to gather enough men. Time for us – for me – to gather men of my own.'

'They may not come at all.'

'Do you really believe that?'

'How many will stand by you in the feud?'

'Not enough.'

I did not answer, and looked again at the land below. My eyes fell once more on that scattering of trees – not forest, barely even a copse. There had been great forests in this land once, but almost all were gone now, cut and burned and they would not grow back again. Those few thin trees were a wealth in wood for an Icelander. I had seen Gunnar sit by the fire at night, listening to the creaking of the wind against the wood, and smiling like a wealthy man looking upon a horde of gold.

'We will cut those down,' I said. 'They will give them cover when they come.'

'A shame to lose the trees. I had hoped to see a forest there one day, when my beard was grey.' He sighed. 'But you are right.'

'The forest would never grow back.'

'It would not?'

'No others have.'

Movement caught my eye. It was Kari and the horse, the boy leading it by the bridle, not yet daring to ride it, circling again and again around the long house. From time to time he would pause, place his hand on the horse's nose or curl his fingers into its mane, showing the patient love that only a child has.

Gunnar scratched at his beard to hide his smile, but I knew that it was there.

'I told him that he was not to take the horse beyond the cattle shed,' he said, 'but I see he has found a way around my command. I expect he will be out there all day.'

'They may kill me as an outlaw, and kill you in the feud in a year. But we cannot change what has been done. And for now, your boy has a horse and he smiles.'

He cocked his head, baffled.

'Poet's talk,' I said. 'Forgive me.'

'I do not understand when you speak in this way.' He touched me on the shoulder, briefly. 'But still, I like to listen.'

'I suppose you must listen while you can. You will soon be rid of me.'

'When will you leave?'

'A fortnight. A few days longer, perhaps, if I am willing to take a chance on the tides. But it would be a pitiful death, would it not? Sitting in a port, outlawed as I waited for the wind to change.'

'I would stand against them, if it came to that.'

'You would fight the entire island? That is what it would come to.'

'I would try.'

I looked away, for there was something in his eyes that I did not like to look upon. A kind of madness that I had no name for.

'Come. We must go back down. There is much to be done. I will help you all I can. But we do not have much time.'

'No. We do not.' He turned away, out towards the sea. We could see it, but not hear it at this distance. Any whispered wisdom it might have had for us, it could not reach us. 'And there is something else for us to plan, before you go.'

'And what is that?'

He looked on me once more, his smile as sudden and brilliant as dawn upon the water. 'A celebration, of course.'

12

It was an early harvest we had that year. A harvest of wood, weapons, promises. For those in the feud, the long days of midsummer are the hardest months, the most dangerous. It is the killer's season, and it offers no respite.

We worked every hour the day gave us: cutting the trees and stripping the wood, gathering stones to build a palisade around the farm. Most days I spent working side by side with Dalla, her dress hitched high and sleeves rolled up, as strong as any man. The children helped as much as they could, and Gunnar too, but he had other matters to attend to. Travelling from one farm to another, bearing wood, ale, meat, silver. Offering gifts, promising a celebration, asking for their oaths in return, to stand beside him when the time came. And at night, we prepared for the feast.

We spoke together of who we would invite, casting our minds back over the years, trying to remember all of those men who might owe us the debt of friendship. For Gunnar had few kin on the island, and I none at all. We thought of men we had traded with years before, exchanged stories with, those who had sheltered me in winters past, whom I thought might be keen to fight. We collected those names by night, repeated them together again and again like prayer, and in the days Gunnar would go to them and ask for their help.

Sometimes he came back with promises, and sometimes even with company, men who came to look at the farm and pledge their loyalty in front of Gunnar's family. But there were not many of them: a pair of brothers who Gunnar had once made a gift to; an old fisherman who liked to hear me sing; Dalla's brother from the north. And too many of those who did come had that doubting look to them that I could not trust. They ate the meat and drank the ale, promised they would return for the feast, boasted of how keen they were for the fighting to begin. But I am a poet, and know a poor performer when I see one.

Once, as we discussed who else we might ask to our harvest feast, I dared to speak a more familiar name.

'You must invite Olaf,' I said.

'The Peacock? He will not come. He wishes nothing more to do with us.'

'But you must invite him. He is a proud man. You do not need him at your side, but he must not turn against you. Invite him and let him say no.'

Gunnar thought on this for a time, rubbing the knuckles of one hand with the dirty palm of the other.

'We do not have many who will stand with us, do we?'

'No. And they have the chieftain, Hallstein.'

'Vigdis's father.' He shook his head. 'It disgusts me. Begging for favours from cousins and cowards. And this is what it comes to, does it not? They have a powerful friend and I do not. Björn, Snorri, none of them could face me in the *holmgang*.'

'But you cannot fight them all.' I paused, then said: 'I will go to Olaf. He may favour me a little more than he does you.'

'I doubt that.' I saw the white of Gunnar's teeth shining in the light of the fire. 'But I think there is someone else there that you wish to see.'

'Of course.'

At this, Dalla spoke: 'Who is that?'

'A woman,' Gunnar said. 'A servant of Olaf.'

'A lover?' she said, her tone carefully neutral. 'You will go tomorrow?'

'Yes.'

'I do not know what gifts we have…'

'We will offer none,' I said. 'There is nothing we could give to Olaf that would not insult him.'

'Very well.' She stood and struck the dust from her dress, and went to tend the fire. When she had gone to the other side of the long house, the children at her side, Gunnar leaned forward and whispered to me. 'Be careful when you travel.'

'They have been watching you?'

'I cannot be certain. But I think so.'

'How many?'

'Only ever one or two. And they could be farmers from another valley. But I do not think so.'

'You believe they mean to strike at us this summer?'

'No, they only mean to watch us, for now. But if they get a chance…'

I raised a hand to silence him. 'Then I will not give them that chance.'

I kept to the high ground, following the ridgelines and staying away from the narrow defiles below. If one knows it well enough, ours is not a country that suits thieves and murderers, aside from the maze of valleys farther to the north. In the daylight, up on the hills, I would see any band of men long before they could come for me. If only the sun would never set – for when the darkness comes, ghosts and killers alike may walk free.

The great longhouse was before me soon enough, the sweet smoke of cooking fires rising from it, the servants working in the fields, the fat cattle wandering, content. The kind of home that all who came to Iceland dreamed of, had been promised, and yet so few would ever have.

I took a moment to measure the point of the sun in the sky, to see how much time I had before the killer's darkness fell across the land. Long enough. I took a breath, put a hand to the axe at my hip, and stepped inside.

There was silence as I entered. It took my eyes time to match the darkness, and no words were spoken. I stood, sightless and soundless, waiting. And when at last I could see, every man's eyes were on me.

There were those who looked upon me as if I were an outlaw, with a hungry, murderous gaze. They must have not been counting the days, and did not know that I had a little time left. I saw one man lay a hand to the weapon at his side and half-rise, but then he looked to his unmoving companions and realised his mistake. I was not yet a man outside of the law.

There were others who stared at me with a kind of pity, as they might favour a dying man. Others simply seemed curious, glad of the entertainment I might provide, for it is good sport to watch the feuds if one lies outside them. But there was only one there who looked on me with hatred. A woman's eyes, for Vigdis sat at the table beside Olaf, her belly heavy with child.

She stood as I looked at her, and a pair of men whom I did not know rose with her. Her kin or those of Björn, perhaps.

She walked past me, her head high. And the silence held after she had left, until Olaf broke it.

'What is this?' he said to his men. 'Are you dumb beasts? Talk! Sing! And offer greetings to our guest.' He came forward and clasped my arm. 'For all men are welcome here,' he said, as the men around us began to talk once more.

'My thanks, Olaf.'

'Will you stay to eat?'

'I must return before dark.'

'Of course,' he said, guiding me to a seat. 'Then what brings you to me?'

'Gunnar holds a feast a week from now, to celebrate the coming of the harvest. He invites you to join him.'

He said nothing for a time. His fingers drummed upon the table.

'I thank you for your courtesy,' he said. 'But I will not trouble Gunnar's patience. The man has little love for me.'

'What matters his love? You would do him great honour to attend.'

'I do not care to honour him.'

'But you honour Vigdis?'

He looked at me levelly and made no reply.

'Will you stand with them, Olaf?'

'I will not stand with them. Or with you. I take no side in this petty feud.'

'Then why was she here?'

'A matter of business. She wishes to sell her farm to me.'

'And what did you tell her?'

'What does that matter to you?'

'I wish to know what she does.'

'It matters not to you. Your feud is with the brothers, not with her.'

'You are not a fool, Olaf. Do not talk as one.'

A nearby warrior stood, his hand to his weapon. But Olaf waved him back. 'Sit down,' he said. 'And do not listen so closely to the talk of other men.' He turned back to me. 'You are right. But you must forget her. There is nothing you can do against her.'

'She has learned that, hasn't she? That is what makes her so dangerous.'

Olaf nodded. 'My sister, Hallgerd… she has learned it too. Two husbands dead and nothing that any man will do against her. There is only one thing that you can do against one like that.'

'What?'

'Leave her no weapon to use against you. Kill every man in her life,' he said, simply and plainly, and took a sip of his mead. I drank, too, and we did not speak for a time. What Olaf thought of, I cannot say.

'It will be your farewell, this feast?' Olaf said, after a time.

'It shall.'

'You should have begun with that. It tempts me more to honour you than it does to honour Gunnar.'

'But you still will not come?'

'No. And I think that it was not I who you truly came to talk to.'

I knew she was there, but I did not look at her once. I wanted to savour the feeling of her eyes upon me. When I turned to look at Sigrid, she met my gaze openly, glanced at Olaf, and returned to her work.

When I looked back on the chieftain, his face held a weary sadness. 'Will you let her go?' he said. 'She is a handsome woman. There are many who might wed her.'

'Better men?'

'Richer men. Men who are not outlaws.'

'It is not my choice to make.'

'You could free her if you chose to. Drive her from you. Some would call it mercy.'

'I will come back for her. We will be poor and we will be happy. I do not expect you to understand.'

'You will not come back.'

'Another of your prophecies?'

'One does not need such a gift to see that.'

'I will come back. I will marry her. I swear to both of those things.'

'In time you will regret that oath, I think. But as you wish.' He clasped my hand. 'Go now. I wish that things had been otherwise.'

I stood, but I did not leave at once. I lingered a moment longer in the hall of the great chieftain, thinking that it might be the last time I stood in such a place. For the first time that I could remember I wished that I might have been such a chieftain as Olaf.

It was not for the food piled high on the tables, the scarlet clothes of Olaf, the tracts of farmland that stretched outside, the great horde of gold and silver that was locked away in wooden chests. It was not for his fame or prestige. It was for the men he had there. The warriors who would stand at his side in any feud.

Had Gunnar and I but half those warriors sworn to us, we would have nothing to fear. When you see a man wearing gold rings and scarlet cloth – what does that matter, so long as one is warm? Why envy a farmer with three hundred head in cattle if one has food enough, or one who owns half a valley if one has a small farm to call one's own? But I understood too late why one might crave wealth and power. For in the feud, they count for everything.

When Sigrid came outside the longhouse, she carried a pail in her hands – her excuse, no doubt, for she cast it to the ground as soon as she was past the threshold.

'There is no need for pretence,' I told her. 'Olaf knows and he will not stand in our way.'

'Oh, I know that well enough.'

I went to speak, but found that I could not.

She cocked her head to the side and said, 'What is it you see, when you look on me?'

'Your eyes. I had not noticed before.' For there was a circle of green within the blue of her eyes that I had not seen. Too faint to see in the darkness inside, and when we met by daylight I had not dared to look so closely, it had not seemed right. Yet now we would be married I could look upon her as I wished.

'A touch of the fey, they call it,' she said.

'I can well believe it.'

'You should not have come here,' she said. 'It angers him to see you. Or it saddens him, I cannot tell.'

'I do not care what Olaf thinks or feels. I came to see you.'

'Why?'

'I am afraid.'

'Of what are you afraid?'

'I am afraid you will change your mind.'

She laughed. 'There is no need. You will keep your promise?'

'I will keep my promise. I will come back.'

'Then you have nothing to fear.' She must have seen some doubt or fear in my face, for she gave a tolerant smile. 'I keep my word,' she said. 'Have no doubt of that.'

'You will wait for me?'

'Yes. I will wait.'

And she stood up on her toes, put her arms around my neck. Her grip was strong, as if she were some warrior, and she stopped my breath with one patient kiss after another.

I knew that there were no others like her. If I lost her, I would not find another woman to take her place.

These are the kinds of thoughts that young men speak and old men admonish. But I am old myself now, as I tell this story, and I can tell you that it is the old men who lie. They have made themselves forget what it is to love, have found a way to lie to themselves, to settle for some marriage of politics or swiftly dulling lust.

But I will not lie to myself. And I will not lie to you. There is love and there are few who truly taste of it. It is spilt once and lost forever.

13

I had seen feuds before this one: petty things, squabbles over cattle, a horse-fight, a wager. Yet I had never been at the heart of one myself, had never known what it was to be hunted. I learned that feeling then as I came back from Olaf's home, the taste of a woman still upon my lips.

As I retraced my steps along the high path I saw the signs of another man's passage. A branch bent back beyond the power of the wind, the shallow hollow in the stream bed that marked where a booted foot had pressed into it.

At first I tried to tell myself that it was some stray animal that had disturbed the ground, some trick of the mind or a wandering spirit of the hidden people that was toying with me. I would rather it had been some faerie than a man, for I feared flesh and iron more than magic. But I knew it was not true. Man and animal are alike in one way at least. They both know when they are being pursued.

It was not long before I saw the men who followed. Moving shadows on the neighbouring hills that froze still when I looked upon them. And I heard them too, the wind bringing whispers and voices of men who did not know they could be overheard.

I looked to the sun and saw that I had less time left than I had thought. Yet I could not hurry, be reckless. I have never been so careful with every step that I made, for it would take so little to leave me lame. A knee wrenched from a slipping patch of mud and earth, an ankle shattered by a misplaced step upon a rocking stone. They would see me fall and I would have to wait for them to come to me like an animal in a pit trap, hearing the heavy footfall of the farmer who comes to take its life.

Every so often I would stop and look back on those shadows in the distance, but they never drew any closer. They went still when I looked upon them. Perhaps they did not know my eyes to be as keen as they were, and thought they might have some chance to surprise me. But I think it was that they felt no hurry. I would be an outlawed man in a few weeks' time, free to be hunted with no consequence.

For now, they were content to watch.

Gunnar must have been running one errand or another – watching the herd, building walls, sharpening weapons, with his children at his side and the sun on his back – for he was not within the longhouse. I was glad that he was not there, would not ask what I had seen. Only Dalla sat there, tending the cooking fire.

If I hoped to keep my secrets to myself, it was an empty hope, soon cast aside. The story must have been written on my face, for as she looked at me Dalla's smile flickered and faded. She gestured for me to sit with a slight motion of her hands, and we shared the silence for a time.

'Gunnar was right, then,' she said. 'They are out there, watching.'

'Yes.'

'Did they try to catch you?'

'No. Only to watch.' I looked at my hands. 'And Vigdis was there. At Olaf's home.'

'I see. On what matter?'

'He says that she wishes to sell her farm to him.'

'Do you believe him?'

'I believe him. Still, it is an ill omen.'

She turned her head slowly and looked about her home, placed her palm against the wall and leaned gently against it. 'I always knew that I would die in this place,' she said. 'But I thought that I would have more time.'

'It will not come to that.'

'Perhaps.' She busied herself about the longhouse and I tended to myself, drinking a horn of water and washing the dirt from my hands and face. I was careful not to wipe my lips, to not lose any remnant of the kiss Sigrid had given me. I wondered how long into exile years that memory, that taste, might last. How long before I would forget.

'Will you do something for me, Kjaran?'

I started a little at her words. 'Anything that I can.'

'Will you take me to see Vigdis tomorrow?'

I did not answer for a time. I stared at her, waiting for her to withdraw the suggestion, to say that she had misspoken. But she held my gaze and did not say a word. Her courage was greater than mine.

'Gunnar would not agree to that,' I said.

'Gunnar will not know.' She leaned forward and said: 'I know you do not wish to keep secrets from him. But there is a chance that I can end this feud.'

'How?'

'A woman's words can matter more than a man's. Has not the feud so far proved this? She is the heart of it, is she not?'

'Yes.'

'You cannot kill her. I may speak with her.'

'It will be no use.'

'Perhaps. But think of Olaf. You had to ask, even though you knew he would say no? It is no different.'

I opened my mouth to speak again, to find some new argument against what she suggested. But it did not come, for there was no case against it, except one: I was afraid to go back to that place. I was afraid of Vigdis.

'I will do it,' I said. 'When do we go?'

'Tomorrow. After midday. Gunnar and the children will be out with the herd. We shall have time enough.'

The silence returned and we listened together to the burning of wood, the wind against the walls, the bubbling of stew in the pot. We sat together and I let myself dare to hope a little.

The mist came from the sea like an invading army, a relentless advance in close formation, covering the land in every direction. And so when Dalla and I made to leave there were no landmarks for us to navigate by. We travelled by our instincts, our luck, and my memories of the way.

'An ill omen,' I said to her as we set out.

'Perhaps,' she said, but she did not seem troubled by it. 'Or a protection from those who might hunt us.'

I felt the chill that any man may feel at the chance of witchcraft. 'Is this your doing?'

She laughed at me. 'No. I do not have the art.'

'It would not surprise me if Vigdis does, for all the trouble she has made.'

'No. If she did, she would have no need of men to do her

bidding, would she? Her curses alone would be enough.' The smile fell away from her face. 'Come. We must hurry.'

The rolling of the wind, the patter of the rain; these sounds kept us company as we travelled. When we began our journey I doubted that I would find the way; perhaps I hoped I would not be able to. That we would wander lost in the mist until it was time to return home.

But though I had not travelled to Vigdis's house since the night of Erik's killing, the way seemed clearly marked in my mind as though we had left a trail only I could see. I remembered the little pyramid of stones Gunnar and I had passed in moonlight, laughing and singing together early in the journey. I remembered the rippled hillside, where we had waited for the clouds to clear from the moon and light our way once more. And I remembered the still tarn on high ground, where we had washed the blood and dirt from our hands after the killing. Soon enough there was a shadow in the mist ahead, a brooding black shape like a whale swimming beneath the waves.

'That is it?' Dalla said.

'Yes,' I said. I saw the blood beating beneath the skin of her neck, saw her pale skin whiten to the colour of bone. 'We may still go back, if you wish.'

'I am afraid,' she said softly. 'But no. We cannot go back. Whatever is said, promise that you will not speak. You and Gunnar have done enough already. You must let me try now.'

'As you wish.'

A farm in peace has a welcoming untidiness to it: pails and tools scattered in the field, animals wandering freely, doors left open and unbarred. In a feud, nothing is left to chance. Animals leashed and tools put away, fences without gaps and horses in the field that are unfamiliar with one another, snorting and circling each other like men in a fist fight. There too, through the mist, I could see a man standing at the door to the longhouse, bored and uneasy.

By chance or by fate it was a man I had seen on guard for Olaf: Ketil Hakonsson. For a moment he seemed to mistake me for someone else, his face half-breaking into a welcoming smile, still fixed in the habits of peacetime. Then he knew me for who I was.

I held my hands up and said, 'Hold. We come to speak, not to fight.'

'It could be a trick,' he said, half-drawing the axe from his belt, licking lips suddenly struck dry with fear.

What stories they must have told him of me, I thought. That I was a murderer in the night. A landless wanderer who brought blood and chaos with him. A man who held the shield of Gunnar the Killer. Some kind of monster, and now he stood face to face with me.

Then Dalla spoke: 'He would not come with a woman at his side, would he?'

He started and looked on her as though seeing her for the first time.

'Who are you?' he said.

'Dalla Egilsdottir. Wife to Gunnar. And I come to speak with Vigdis.'

'Very well,' he said. 'I will ask her.' His eyes danced over the blade at my hip. 'Will you agree to leave your weapon here, if she says yes?'

'I mean you no harm, friend. But I shall not walk into that house without a weapon. I am sure that you have many men in there. If you choose to murder me, I cannot stop you. But I will die with a blade in my hand. And there will be blood on it, before the end.'

He shivered a little and I could not help but feel a little pity for him. He had no place in the feud. I hoped that I would never have to fight him.

'But listen,' I said. 'I swear to you on my honour that I shall not be the first to draw iron, if it comes to that. We came to talk, not to die.'

He swallowed and nodded, and went inside. We waited.

'My thanks to you, Kjaran,' Dalla said.

'Why?'

'I see now the risk you took in coming here.'

The door opened once more and the young warrior appeared to us again. He looked more afraid than he had before. He tried to speak, but could not. He merely beckoned us to enter.

I pressed one hand to my eye before we entered, giving it a chance to adjust to the dark. With that eye, I counted the men within and marked where they stood. Five, and none of them men I knew well, but if anything it made me more wary than before. Had there been ten of them, they would have had the confidence of their numbers, would have had nothing to fear from me. Five was too many to fight, too few to trust.

Vigdis sat in the high chair: a queen of her little kingdom, an heir growing thick in her stomach. She kept us waiting there with royal contempt, even as the men eyed us fearfully, lost in that silence.

Perhaps she thought we would turn to bloodshed for lack of anything else to do; had it been I alone, she might have been right, for men fear the silence. But Dalla was her match in patience. She stood, her weight evenly balanced and her hands clasped in front of her, and waited for her host to speak.

'Dalla,' Vigdis said at last. 'Or are you called Flat Nose? Why have you come here to insult me?'

'I did not come to insult you.'

'You come with a murderer at your side.'

'He knew the way. I would have come alone.'

'Your husband knows the way. Why not bring him?'

'I think it is better that he is not here. Don't you?'

'I suppose that is true. Very well, I give you my hospitality.'

The low fire hissed at us; the mead was warm and strong against my lips. I heard men moving behind me and fought the urge to turn and watch them. One brushed against me, perhaps hoping I would do something foolish that might justify a killing. I kept my eyes ahead, on Vigdis, and watched her restless hands return again and again to her stomach.

'You have not had a child before?' Dalla asked.

'It will be my first,' Vigdis replied.

'It is a wonderful thing.'

'It is the greatest thing. Do you not agree?'

'No. There are other things that make me happier. But I am glad of my children.'

'What can be better than a child?'

Dalla bit her lip and looked to the table.

'Why have you come here?' Vigdis said.

'I come to seek peace between our families.'

'Blood has been spilt twice on our side. Erik and Hakon. And you have suffered nothing.' She pointed to me. 'This slave's son will be an outlaw for three years, and you think that justice?'

'The law calls it justice.' She drank and placed the cup down with a careful motion. 'But no, I do not call it justice.'

'Then what can you offer me?'

Dalla looked to me, but only for a moment. I understood then.

She meant to give me up to them. That was why she had brought me here. She would give me up to save her family.

I let my hand wander, slowly, slowly, to the weapon at my side. I would kill one, at least, when she made the offer.

'You asked something of me before,' Dalla said. 'Of my husband. That he would cast me aside and marry you.'

Vigdis cocked her head to the side. 'Yes,' she said. 'I remember.'

Dalla faltered for a moment. Unable to hold the other woman's gaze, she looked to the ground. 'If that is still what you want. You may have him.'

She could not look at me either, but she must have sensed my movement. For without looking she raised a hand, palm towards me, telling me to wait.

Vigdis sat in complete stillness, as if she were a carving of stone. 'You would do that?' she said.

'If it would bring an end to the feud. Yes.'

'Gunnar would do it?'

Dalla raised her head once more, and there was pride in her voice. 'If I asked him, he would.'

Vigdis paused for a long time, considering what had been said. The low hum of other men's talk had ceased entirely, warriors and servants alike looking and listening to our conversation alone. Their faces uncomprehending, for we might have been speaking another tongue entirely: this strange duel was one that they could not understand.

'That time has passed,' Vigdis said. 'That is not what I want.'

'What is it you want of me, then?'

'I want you to die.'

Dalla gave no response – not a flinch, nor even a blink. Not at first. But then her head dipped a little, her shoulders rose a little, as if some iron weight had been hung from her neck. Yet her expression did not change, even as she simply asked: 'Why?'

'He said that he would kill my child, if he could. What forgiveness can there be for that?'

'A man may say many things when his blood is up.'

'Oh, he meant what he said. I saw it in him. There will be no settlement. No trading of blood for silver. Only of blood for blood.'

'You could end this whenever you wish.'

'Yes, I could. But I do not want to.'

I have seen men when they are about to die in battle. Cut and wounded, shield broken and no ally to help them. They always come forward, make one last attack. Even if they know that it can do no good, for there is nothing left for them to do. Many do it smiling, thinking of the glory that waits for them in the next world. Others go with a studied seriousness, focusing only on that moment, that last moment, and thinking of nothing else. And so it was that Dalla raised her head and said: 'Your first husband, Hrapp. He must have been as evil as they say, to have given you such hate.'

'No,' Vigdis said. 'I think it was I who made him that way.'

We did not speak for a time, after we left the longhouse. We moved fast, to get to the higher ground where we might not be taken by surprise. Before, I would not have thought that they would attack us, that they would dishonour themselves by murdering a woman. After hearing Vigdis speak, I did not know what I believed.

We pushed hard, lungs burning and legs heavy, until we reached the tarn. There we rested and drank, and soaked water into rags that we held to our skin.

There was every reason to hurry and none at all to wait. Yet when we had finished, I found that I did not want to leave.

It seemed that Dalla felt it too. We lingered. I waited for her to speak.

I thought of the winter past. Of all the times I had lain awake at night and listened to Gunnar and to Dalla, listened to their lovemaking.

For there is no privacy in such a place – no privacy except the darkness. In such a home, especially in winter, there is not a thing that one does not know about the other.

There are some who would have a fascination for listening to the practices of a husband and his wife, or lonely men who might nurse their jealousy and resentment like a man sharpening a spear. It meant nothing to me.

But I remember once that I wished to look upon them, like those heroes of the old stories who long to look upon that which is forbidden. And I remember seeing that she looked back upon me. Just the white of her eyes, glinting like silver in the night. And a thing unspoken passed between us, though I could not say what it was.

'Taking me there cannot have been easy,' she said.

'What do you mean?'

'You could not feel it?'

'I do not understand.'

'It was not a ghost you killed that night,' she said, 'but that house is full of them. You truly did not feel it?'

'No.'

'I thought that a poet would see it even better than I. No matter. Perhaps it takes a woman to know it.'

'To know what?'

She shook her head. 'I do not want to think of what has happened in that place. What has been said and done there. It is a place of horrors.' She clasped her hands together. 'What will we do now?' she said.

I did not reply for a time. Then I said: 'I thought that you meant to offer me up to them. That you thought to buy Gunnar's life with mine.'

'I would have done, if I thought that it would do any good. Does that surprise you?'

'No. I would not blame you for it. We would both do anything for Gunnar.'

She nodded. 'Yes. We have that much in common.' She rolled a hand through the waters of the tarn and watched the ripples run. 'May I tell you something?'

'Of course.'

'I met Gunnar when he had just come to this land,' she said. 'A Viking bearing a small hoard of gold and silver, looking for a home. He came to my father's hall, seeking a wealthy man's favour. He saw my broken nose and asked what man had done that to me, so that he might avenge the insult. My father said that he was the one who had done it. And Gunnar told my father that he would either marry his daughter or kill him in the *holmgang*. And so we were married.'

'He never told me that story. You are well matched to Gunnar.'

'Yes, I am. But I would have given Gunnar up to her, to save him. To save our children.' She put her scarred face into her scarred hands, but still she did not weep.

'You must have loved him from the beginning,' I said.

'No.' She shook her head. 'I wanted to leave my father's house. I would have married any man who would have taken a flat-nosed girl. I did not love him for many years. I taught myself that art.' She picked at the grass at her side. 'Tell me how you met him.'

'I was at Olaf's hall two winters past. Gunnar came to visit his chieftain. He brought a few grudging gifts, hardly said a word to any man there. I thought him to be just another arrogant troublemaker. A bully with a fine sword. Yet when I sang, I saw him smile. He sat down on the ground and spoke not a word until he was certain that I had finished.'

'And you believed that was who he truly was?'

'Of course. If there is magic in song, it is that. When I sing to them, I see who men truly are. Women too.'

'I remember when he came back from Olaf's hall and told me of you. Still smiling then, his eyes alive. It was as if you were some woman he had fallen in love with.' She hesitated. 'I wish that he had not met you. So much might have been different.'

'You hate me, I think.'

'I do not hate you. I see you carrying my death with you. It is hard not to hate such a man. But I try.'

I could not think of a word to say to that. She noted this and smiled. 'A poet struck silent. At least I have seen that in my time.' She stood. 'Come. Let us go back. Gunnar will be back soon and I do not wish to answer his questions.' She paused, then said, 'I want to forget that I ever spoke to that woman.'

'We will fight.'

'I will get ready to fight. You must be ready to run.' She smiled then, that same awful, hopeless baring of teeth that I had seen Gunnar give at the Althing. A warrior's smile. Had she learned it from him or had he learned it from her?

'But first,' she said, 'we will have our feast. They will not take that from us.'

We are in the deepest part of the night now, are we not?

No moon tonight, and clouds are knotted thick as the rings on a mail shirt. The black air surrounds us. We should be long asleep, but there is much more for me to tell. There will be no sleep for either of us tonight. We shall have to have waking dreams, instead.

And so now, in this darkness, when we can see so little of our own country – let me tell you of other lands.

For you have never left Iceland, have you? You have known no place but this. You tell me you never wish to leave. But you are young and the time will come when you tire of this island, when you dream of some other place that might make a better home. Some place where you might be born anew.

Perhaps you will travel to Norway or Denmark, the old kingdoms of your ancestors. You will see great cities and know what true power looks like in this world. One such as you would catch the eye of the king, and I know you would find favour there. Gold, women, war – all the things that men desire, they would be yours.

But everywhere you went, you would feel the cold hand of the king on your shoulder. You would come to see the gold you wore as a yoke, as chains. And you would dream of Iceland, where there is no king demanding you kneel before him. Only brave men, demanding that you fight beside them, or against them.

Perhaps you will not go so far as that. You will travel a little way to the south: to Orkney or Scotland. A little further, to the land of the Irish or to England. You may make your fortune there, with a merchant's skill or warrior's sword. But they are not your people. The clans and tribes are no kin to you, and you will find no welcome there. A tolerance, yes, if you bring them gold and iron, but no friendship. You will settle there, hoping that things will change. They never will. And you will die there alone, dreaming of Iceland.

Or perhaps you will go further still, to the ruins of old empires in distant lands, to lands that burn beneath the sun, cursed by the gods. You will find no quarter there, only desolation and treachery.

For there is no country as beautiful as this. You must know this. We came to make a new world with all things set right. We failed, for we are weak and foolish and cruel. But there is still something of the dream left here, some power in that spell. And there is none of it to be found in the rest of the world.

Promise me this. That if you decide that you must leave, you will sail not to the south or to east. For there is nothing there for you, no country to match your home. Promise me that you will go to the west instead.

Do not speak, for I already know your answer. You will tell me there is nothing but endless ocean there for a ship to wander lost upon, for a crew to starve in. Perhaps this is so, and it would be a hero's death, have no fear of that. The bravery of the sailor in unknown waters is greater than that of the swordsman on the battlefield. But there may be another land out there. And if it is there, it will be a country untouched by men.

For that is the only country that could be better than our country without kings. A country without men. An empty land, waiting for a new beginning.

If you must leave, you must go west. To die on the empty sea, like a warrior facing down hopeless odds. Or to find a new land to call your own.

14

The night of the feast. The air still, the sky clear. Gunnar's family stood side by side, washed and anointed like those gone to sacrifice in the old country, Kari holding the reins of the black stallion, the horse a brother to him now. We all stood together and looked to the hills.

It was the first time that day that we had been still and waiting. The cooking fires had been burning all day, the smoke so thick in the longhouse that one had to crawl across the floor to breathe. Gunnar and I had become things of blood, butchering animals from the herd one after another without pause, our arms and faces marked with gore. Always casting our eyes on the descending sun, worrying that we did not have the time.

Then we were in the river together, scouring our skin with sand and grit. On the bank, skin drying in the sun – yet still we worked, stitching our torn clothing, braiding hair and beard. It was only when the sun had fallen low, after we had lit the fires and let the torches call silently out into the night, that we could be still. That we could wait, and hope.

Would any come? More than a dozen had made their promises, some strong, some weak. But there were none whom I could believe in without question. We might stand there waiting all night, with enough meat cooked to feed twenty families and not see a single visitor. No doubt we would lack the heart to eat any of it that night if no one came. Some would be salted and put away, the rest cast out to rot, left as carrion like the dead of a defeated army.

An hour passed and I felt Gunnar's hand grip mine a little tighter, as if it were a sword hilt and he were facing fearful odds on the battlefield. It seemed as though the worst of our dreams had come to pass. That all of his restless wanderings had been for nothing, all the pledges of allegiance empty.

But then we heard a drum begin to beat.

Distant, steady, unmistakable, and coming towards us. A shiver of joy passed through me as I heard the drum joined by another, and another. And then there was fire on the horizon. The torches and the music coming towards us.

We had no instrument to answer them but our voices. We howled like wolves, baying at the moon, calling them to gather around. And they came, ten families from across the Salmon River Valley, men and women and children all together, drunk and laughing, come to join us for the feast.

What manner of men they were. Those like Narfi Thorkelsson, who cared not for honour or kinship, longing only for the glory of a fight against greater numbers. Desperate men such as Odd the Fox, who had no hope of winning favour with a chieftain and were willing to stake their loyalty to a warrior like Gunnar. Reluctant men like Kormac Bersisson, called upon by the debts of blood to join us against his better judgement. These were those we had to stand beside us in the feud.

Since the killing I had forgotten what it was to feel a kinship to any man but Gunnar. Now I felt the strength that only comes from a gathering of warriors. Let me be outnumbered and doomed to die, but so long as I still have a good man standing on every side, I know that I will feel no fear. I will go to death content. For the people of my country do not fear death. We only fear that we will die alone.

I remember many things of that night. Narfi and Gunnar speaking together, then suddenly furiously grappling with one another, pausing to talk calmly for a moment, and then wrestling once more, as others looked on and laughed. The children running wild around us, forming and breaking and wheeling like flocks of birds in the sky. The women talking together, some having not spoken in years in spite of living but a few miles apart, lost in the labyrinths of their homes. Though I looked and looked again, hoping anew each time, I did not see Sigrid amongst them.

We talked for hours, on every subject except that of the feud. We sang our throats hoarse; I spoke my poetry; we laughed and cursed together. But to my memory, it was as if the whole night passed in silence, like a wordless prayer. I remember no words that were spoken.

I remember being filled with a sudden restless energy, and saw, too, Kari standing hesitant on the edge of the circle. I gave chase, lumbering after him, rolling my shoulder up into a hunchback and twisting my face. He ran from me, laughing, and I heard the others jeering and laughing at me in equal measure.

Perhaps they thought it a shameful thing, to play a child's games when one was a man. But perhaps they too wanted to forget as I did, to live fully within the game or the song, if only for a moment. If only ours was an island of children, we might know peace. For children feud – of course they do, quarrelling with more eagerness than any warrior. But they know how to forgive. And it seems that as we grow old, and learn of honour, that quality is what we lose.

Later, those who lived close began to stumble towards their homes, still laughing and singing. Others went to the longhouse to sleep wherever they could find a place on the floor, their children lying outside, piled together like sleeping beasts, immune to the noise and night air. We threw blankets over them and let them be.

I went out into the air, and I saw Dalla saying farewell to Kormac Bersisson and his kin.

'I did not think to see you here, Kormac,' she said.

'I did not think to be coming.' Kormac scratched the back of his head and looked down at the son who stood beside him. 'But your husband is a brave man, even though he is unlucky. Perhaps there is better fortune in your future.'

'Let us hope so.'

And he was away then, into the darkness. Only Dalla and I remained.

'I did not think that anyone would come here,' she said, her eyes bright.

'You have more friends than you thought.'

'We have nothing to offer them.'

'Only honour, the promise of blood. For some that is enough.'

'True,' she said. Her foot scratched at the ground. 'You will go tomorrow?'

'Yes.'

'I am glad you saw this. A little hope, before you go.'

'There is much hope here. If the men stay loyal, there is little for you to fear.'

'They will still outnumber us.'

'But they will fight on your ground. You must merely watch and wait.'

'Wait for what? For Björn and Vigdis to grow old and die?'

'Wait for me to come back. Let them grow bored and stupid. I will come back and I will settle this feud.'

'We will settle it together,' she said.

'Aye. We will settle it together.'

She grinned at this – not the awful warrior's smile I had seen before, that greets death as a boon companion. For a moment I think that she forgot all thought of killing.

Then she looked out in the darkness and the smile froze upon her face.

'What do you see?'

'There is someone out there,' she said, her voice flat, her body still.

I followed her gaze, but I could see nothing in the darkness. 'Where? I cannot see.'

'Do not move. We cannot let them know.'

'Björn and the others?'

'I cannot tell. Wait.'

Her eyes hunted through the darkness, one hand drifting to the knife at her side. I waited – for the command to run or fight, for an arrow or a spear from the darkness.

She said: 'We have nothing to fear.'

'Who is out there?'

She laughed. 'You still cannot tell?'

'No,' I said, for she spent most of her life in the dark of the longhouse and her eyes were better than mine at night. But I saw it then: a moment of motion, grey cloth catching under the light of the half-moon. I knew what was out there, then, and I gave chase without a word, Dalla's laughter following me into the night.

There are stories my father used to tell me, about the hidden people. Women whom one can see but not touch, beautiful and terrible, leading men into the darkness, into the sea and over high cliffs. And there were times, on that night of the feast, that I thought I might be chasing such a creature.

That winter I had hunted a ghost in the night, only to find it to be a man. Now I pursued a woman; would she truly be a ghost this time?

Many times I almost caught her, but she was quick and saw better in the dark than I did. Many times I thought I had lost her, only to hear a silvery laugh echoing back at me that I chased after once again, through the fields and rivers, the remnants of the woodland.

I could tell no pattern to where she took me, though we never ventured beyond sight of the farm, the fires of the feast always nearby. She seemed to be leading me no place in particular, for I retrod the same ground many times in pursuit of her: again and again we passed through the cut-down remnants of Gunnar's wood, the shallow waters of the river, the broken stones on the high ground that marked the borders of Gunnar's land.

It was only when I stood still for a moment to catch my breath and saw her pause in the distance to wait for me that I at last understood the rules of the game.

I turned my back to her and walked towards a turning of the river, where the hills on each side might grant us some measure of privacy. I put my hand on the ground; the grass was wet and I laid my cloak down upon it. I sat on the ground and waited.

I saw her at the top of the hill, but she did not come to me at once. She moved slowly, pausing every so often to see if I would lose my patience and give chase once more. She was testing me, but I remained still. I knew what it was that she wanted.

She did not want to be caught. She wanted to catch me.

She walked upstream towards me and knelt upon my cloak. We looked at each other, she close enough to me that even in the half-light I could see the mark of the fey in her eyes. I still could not quite believe that it was her. I reached out, to truly know, and a moment later felt her lips against my palm.

We stood for that moment together, listening to the whispering river. I could see her trembling a little – a quiver in her shoulders, a tremble in her hand. But her eyes were clear and a smile danced across her lips.

'I could not wait,' Sigrid said.

And there, in the darkness, we found each other.

15

After, she lay on her side, her head turned from me, and I watched as she let one hand trail in the waters of the river beside us.

'I could not come to the feast,' she said.

'Olaf forbade it,' I replied, coiling a strand of her hair around my finger.

'Of course.'

'But you came here tonight.'

'Of course.' I reached out from the cloak to where my belt lay. I drew my knife and cut away a lock of hair.

She rolled back to face me then, and in the darkness I could see the white of her rolling eyes. 'Of course, a poet would do such a thing.'

I kissed her. 'You must go back. There is not much night left. Olaf will be angry if he finds you away. I must go away tomorrow. But I will have this to remember you by.'

'And what will I have? I want no token part of you. I shall have all of you or nothing.' She stood from the cloak, naked and unashamed. She washed in the river and dressed, and when we stood together once more, she touched the two silver arm-rings that I wore. 'One of these buys you a place on a ship. The other buys us a place at a farm, when you return.'

'That is so.'

'You will come back?'

'Yes. I will come back.'

She dropped her head, and so if there were tears I could not see them. She was as proud as any warrior.

I watched her go, a shadow in the darkness, and I tried to mark her in my mind – every word, every touch that she had gifted to me. They would be all my company in exile. Within me, the aching hope that she would wait for me.

I wandered back towards the farm, uncaring for anything else. For I was young and foolish, and I loved. Yet it did not last long. The beating of five hundred heartbeats, perhaps. The time it took for the moon to sink only a fraction in the sky. However long it took to lay eyes upon the farm and to see that the torches were out.

Perhaps, I thought, they had simply burned out of their own accord – there might be no more to it than that. Yet some instinct made me come forward as quietly as I could, waiting for the wind before I moved, watching and listening as if I were a hunter close to the wolf, not a man returning to his home. Some wrongness seemed to seep from that place, though I could not say what it was.

I drew closer and saw that the door was open, swinging and creaking softly in the wind. There was no light from within. They have put out the cooking fire, I thought, and a coldness stole through me.

It looked abandoned, like one of those farms emptied by disease and roamed by haunts. As if some strange witchcraft had passed out in the dale, and Sigrid and I had lain together for half a hundred years. But then the wind blew hard, caught the door and almost swung it closed, and a pale hand stole out of the darkness and held the door open. There was still someone inside.

I drew the axe from my belt, crept closer to the wall. I felt it with my free hand, searching for the places where I might place my hands and feet. I tried to remember when I had helped build this wall, what stones I had chosen and what order I had laid them in. My poet's memory served me well; it had been a hot day three weeks before when I placed those stones. My lack of craft was my undoing, for as I came down the other side my foot struck loose a poorly placed rock.

It danced and chattered across the wall, rapping out a soft alarm call. I crouched down, hoping that I had not been heard. A whistle came to me from the doorway: the tune of a song that I had sung that night, of Odin and the Poet's Mead. I whistled back the same set of notes.

'Kjaran?' It was Gunnar's voice, coming from the doorway.

'Yes.'

'Come inside. Quickly.'

I ran across the open ground, expecting at any moment the thrum of a bowstring, the whistle of a thrown spear. But I was through the door, Gunnar's hand on my back.

'What—?' I said, but Gunnar grabbed my arm and put his finger to his lips. I stood in silence and waited for my eyes to adjust to the darkness.

When they had, I wondered if some madness had stolen over Gunnar, for I could see nothing awry. The guests were asleep, lying on the ground in every part of the room. The children had all been brought inside, but they slept too, exhausted and content. I saw no sign of wounds on anyone; no one save for Gunnar and his family were still awake.

But Freydis was crying, sitting in her mother's lap and

sobbing against her, as Dalla bounced the child on her lap. And Kari not quite weeping, but blinking back his tears, his mouth agape.

'I thought that you might have been ambushed,' Gunnar said. 'I would have come out, but I could not leave them alone.'

'I do not understand,' I said. 'What has happened?'

Gunnar did not reply. He pointed outside.

I saw nothing at first. The remnants of the feast, the ground marked by many feet. The barn, the hitching posts, the stockade – all was as it should be. Then the wind came once more and I saw a strand of rope dancing in the wind. One end knotted to the hitching post, the other wandering freely.

'The horse is gone,' I said.

'Kari woke me. He says he heard men speaking, the sound of the horse crying out. When he came out, it was gone.'

'It could have broken its tether.'

Gunnar snorted in disgust. 'Do you really believe that?'

'We must see for ourselves.'

'I will go with you,' Kari said.

'No.'

'I will go!'

Gunnar struck him – a measured, backhanded slap. 'I told you, no. Do not make me say so again.'

Dalla pulled the boy close against her, and her daughter too. I could not meet her gaze, and so I took up a shield and looked to Gunnar. He nodded to me and we stepped out into the dark, our shields held high.

Out there in the summer night the land seemed alive with motion. My eyes made a nightmare of it all. A startled bird rising from the moor became an arrow flying towards us. A lumbering sheep, for a moment, changed to a man hunched over and walking on all fours. We walked amongst monsters in the darkness.

'I wish it were winter,' I said.

'I do not,' Gunnar replied. 'I have always wanted to die in summer.'

I crouched beside the hitching post and in the blue half-light I tried to read the story of the ground. There were so many footsteps of men and horses that it seemed a hopeless task. But I studied the tracks like a priest reading an omen, listening for a voice from the gods that might guide us on the way.

'What do you think?' I said.

He ran his finger over the clean cut in the rope. 'He did not break his tether.'

'You believe that they are still out there?'

He looked at me. 'Oh, that I know for certain. But we must still go searching for them. I'll not hide in my home like a coward.'

'I do not think they will fight us. If they wanted to kill me, they have but to wait a few days. They want to scare us.'

'Then we shall not be scared. But keep your shield up. They may have an archer with them.' He shook his head. 'I wish we had armour.'

'I have never worn mail. I would move like a fat old man.'

He laughed and I took what comfort I could at the sound. Even if we had the light of day and a horse of our own to search on, we would have had little chance of finding a runaway horse – and none at all if it had been stolen. But there was nothing to do but try. To wander in the dark, stumbling over rock and tussock, the weight of the shield burning in my arm, mouth dry as a stone. To wander into whatever trap might be laid for us, for the sake of honour and nothing more.

We circled the farm, always keeping it in sight on our left. Gunnar insisted on walking on the outside, his unprotected right side exposed to the open countryside and whoever might be waiting there. I listened for the whispering sound of footsteps in the darkness, the creaking of an unseasoned spear, the accidental rap of a blade against a shield.

'Wait.'

I raised my shield when Gunnar spoke, and laid my back against his.

'I heard something,' he said.

We stood and listened. I heard nothing except the wind against distant trees, Gunnar's steady breaths in and out. Yet I could feel his sweat-sodden tunic pressed damp against my shoulders. It seemed he could feel fear after all.

'What did you hear?' I asked.

'Laughter.'

We waited, and I do not know how long we listened for, waiting for the sound to come once more. But it did not and we slowly resumed our circle.

We returned to where we had begun and saw no sign of men or of the missing horse. There had been no trail that I could read upon the ground. The creature had vanished.

'Does that satisfy your honour?' I said.

He nodded, exhausted. 'Yes. Daylight will reveal the rest.'

Imagine a warrior waiting for a battle, knowing that the morning will bring his death. Yet the sun rises and, as he readies his arms, he is told a truce has been struck and there will be no battle that day. Or a man condemned to die at the order of some foreign tyrant, readying himself to be sent to the headsman's block and given a coward's death, only to find himself pardoned at the last moment. That was how I felt as we came back to that farmhouse.

Perhaps I would have met my death well, having known the woman I loved that night. But in that moment I knew it could not be true. I felt no peace, no readiness for death. For mine was a greedy love.

We passed through the door, back to the welcoming darkness. And the moment we stepped through, I knew that I had been mistaken. For Dalla came forward, her eyes rolling like a spooked horse, and she gripped her husband by the shoulders.

'Where is Kari?' she whispered. 'Is he with you?'

'Why would he be with us?' Gunnar said.

Her mouth gaped in grief and she made no reply. She did not need to. We knew it then, without another word being spoken, even as we hunted with our eyes a boy who was not there.

Kari had gone.

It was behind the boards of his bed. I found it by passing my hand over the planks, feeling the wind against my skin. I rapped the wood, found it hollow, and lifted up the loose plank. And behind it a tunnel, cut through the turf wall, just big enough for a child to crawl through.

'He said he wished to sleep,' Dalla said. 'He went to his bed. When I looked again, he was gone.'

I saw it all then: a bored child, trapped inside by the long winter, giving himself a project. Turning his home into a place to explore, a world of wood and earth given life by the mind. A child's secret. An innocent thing, but he had found another use for it now.

'I always thought this house was too cold in winter,' Gunnar said. He spat in the embers of the fire and I heard it sizzle.

'How could we not see him?'

'He went along the riverbed, upstream or downstream. That is the only way that he could have gotten away without us seeing him.'

'We must go back out.'

'I will go with you,' Dalla said. 'If they are out there, they will not hurt a woman.'

'We do not know what they will do,' Gunnar said. 'And you must stay here and guard our home.'

She looked at her daughter, lying in fitful sleep by the fire, and her mouth twisted with anger; a killer's look stole across her face. She took up an axe and knelt down beside Freydis. One hand stroking the golden hair of her daughter, the other gripping the handle of her weapon, as if she were some kind of loving executioner.

We left her like that, back into the blue air of the summer night, following the sound of running water down to the riverbed.

'I will go upstream,' I said. 'You go down. We return to the farm at first light.'

Gunnar glanced upstream and shook his head.

'Björn's farm lies that way.'

'And Vigdis lives downstream. They could be waiting for us either way. Or both.'

'The danger is equal. Very well.' He paused for a moment. 'Be lucky, Kjaran.'

'This will be a good time to start.'

He nodded. 'Call out if you see them. I will come to you.'

'What signal should I expect from you, if you need my help?'

He rapped his sword against the boss of his shield. 'You will hear that, and the sound of the killing.' With that, he slipped away, swift-footed in the dark and dancing from rock to rock down the shallow river. I watched him go and turned to follow my own path.

Alone now, I moved up beside the river, feeling the wet ground against my feet where the boots had worn away. I should have been more afraid, but I was not. My life was in my hands, and my life alone. I did not carry the lives of Gunnar or of his family. And so I was a weightless, grinning creature as I ran through the dark, scouring the hills for the shape of a boy. I could not risk calling his name, but I listened for his voice. For I could not think his courage would last long, alone as he was.

But I heard nothing. The wind, the trees, the river, and nothing more than that. I drew close to the boundaries of Gunnar's land and had found no further sign or sound of the boy. I told myself that he must have gone downstream in search of the horse – perhaps Gunnar had already found him.

I turned back – hurrying, and more afraid now that the danger seemed to be passing, for no man wishes to be killed when the end of a battle is in sight. A little longer, a few hundred footsteps, and I would be back to warmth and safety.

But something was wrong. I knew it, and yet I did not know it. It was as if my mind were screaming a warning at me, but in a language that I could not understand. Nothing had changed: the night was still, no sight or sound of anything amiss. I stopped and listened, trying to understand, but heard nothing but the wind and the creaking of the trees.

Then I knew what it was. The ghost of a sound, a memory of the spring. For we had cut down that little wood on Gunnar's land. There were no trees left. I did not know what the creaking was, but it was not the wind against the trees. A slow, dull, wooden creaking, that came and went with the passage of the air.

I went to my hands and knees. I closed my eyes. I listened again.

To the west. In a dip in the valley, hidden from view. That was where the sound came from.

I made my way there. Slowly, as slow as ice spreading over water. Each foot placed where it would make the least noise. Not a single thing left to chance, for there is no patience like that of a man hunted by other men.

Moment by moment, the sound seemed to change. It sounded like the cawing of a crow, then the groan of a tree, then the turning of an old cartwheel. Even when I was almost on top of it, lying on the grass of the hill with the sound just beyond, I still could not tell what it was.

I waited there a time. I had always thought that, in such a place, I would feel the touch of a god on my shoulder and know that it was time to fight or die. But I felt no sign. And so I counted ten breaths, then leapt to my feet, shield in front and axe held high behind.

A monster. That was what stood before me. A shape taller than a man, a distended head that leered, tongue lolling and open mouthed, teeth shining in the darkness.

That is what I saw for one heartbeat, for two, for three. Then my mind made sense of what my eyes could see. I saw the wooden pole thrust into the ground, black with blood. I saw the horse's head thrust on top of it, shifting and creaking with the wind. And I saw the runes marked on flesh and wood. A curse. A warning. A promise of the killing to come.

I turned around, expecting to find the men who had done this behind me. But there was no one. They would be long gone, back to their homes, their curse behind them. They had left their message, written on the body, mounted on the pole. That there would be no forgiveness, no ending of the feud. That what they had done to that horse, they would do to men.

The wind stilled and I heard another sound. The sound of weeping. And I saw another shape in the dark, knelt at the base of the pole, a worshipper prostrate before a hateful god. It was the boy.

'I thought it was him,' he said. 'I saw him. I thought I heard him call to me.'

'I know.' I sat beside him and put my arm over his shoulder. 'It is nothing. Nothing but a scorn-pole. The tool of a coward.'

'Will it curse us?'

'No. They think to insult us, and scare us. But we are too brave and clever for that, aren't we?'

'You will not tell my father I wept?'

'That is not what I saw. You were watching bravely to see if they came back, weren't you?'

He nodded dumbly.

'Come on. Let us go home.'

He got to his feet and walked in front of me, tottering like a child half his age. I followed him, but as I did so I looked back once more at the scorn-pole, looked on that face of the horse. It was as though it was laughing at me.

I could almost hear it, and I wondered if they were out there too, watching and laughing. I felt the killer's longing rising in me as I never had before. I had stood beside Gunnar at the *holmgang*, had looked into the eyes of men who wished me dead and had felt no violence stirring. Yet the thought of that mockery, of being toyed with for sport – that was what brought the murderer's rage to me. I wanted nothing more than to hunt those hills, to kill every one of them.

But I did not have enough time. Tomorrow I would be gone.

16

'It was one of them, was it not?'
    'What?
'One of our guests, at the feast. Who took the horse.'
I did not reply. There was no need to.

Gunnar and I were sat on the high ground above the farm, looking down upon it. On the sheep wandering in the fields, the high wheat almost ready for the harvest. The place that I would not see again for many years. For that was the day I would leave.

The guests had gone home at first light. Gunnar had smiled well enough and played the happy host. No one asked why his children sat dead-eyed in the corner of the house, refusing to speak. Or why our flesh was grey from our sleepless night. They had gone and we remained. To speak together and say our goodbyes.

We had gone out once more in the night, to take down the scorn-pole and burn it. The body we could not find. Perhaps they had butchered it for meat and split it amongst themselves, bloody reward for the hard night's work. Or left it for scavengers to take.

At last, Gunnar spoke again. 'At least now I know that I cannot trust them. Better to know that now.'

'You will find out who it was, soon enough. There are no secrets in this place.'

'As we have both learned.' He looked back over the dale, towards where the scorn-pole had stood. 'Do you think it is true what they say? That it is the worst of curses?'

'I do not know.'

He nodded absently. 'And who is it you sail with?'

'Ragnar Ragnarsson. The one they call the Keel-farer.'

'His kin call him that. I have heard him nicknamed the Coward.'

'That is what most men call him, yes.'

'I would not trust such a man to captain a boat.'

'Oh, he may tremble on the shore at the first sign of blood-shed, but there is no calmer man on a restless sea. Or so I have been told.'

'And where will you go?'

'I do not know. Dublin, perhaps. I have always wanted to see Ireland. Perhaps I will find kin there. Or Jórvík.'

'You will like Dublin, I think.' And then he drew his sword and held it flat in both hands, the blade against his palms, a man in prayer to his god. Then he turned and held it out to me. Wordless, perhaps not trusting himself to speak, he gestured for me to take it.

I said: 'That is too great a gift. I have no need of it.'

'You have every need of it.'

'They may mistake me for some great warrior. I do not have the skill to fight the men who would be willing to stand against this sword.'

'You will take it or I will cast it into the sea. You may choose.'

I lifted the sword and held it flat, placed one palm

underneath the top of it. I looked down on the blade and saw there the name of some craftsman whose story was long since forgotten. I ran one finger down the centre of the groove that was carved there to make the weapon lighter, to let the blood run freely from the blade, and I thought of how much must have poured down that mark. No mighty river's worth, but perhaps, somewhere in Iceland, there was some brook or rivulet that had washed the ground with as much water as this blade had seen blood.

It was beautiful, in the way that killing can be beautiful.

'How did I earn this?' I said.

Gunnar thought upon this for a long time. 'You are kind,' he said at last. 'Perhaps it is as simple as that. Most who are kind are cowards. They think to buy with words what they cannot earn with courage. But you are not like that. I think you are the only man I know who has that quality.'

'Another name for me. Kjaran the Kind. If I were to make a song of that, none would listen.'

'I cannot learn it from you. I wish that I could. But I am nothing but a killer. Men love me for it. But it is worthless. I am tired of it.'

'That is not why men love you, Gunnar.'

'What is it, then?'

'Because you are not afraid to die.'

He looked at me, his eyes disbelieving. 'You think that such a precious thing?' he said.

How much we discover of someone, when we are so close to leaving them. What a cruel trick that is.

I would have pressed him further, but I saw them then, coming from Hjardarholt. Olaf and his men, a convoy of warriors and horses. My escort to another world. He had business in Borg, family to visit, and had offered to take me to the coast. One last favour. Doubtless it would dishonour him if I were murdered on the road. He would see me safe to a ship and his part in the feud would be ended.

'You go to the ship here?'

'No. South, to Borg. Ragnar has a shipwright there that he trusts.'

'Will you say goodbye? To Dalla and my children?'

'It is better that I do not.' I looked away. 'You could come with me,' I said.

'What?'

'Sell your land. Olaf would give you a fair price to be rid of you, rid of the feud. Take your family, find a new home. You have silver enough and no kin to keep you here. I do not know why it is that you stay.'

I watched him think on this. It is not as they say, that we poets can see into the hearts of men. The world would be a simpler place if we could. There would never be another feud, or a true love that remained unspoken. I cannot see into the hearts of men. But I think that I could see him tempted, in that moment.

He spoke. 'Do you know how many places I travelled to, before I settled here?'

'I do not. You never tell me of that time.'

'I have been to lands to the east where there are deserts greater than this whole island. I have been to the courts of kings where even the whores wear gold. Seen wonders that you could not imagine, poet that you are.' He turned a palm towards the sky, gestured to the valley as if he were toasting it with a cup of wine. 'But this is the finest land of them all. I would never leave this place. I love my children, my wife. I…' He fell silent for a moment. Then: 'But I love this country more than anything else.'

'Then you would have me stay?'

'No. I want you to go. To stay is to die. But I wish that you could.' He stood and offered his hand to me. 'I will see you in three years. Promise me that.'

'You have my word.' I laid my fingers against the sword. 'I will return this to you.'

'If I am still here.'

'I am the one that they want. They will leave your family in peace,' I said. And he smiled in such a way that showed he knew that I was lying. But we wanted to believe the lie.

I made to put the sword in its sheath, but some omen stopped me. I put my free hand against the blade, felt the sharp line against the back of my hand. I pressed it there, until I felt the blood run free. I held forth the sword, and my bloodied hand.

'Would you become my brother?' I said. 'Swear an oath in blood with me.'

It has always been done amongst my people. Where a man finds a brother in battle rather than kinship, and seals the bond in blood. I could not think why we had not done so already.

There had been no fear in him on the night he hunted the ghost, when we stood accused upon the plain, when he fought in the *holmgang*. But I think that, for a moment, I did see him afraid. Of what, I could not understand.

'No,' he said, his voice cold. 'I will not do that.'

There was something more that needed to be said, but I could not find the words to say it. I heard the horses come up to us, heard Olaf calling my name.

That is how I left Gunnar. With words unspoken, a debt unpaid. The worst of partings between friends.

★

Two days remained. I would be a man of the people in that time, protected by the spoken laws that bound all of us together. Once that was over, I would be an animal to be hunted for sport or for revenge. But if Olaf and his men thought any differently of me, they did not show it. I did not travel set apart from them, but as just another member of the company. Perhaps even as the last moments were counted away, they would still laugh with me, urge me to sing another song, hand me one last cup of ale. Then, as the sun touched the horizon, they would take up their blades and murder me without a moment's hesitation. Such was the power of the law that bound us. And such was the outlaw's fate.

We rode down through the valley to the south, passing mountains that held their snow even in the height of summer, listening to the calling of the waterfalls. We came to the open plains, scarred and marked by the black rock where the earth had cracked and bled many years before.

It was then that I saw them. Always behind us, another group of riders. My second escort, trailing us the way that wolves will trail a deer abandoned by its herd.

They kept a respectful distance, never close enough to be a threat, always close enough to keep us in sight. They made no attempt to hide, for they did nothing wrong. A band of men, travelling towards the sea. Björn, Snorri and the rest of his kin. I wondered if Vigdis rode with them.

They were there to see that I truly left the country, that I played no sorcerer's trick. And if we found ourselves delayed – if a sudden storm trapped us on the land or the tides went against us – they would take their opportunity for revenge.

Not a man that I rode with spoke of the people who followed us. But from time to time, when they thought my eyes were not on them, I saw them twist in their saddles and glance back. Perhaps gauging the distance, checking that they were not riding any closer to us. Perhaps counting for numbers, to see which side would have the advantage if it came to a fight. Perhaps wishing that they were with that second band, that they rode with the hunters of men. I had no doubt that if I remained in Iceland as an outlaw, there would be plenty amongst Olaf's men who would come looking for me.

We left behind the plains, and before us lay the fjord, the harbour, the open sea. The place they called Borg.

A coffin cast into the open sea had guided the first settlers to this place, and the dead had chosen well. A natural harbour, and farmlands that stretched far inland. We came to that first farm, where Egill Skallagrímsson now lived, and it was there that Olaf parted from us. He strutted and preened himself for the laughter of his men, preparing himself to face the most fearsome of the warrior poets as though he were wooing a lass that he loved. Only when his eyes passed over me did they dim for a moment.

His men soon scattered to attend to their own matters: visiting the traders at the docks, looking in on old friends, visiting new loves. Ragnar and I alone made our way to the docks.

He was so nervous and uncertain on land, tripping and hurrying like a clumsy child as he made his way down the rocky path to the sea. Yet the moment he laid his hand to the hull of the ship, smiling like a shy lover, he seemed to right himself: set his feet and stand tall, a man born to be upon the water.

No doubt his life would have been ended a long time before in one quarrel or another had he not shown such courage on the sea. For the people of Iceland hate nothing more than a coward, fear nothing more than the open water in a storm. For Ragnar, a man inverted, they held a kind of wary respect.

For I had heard the stories: of waves that seemed like mountain ranges, of lightning dancing across the sky and thunder striking men deaf. Of the bravest warriors shaming themselves with fear, and there was Ragnar at the tiller, entirely unafraid, guiding his ship without loss through the worst of storms.

'How does she look?' I asked him. 'I know nothing of ships.'

'My shipwright has taken good care of her,' he replied. 'We should go tonight.'

I hesitated. 'I had thought we would leave in the morning.'

'Why wait? The tide will be with us, and the wind too.'

'Where do we sail to?'

He looked at me and grinned. 'Where do you want to go?'

'Too great a privilege for me to choose. A mere passenger.'

'It matters little to me. There is trade wherever we go.'

I did not answer for a time. 'I will not choose,' I said.

'Why not?'

'If I asked you whether I should cut off your hands or pluck out your eyes, what would you answer?'

He went pale at my words. 'I am sorry,' he said. 'It is one thing to choose a journey. Quite another to have it forced upon you.' He ran his hands over the hull once again.

'I have always wandered across the land. Perhaps you can teach me what it is to wander the sea as well.'

'I have never cared much for the land. The men may tolerate me, but I know what they say: no woman would choose a coward for a husband. It is a lonely place for me. And out on the water I am not alone. I am not a coward.'

'Your body is a coward. Your mind is not. I know that of you and I have not even seen you on the sea.'

'It is kind of you to say so. Very kind.' He blinked and looked away. 'I will come and find you, when it is time to go. You should say goodbye.'

'Goodbye? Goodbye to who?'

'To the island, of course.'

I wandered alone, picking my way across the rocky paths and listening to the calling of the gulls until I had made my way to the end of the land. It seemed a fitting place to say goodbye.

The sea was not empty in front of me. There was one islet in the water; local stories spoke of it as a boulder thrown at a witch. I sat down and wrapped my cloak tight around myself, for a cold, sharp wind came from the sea. I looked out across the open ocean. I looked towards the west.

There were stories of untouched lands out there. I did not know if I believed them. For all I knew the ocean I saw was empty, perhaps even endless. Unless the songs were true and out there somewhere lay the serpent that encircled the world. I looked on the ocean and found that I was afraid of it.

No, not of it. But of what it meant, what lay upon it, and beyond it. Of countries that were not this one, of people who were not my own. Of losing my home. Of exile.

I tried to think of all the wonders that I might see. Great cities, the courts of mighty kings. Forests where the trees stretched high above the heads of men and went on as far as the eye could see. I had sung of so many places, yet I had known nothing but this island. Known long winters and brief summers, known farms and never a city, the sea but never a desert. Now I would have the chance to see the world beyond.

I looked back on the mountains, snow-touched and towering above the pale hills. I thought of the long winter ahead, the men who waited to kill me, their longing for blood, that feeling that is more than a little like love.

I heard the footsteps on the path and saw Ragnar walking

towards me. Light-footed and happy, and I knew from his smile that it was time to go. That he could not wait to set out to sea, to be in the only place that he felt as a home.

He looked on me and I saw the smile fall from his face.

The oars beat the water, the sail spread like the war banner of some great giant. The sea slapped the hull and the wood moaned like a lover.

That is what I saw and heard, as I watched the ship go.

I remained on that same rocky outcrop, looking out on that same little islet, as the ship was loaded, cut its ties and went out to sea. Time and time again I saw Ragnar look towards me as he paced the deck of his ship, but I did not meet his eyes. And I did not move from that place until the ship was far out on the water.

As I stood, for a moment I felt horror at what I had done. Felt the urge to run to the dock and dive in the water, to cry out for them to wait, to take me with them. But I would have to be one of those shape shifters who can take the form of seal or fish to catch them now. Already they were drawing close to the horizon. Already it was too late.

It was a passing sensation, like a cold breeze that blows once and crawls across the skin and then is felt no more. After that I did not feel fear, though I knew it would come in time. I felt nothing at all.

I traded the first silver ring I had for food that would not spoil. I paused for only a moment before I handed over the second, the one that Gunnar had given to me, for a strong horse. I was going to a place where silver and gold meant nothing. Only iron and flesh had value for me now.

I do not know if those tradesman knew who I was or the

sentence that was about to be passed. That today I could trade with them like any other man, but tomorrow I would be an outlaw. Perhaps they were men of the sea like Ragnar, who knew nothing of the feuds of landlocked men. Perhaps they thought that I must be taking some later ship, that I was buying supplies for the voyage itself. Or perhaps they simply did not care.

I rode out from Borg and headed to the east. I knew they would come for me soon.

OUTLAW

17

It was on the fifth day that I saw them. Black dots on the horizon, small enough that I thought them some trick of the light at first. But the truth was clear, soon enough. Riders in pursuit.

I had thought they would come sooner. No doubt they had believed that I would run, that I would not be fool enough to stay as an outlaw. Word must have reached them from Borg that I had not taken my place on the ship. That the sun had set on my last day as a free man.

Those five days had been days of peace. I still had enough food, and had yet to shame myself by stealing from a shepherd's shieling. I travelled in the day, singing my songs to keep myself company. I slept at night with my head against the flank of my horse, soothed by the gentle rise and fall of his chest, the heavy beat of his heart. For one last time I could be a happy traveller, could fool myself that I still had some kind of freedom.

On the day that I woke and saw those figures on the horizon, I set my heels to the sides of my horse. The chase began in earnest.

Many were the times that I thought I had lost them. I sought the valleys and narrow defiles to hide from their sight, pushed my horse as hard as I could. If the day of my exile had been but a month later, perhaps I might have succeeded. I could have travelled by night and hid in the day, and they never would have been able to follow me. But the late summer days were still long, the nights too short. I could not travel as fast as a free man, for I had to pick my way round the borders of every farm that I rode through, or take to the rocky, unpeopled terrain that slowed me down. Any man I saw might know me for what I was. Any man I saw might choose to kill me.

On some days I managed to get away from my pursuers for a time. A hard morning's ride, an unseen valley with branching pathways, and those figures on the horizon would vanish for a time. Whatever tracker they had convinced to join them, he knew his trade well. If there was an evening where I could no longer see them, inevitably that next morning I would rise to see those shapes on the horizon once more. And my horse was beginning to tire.

How long would they follow me? How far would they go? They were men with farms, families, a winter to prepare for. Would they be willing to risk all of that to hunt down an outlaw?

All depended on who was with them, how strong their loyalty was. Björn would lead them, Snorri at his side, and those kinsmen he had rallied for the chase. There would be others there, tempted by something other than revenge and kinship. Some bought with silver to join the band, and there would always be those who hunted for the pleasure of killing. Half-tamed men who longed to murder, and who would take up arms in pursuit of any outlaw, no matter who that man might be.

My hope was the mountains, the winter, ice and snow and

stone the only allies who might come to help me. And so I made my way towards the heart of our island, a tomb of ice and snow where no man could live for long.

I pressed on towards the mountains, praying for the snow to fall.

I could not say on what day it was that I came upon the river. A week after I had begun to run, perhaps it was more, for already the days ran into one another and I slept little.

It was angry, fast-flowing, high rocky banks on either side. Impassable for much of its length, though I knew where it could be forded. For I had come this way long ago, as I came up from the south to the west. Further south, there was a turn in the river where it grew slow and a brave man might force his horse through before the cold stole his strength. I could only hope that my followers did not know of that place.

I found it, that place where the river turned shallow. I had crossed it six years before, fleeing a part of the country that I could no longer call home. Now I crossed it again, running again, and turned my horse towards the north.

The mountains grew tall in front of me and I dozed in my saddle as I rode, for the sun was warm and the air still.

'Kjaran.'

I shuddered at the sound, thinking it a word from a dream.

'Kjaran!'

My name repeated. I lifted my tired head, looked across the river. They were there: a dozen men on horseback, the war-band that pursued me.

I sat upright, reaching for the sword at my side, the taste of iron in my mouth. Yet they were on the other side of the river. A little more than a bowshot away, but it would take them half a day's hard riding to reach me. I could not quite believe: it seemed impossible for danger to be so close, yet so far away.

It was Björn who had called to me, and now he did not seem to know what it was that he should say next. One goes on the hunt to kill a murderer, not a tired rider half-asleep in his saddle. Björn rode one of the largest horses I had ever seen, yet it was as though he were riding a colt, so small did it seem under him. He was not quite as tall as Hrolf the Walker, the great Viking whom no horse could bear, but there was something absurd in seeing his heels almost clip the ground as he rode.

They drew up on the banks and I saw one of them look down into the water to see if it might be crossed. I knew that a roaring torrent would greet him that no man could hope to swim through alive, sharp wet stones that no man could climb.

'Come here, Kjaran,' Björn said. 'Let us speak.'

I saw no bow amongst them, but I came forward carefully. One of them might have a good arm and a spear to hand, and they did not need to strike me to kill me. They had merely to wound my horse and they would have me soon enough. And so I did not come to the bank as they did – merely came close enough to speak.

Yet still, we did not talk for a time. Merely stared at each other, while they drew no closer and I drew no further away, the only sounds the water and the wind. I had the thought, the mad, hopeful thought, that somehow we might both stay there. Found a settlement on each side of the river, ever watchful, unable to harm one another. That we would grow old looking across the divided land.

'You go north, then,' Björn said. 'You think to go around the mountains?'

'That is right,' I replied. I looked beyond him, to the men

who followed him. 'How far will you go for another man's feud?' I said, and I saw Ketil Hakonsson there with them. 'I am sorry to see you here, Ketil. I thought you a better man than this.'

Ketil shook his head. 'You should not have stayed, Kjaran. Why did you not go when you could?'

I made no reply. I was not certain that I could have answered him.

'A shameful thing, to run like this,' Björn said.

'A shameful thing,' I said, 'to hunt one man with a dozen.'

'We should not speak with him,' said Ketil.

Björn turned to him, his face red with anger. 'I will speak if I want to!'

Ketil shook his head and looked at the ground. 'We should not speak with him.'

'He is right,' I said. 'We should not speak. Go home. There is no honour in this.'

'No,' Björn said. 'But there is revenge.' He turned to the warband. 'I would speak with him alone. I would speak with the man who killed my brother.'

The others turned their horses and rode away. Björn dismounted, drew his hand-axe and knife and laid them upon the ground.

He came to the bank open-handed. 'Let us speak. I have no weapon.'

'You still have your sword.'

He spat on the ground. 'You think I will throw that at you?'

I tugged on my horse's reins, turned him away, and touched my heels to his flanks.

'I want to speak to you about Gunnar.'

I should have kept riding. I should have spoken with him no further. But already I had stilled my horse and he knew that his words had found a mark. And so I swung down and walked to the bank.

'What would you say to me?'

'Vigdis told me the truth,' he said.

'What do you mean?'

'You lied at the Althing. I know it was not you who killed my brother.'

I hesitated. 'Then why hunt me?'

'You played your part. There is no mercy for such as you. But I will kill Gunnar.'

'You may kill me. If it comes to that, so be it. But you cannot stand against Gunnar. And I may not die so easily.'

I half-drew my sword, Gunnar's sword, enough so that he could see the colour of the metal, the familiar marks on the blade. He tossed back his head, as if struck by the sight of it, and I wondered if he feared it. It had killed two of his brothers. Perhaps he still believed in fate, and curses.

'You shall die upon this sword as well, I think,' I said.

'No.' He shook his head. 'You still think you will die like a warrior, like a poet. That you will die well. When we catch you, you will be torn to pieces like a hunted animal.'

'Perhaps. But Gunnar will avenge my death.'

'No. He will not.'

He turned from me – disappointed, I thought. I do not know what he wanted from me, but I had not given it to him. As he walked away, I searched for something more that I might say. Some words that might put aside his hate or inspire fear. But I could not find them.

I took to my own horse, rode north, and every so often I looked over my shoulder to watch them ride south towards the ford, to watch them disappear from view.

By the morning, they were in sight once more.

It was time, then, to take my chance. To break free of my pursuers or die in the attempt.

For weeks they had pursued me and we had barely stirred our horses beyond a walk. At the end of a battle, when men are too tired to run, I have heard there are many such chases. Walking men stumbling after other walking men, dragging one foot in front of the other. For the pursuit of men on horseback is not settled through galloping speed, but mere persistence. A horse that stumbles and breaks a leg or throws its rider into the rocks – these are the things that may end a chase across the land.

But that morning I broke with that tradition. I put my heels to the horse and we tore across the land.

When I looked back, I saw the figures on the horizon recede a little. They too stirred their horses, but they were content to lose a little ground, knowing that I was riding a tired horse too hard. No doubt they thought that I had panicked, that they had merely to wait for my horse to be exhausted. I had no second horse and no man would trade a mount to an outlaw. They would wait and have me soon enough. But they did not understand my purpose.

I rode like that until I was at the base of the mountains, until I was stood beneath some great, nameless piece of stone – who would waste time giving names to such things?

I swung down from the saddle and my horse seemed to gasp in relief. His head bowed, spitting gobbets of rank phlegm to the ground, the sweat rolling off his hide like waves in the swell. In the last few miles he had favoured one leg, and now I saw that he could barely stand on it. Yet still he stood: brave as he was, he would not go to ground unless I gave him leave.

I put my head to his, embraced his neck with my arms. I felt him lean forward, lean against me, like a weary old man leaning on his son, as though he hoped that I might be able to take some of his weight.

'Thank you,' I said. I took my knife and opened his throat and let him go to the ground. I held him as he died.

I had no time to butcher him properly. I took only the quick cuts across the top of the back, wrapped the bloody meat in cloth. Then I was away, running up the scree as fast as I could, the loose stones biting my feet. Three times I fell, striking skin from my palms, digging in my knees and elbows to stop myself from sliding further. A wrench of the knee, a breaking of bone – either of these would ruin me, leave me helpless for my followers. But I had to take the chance. I could not be caught on that slope.

Distant, I thought that I heard a cry, carried to me on the wind. I looked back and saw the figures moving faster in the distance. Stirring their horses, realising at last what it was I intended. I did not look again until I reached the top, gasping and retching, looking down to see the warband milling at the bottom of the mountain, shouting and arguing with each other.

I did not have to hear them to know what they said to one another. They had not thought that I would be so desperate as to go into the mountains. Would they follow me there? Or would they trust to the ice and stone to settle the feud for them? For no man could hope to pass three years in such a place.

'Go home,' I whispered to myself, willing it to be so, a heartfelt prayer.

And yet it seems they heard me. For they leapt from their

horses, took their weapons and supplies from their saddlebags, and began up the slope.

I turned away and looked to the east, to the heart of our country. And it was there that I saw a more dangerous sight than a conquering army, a fleet of warships, a mountain spewing fire.

I saw – nothing. I saw a land in which nothing lived, in which nothing could live. And I walked into it, the dead snow breaking beneath my feet, and moved as fast as I could over ground that no man had walked on in a hundred years.

They would not be far behind.

18

There are those who come to Iceland – newcomers, merchants from distant lands – who have never seen our country before. If the sea mist hangs thick in the air when they arrive, they may only see the rich farmlands along the coast, the rivers teeming with salmon, the grazing pastures on the low rolling hills. They may wonder how this country took such a hard name at its birth. How any man could look on this place and call it a land of ice.

Then the wind blows from the sea, the mist clears and they see the great mountains at the heart of the country. The endless fields of snow and ice, the black stone, the dead soil. And it is then that they understand. We live at the edges of this land, holding fast to what green country we may find. The rest we leave to the ice and snow, to the beasts, the monsters and the outlaws.

We look watchfully towards the centre, as if fearing that one day the mountains and the ice will march towards us like a conquering army, consuming the pastureland and freezing the rivers, driving us out into the sea.

Nothing may live in that place. Nothing grows. A world of ice and snow, that only the desperate, the hunted, will call home.

They followed me into that maze of stone and ice. Their numbers diminished: eight of the twelve now remained, for the others must have taken the horses back. They would not have cut down their horses as I had. These were still men with something left to lose.

Before, our chase had been almost sightless. Specks on the horizon following another speck on the horizon, walking our horses across the empty land. But we were on foot now and on ground where a few miles might take a day to cross.

When they shouted I could hear them clearly, and sometimes they did not need to shout. The twisted rock faces brought their voices to me – idle conversations about cattle and crops, muttered complaints about the cold. At night I sometimes felt as if I were at the campfire with them, and had to catch myself before I spoke in answer to them.

Not a day passed without us seeing each other. When I was on a high path and looked back to see them on the rocks beneath me. When I had passed through a thick snowfield, the cold whiteness up to my thighs, only to hear the soft crunch of breaking snow behind me, see the warband struggling half a mile from me.

I had no time for a fire and could not chance it, and so I ate my horsemeat raw – wolfish, blood running in my beard, soft meat slipping down my throat. Perhaps, I thought, it would be sickness that would kill me rather than the men who hunted me, for already my throat was raw from coughing. But if it seemed that it might come to that, I would turn back to seek out my pursuers. I would rather die fighting than be consumed by disease. I would rather taste iron than starve to death.

I knew no paths through the maze. At any moment I might come to an impassable blankness of stone, with no time to retreat. I turned each corner in fear, came over every rise in the terrain expecting to see the place where I would die. But the gods were kind, or perhaps they merely wished to toy with me a little longer. I always found a path through. Yet always, I could hear them close behind.

Weaker day by day, chewing snow in place of water, feeling the cold settle within me like a piercing arrow, a deep wound that I could not heal. Once I had run out of meat I scraped moss and lichen from the stone, hoping the pretence of eating might quiet my hunger for a time. I waited for some change, some way that I might escape.

Then, one morning, I felt a touch upon my face as I slept.

A gentle touch, like a lover's hands that seek to trace across skin without waking the sleeper. And I sat upright, one hand pushing forward and seeking a tunic or hair to wrap my fingers around, the other taking up the blade at my side, for there could be no lover here to wake me. My hands found nothing but air and I thought at first I had merely dreamed that touch.

Then I felt it again. A cold, scattering touch that seemed to be everywhere at once. It was only once I had come fully out of the world of dreams that I understood. It was snowing.

I put down the sword, held my hands upright and felt the coldness against my skin. What had begun as the lightest of touches was already becoming something else: a thick flurry of white that had already covered my legs, that swept over the mountainside all around me, that blocked the rest of the world from view. I looked on it and I began to laugh.

Silent laughter, for I could not take the chance of being heard. My shoulders shaking, biting down on the web of skin between thumb and forefinger, as the snow fell around me like the answer to a prayer. I got to my feet, already shivering yet still laughing, and stumbled forward into the snow, one hand held high to shield my face.

This was the time. There would be no more hunting, no more running. I would lose them in the storm that day or I would die in the attempt.

They were close to me. I could hear them calling in the storm, trying not to lose one another. They were stronger than I was, well fed around a fire each night, moving faster than I could. Wherever I placed my feet I left marks upon the snow. Wherever I went, I broke a path for them to follow.

And yet we could not see one another – the storm was too thick for that. The blind hunting the blind, by touch, by sound, by voice, fighting through the heavy snow one aching step at a time. Of all the ways I had thought to die, I had never foreseen this.

Out there, on the high mountains, I came to a flat, open field of snow – beautiful, in its own dead way. Like a well-tended field, as though the mountain spirits had chosen this place to harvest snow and ice.

The storm swirled into stillness for a moment, and on the other side of the snow field I saw something. A glimpse only, so brief that it might have been a trick, but I had to believe it to be true.

A pass leading down from the mountains. A valley beyond, green fields and rivers. A place of life, not this open-air tomb that I had trapped myself in. The snow closed off that vision once more, but I knew it to be there.

I moved across the field as fast as I could, towards what I had seen. And it was not long before, behind me, I heard them coming. The crunch of snow, the curses of tired men. They sounded so close to me, yet I could not see them.

I moved as in a dream, those trapped, sluggish motions. Pulling my legs free of the snow with numb hands, taking in the sharp air in great gasps that seemed to cut at my lungs, the tip of my belted sword catching with every step that I took. Waiting for the touch of a hand upon my shoulder, the feel of iron inside my skin.

But it did not come. There were rocks beneath my feet, in front of me the vision I had seen before. I could leave this place, go down amongst the living once more. But it would not be for long.

I turned to my right and ran across the rocks, crouched low, my ragged cloak flapping about me like a raven's wings. When I had gone far enough, I turned again, back towards the field of snow. I stepped on to it and I began to walk back.

I moved slowly now, caring more for silence than speed, waiting for the wind to gather up before I took each step. I could hear them drawing close. If they were spread out across the snow, they would catch me. I would see the shadow of a man in front of me and know it was too late, that my ploy had failed. He would see me and call to his companions. There would be no rush to it, for I could not run in that thick snow. It would be a patient killing.

But there was no man in front of me. They must have been gathered together, like a troupe of blinded slaves navigating as one. I heard them draw level, deep breaths and heavy footsteps to my right. They could have asked a question of me and I could have spoken softly in answer, we were so close. Then they were past, the sounds of them receding. Distant, I thought I heard one of them cry out as they reached the edge of the snowfield, when they saw that path down from the mountains.

A quickening joy in my heart. How long before they realised their mistake? Before they turned back and found that second trail through the snow? Long enough for me to vanish back into the mountains. Most likely to freeze or starve, but in that moment I did not care. I felt only the trickster's joy, Loki's joy.

Then I saw a shadow in the storm. The shape of a man, passing close by.

I crouched down, the snow slackened and I saw him. A man, pulling his cloak close around himself. Bowed over, staring at my tracks in the snow, trying to make sense of them. Just for a moment, then he was gone.

Carefully, gently, I dug at the snow at my feet. Clearing a hollow, like a madman digging his own grave. And I crawled into it, pulling the snow back over me. I took my knife in my left hand, and I listened.

For a long time, there was nothing but the howling of the wind. My right hand held close against my chest as if to quieten the beating of my heart, my left hand burning in the cold, fingers locked tight around the handle of the knife. The pain of the cold was akin to nothing I had felt before and I bit the folds of my cloak to keep myself from crying out. Then, abruptly, like the striking of lightning against the ground, I felt nothing at all.

I heard him then: the heavy tread of footsteps drawing closer. And a voice calling out – too hoarse for me to know who it was.

'Björn! Kari! Can you hear me?'

He was lost. Calling to his companions, mistaking my tracks for theirs.

What strange stroke of chance had brought him here? A twisting in the bowels that had set him behind his companions.

A stone working its way into his boots that he had taken a moment to remove, then looked up and found himself alone.

He wandered closer and closer, until he was near enough that I could have reached out and touched him from my hollow in the snow. But he had no eyes for the ground. He was trying to pierce the storm, to catch the sight of his companions.

'Björn!' he cried once more, the wind swallowing the sound. Then, 'Kjaran.'

He did not cry out my name. He said it quietly, to himself, a realisation. Then he looked down and his eyes met mine.

The snow flew from me as I rose, my shoulder into his knee, the knife searching and cutting at his leg. He fell, his body taut with horror, his lips moving but saying nothing. I crawled up him like a man climbing a mountain, and placed my fist into his mouth before he could cry out.

It was Ketil. Here for some duty he owed to Björn, some debt to be repaid in blood. No killer's longing for him, a mere discharge of a duty. And of all the people I might have faced, the gods had brought him here to die at my hand.

I rolled back from him, scrabbling along the snow on all fours. He stared at me, disbelieving, and he tried to stand, his hand reaching for the axe at his side. He tried to stand and his ruined leg gave way beneath him. I had felt the skin part deeply under the cut I had given him, but he did not know his wound until that moment. I could see the white of bone, the cords of his leg exposed like cut worms.

He embraced himself, arranging and rearranging his arms again and again over the wounds I had given him, for there were too many to cover. He was lost for a moment in his pain – eyes closed and teeth bared. Then it seemed that he remembered me.

'Do not shame me,' he said.

I looked beyond him, into the storm. Thinking that I had heard distant sounds, drawing closer. That they were coming back.

'Do not shame me!' he cried again.

But I turned from him and ran back across the snow. Back to the rocky paths at the heart of the mountains, leaving a dying man behind. And, before all sound was stolen by the wind, I heard him plead with me one last time.

I heard him plead with me to kill him.

I wandered, lost in the storm, looking for a place to die.

Every step I could feel the life pouring out of me, like blood from some deep and terrible wound. All I wished for was sleep, to lie on the snow and sleep.

There is a longing of a man who faces hopeless odds in battle. It is the longing to kill one man at least, to not die without spilling the blood of one who has come for you. You have killed one, the mind seems to say, and that is enough. Lie down and die if you wish, for you have done enough.

The snow fell thicker and thicker, the memory of the blood the only warmth that I had. And as I took another step I knocked loose a rock, heard it dance and scatter down towards my left. I followed that sound, and beneath the snow and stone I saw something. Not a path, but a gully that seemed to lead down from the mountain.

I stumbled down: careless, clumsy steps that were buried in snow, slipped across icy stone. I fell, time and time again. Slumping against the white blanket on the ground, closing my eyes for a moment of exquisite rest, then coming to my feet again.

'One more step,' I whispered to myself. One more step.

And then the ground levelling before me, the storm growing weaker and weaker until the way was clear and I could see where it was that the gods had taken me.

It was another world of black stone. A bare and empty valley, no shelter to be seen, no grass. No man had walked in this place for a hundred years at least.

I fell and could not get back up. Again and again I tried to stand, but I could feel some great, unseen weight upon my chest. I knew that I had gone as far as I could. At least I would not die in the mountains. At least I would not die at the hands of those who hunted me.

I looked out at the hand that had held the knife, that had maimed a man I had once called a friend, and I could feel nothing from it. I lay down in the snow and I waited to die.

I wandered from sleep to waking, time and time again. I had hoped to dream of Sigrid, but I dreamed of nothing at all. Only a silent dimness, like being under deep still water.

I woke one more time, and before me there was a figure in the darkness. He was no trick of the mind, for I could feel his heavy tread against the ground. I thought, for a moment, that he was one of my pursuers, that against all odds they had followed me to this place. But it was a man I did not know.

A ghost, perhaps, of another outlaw who had died in this place, come to guard his territory from the living. His clothing a patchwork of rags, his eyes rolling wild, a chipped axe held in his hand. Yet there was a dripping carcass slung to his back – a fox, skinned and bloody, and I knew that he was no ghost. For the dead do not need to feed.

He knelt beside me, unstoppered a leather skin that he slung around his neck. I could smell the sweetness of mead. Life was in that smell, and poetry and love. The strength to stand and fight again. I ached for it and reached out, but he drew it back from my hand.

He gave a bark and a cough – a man remembering how to speak. Then he spoke.

'Why should I save you?'

I could not understand and did not answer. He grabbed my chin and shook me.

'Listen! Tell me why I should save you.'

My lips moved, but no words came. He sat back, preparing to stand, preparing to leave me in the snow. And, his voice marked with regret, he spoke to me one more time.

'What can you do?'

I knew then what I had to say. What it was that I had to offer this man, the only thing of value that I had in that waste of ice and snow.

'I can sing,' I said.

I remember nothing more after that.

19

When I woke there was no sky above, no mountains surrounding me. Only shadows dancing on the walls of a cave. And, close by, the sound and the feel of a fire.

I shrank from it as the first man to strike fire must have done, fearing his own creation, believing that he was going to burn the world away with his strange, flickering gift.

It endured only for a moment. Then I had a hunger for the fire, crawling as close to it as I could stand. I held my hands out to it and could smell the hair burning, yet I could feel no heat in my fingers.

As I moved, something stirred on the other side of the fire. A great shadow moved on its hands and knees to my side, for he was tall and the top of the cave was close to me.

I saw him better now than I had out in the snow. His hair was the colour of wet iron, tied back tight against his head, yet his eyes were alive with youth, or madness. When he turned his head to face me, by the light of the fire I saw that one ear was gone, a ragged lump of flesh and scar all that remained on the right side of his head.

He gave me a sip of water. I gestured for more, but he withdrew it after I had barely wetted my lips. He rested his head against one palm and stared at me for a time. Then he said:

'I think you will die. A fever, most likely.' He turned away, stirred the fire, then looked back to me once more. 'I will give you a little food and water. I do not have much and I will not waste it. If you live a week, I will give you more. Do you understand?'

'I understand.'

'Do not foul this cave. Call me when the need takes you and I will carry you out.' He paused. 'It is a long time since I have shared a place with anyone. I will try to remember. But do not test me.'

Blackness came again – as swiftly as river ice breaking, cold dark water swallowing me. When I woke again, he had not seemed to move.

'You are an outlaw?' I said.

'You think that a free man would choose to live in this place? You are as well, I suppose.'

'Yes.'

He leaned forward, close enough for me to smell the stink of his breath. 'Do you know who I am?' he said.

'I do not know you. Are you from the north?'

He leaned back, seemingly satisfied. 'Yes. And you have come from the west?'

'I lived in the south, once. Then in the west.'

'And now, here.' He leaned back against the wall of the cave and his eyes followed the dancing flames. 'My name is Thoris. They call me Kin-slayer.' He paused. 'You know me now, I think.'

I had heard the story. 'You killed your brother,' I said.

'Yes. I killed my brother. I wanted to marry his wife.'

He lapsed into silence. There was nothing else to be said.

For a man may kill for many reasons. To answer an insult, to take revenge, to avoid shame. For silver or land or power. But our people hold no honour in killing for love.

'When I found you. Whose blood was on you?' he asked.

'A man who hunted me.'

'An enemy, then.'

'No. I would not call him that.'

'You gave him a warrior's death?'

'No. I left him maimed in the storm.' I turned my head away.

'You need feel no shame,' he said. 'Not here. That is the secret men like us know.'

'What secret?'

'That there is nothing we will not do. Eat a man, kill a child. I have seen the outlaws do it all, and worse. To survive.'

Exhaustion came over me and I knew that soon I would have to sleep again. I lifted my hands towards the fire – not for the heat, but to look upon them.

The fingers of my right hand were pure white. On the left, they were grey and black at the tips. Both were utterly unfeeling.

He noted them and said, 'I will help you, when a week has passed.'

'If I live.'

'If you live.' Then, almost shyly, he asked, 'When will you be able to sing?'

'Soon,' I promised.

For the first time I saw a smile dance across his lips. Just for a moment, like a falling star, and then it was gone.

The fever came, as he said it would. Days of waking madness and nightmares in the dark. Despite his instructions, I fouled myself time and time again in the dark. And I remember him

screaming at me, striking me about the face, dragging me out
to the mouth of the cave, where I used snow and rags of cloth
to scrub myself clean. The fever filled me with a feeling like
hate, a mad, screaming hatred. But it could not kill me.

I came through it as thin as cattle at the end of winter:
hollow-bodied, bones sharp against the skin. I could see Thoris
look doubtfully on me. Yet I could feel, deep within me, that
it was not my time to die. I have seen men and women die of
sickness, and they have always known, sometime before the
end, that it was coming. I knew that I wanted to live. I thought
of Sigrid and I knew that I would live.

My right hand had returned to life, though the pain of it
had been like nothing I had ever known. Even in the depths of
the fever, when all else was lost to me, I could feel the burning
of those fingers coming back to life. Yet on my left hand, the
hand that had held the knife, there was nothing. They grew
soft once more, but no feeling returned to them and they gave
no motion. They had turned from grey to black.

I did not know how many days it had been since he had
found me in the snow. Perhaps it had been a week, perhaps
longer. But on that day, when he came back from his morning's
foraging, he gave me a piece of his flatbread. Just a small piece,
but always before he had eaten, then left once more, without
offering me anything. He had given me food in the evenings
alone, leaving only a bucket of snow that would melt to drinking water in the day.

On that day, when the heat of the fever was falling from my
skin, I felt a different kind of warmth. There was no fire in the
cave and yet beneath me I could feel that the stone was warm
to the touch.

'Is this magic of yours?' I said.

'It may be magic. But it is not of my doing. I do not possess the art.' He leant down and spread his fingers across the stone. 'Perhaps something sleeps down there. A dragon or some other beast. And while it sleeps, we may live. And if it wakes, we die.'

'I will speak softly, then, so as not to wake it.'

'No. You will sing loudly. Let it wake. What does it matter?' He paused. 'How long are you outlawed for?' he said.

'Three years.'

He turned his head from me. 'I am glad for you,' he said. For I had heard that he had been outlawed for the rest of his life.

'How long have you been out here?' I said.

He did not reply. I waited, for I had learned that after spending so long alone, he was accustomed to silence. Many were the times I would ask a question, hear nothing from him, only to receive an answer hours or days later.

'Seven years now.'

'You did not think to go abroad? Why did you stay?'

'A woman. The woman I killed my brother for. She came with me, to this place. This was our home.'

I looked around the cave for some trace of her.

'She died,' he said. 'A fever. Three years ago. She was why I have survived longer than any other. I have seen many outlaws come and go. Stronger men than me, better hunters, better thieves. And they all die. For what else is there for a man to do in a place such as this? What else is there to do but die?'

'They kill themselves?'

'No. But they grow forgetful. They do not prepare enough for winter. They wander openly in farmlands and the hunters find them.' He tore another piece of bread and gave it to me. 'They die, without knowing that they want to die.'

'Do you still have men hunting you?'

'They still come. Every summer. My kin, bearing the duty

of revenge. They have seen me from afar. I expect they will find me, one day.'

'I have never heard of an outlaw living as long as you have.'

'There is pleasure in it. To live, when an island of men all wish you dead.' He smiled that faint, twitching smile once more. 'I feel powerful.'

I laughed then, as much as I could, hearing his words and looking on the pair of us: half-starved, ragged and filthy. Worse than beasts, for even a horse or a sheep had more protection under the law than we did, and yet he spoke of power.

'You will see,' he said. 'Perhaps you know it already, but choose not to believe it yet. Now tell me, why did *you* not run? Perhaps you did not have the silver.'

'A ship waited for me. A captain to take me away.'

'So why not take it?'

I did not answer.

'You have a woman?' he said.

'Yes.'

'I see. That is why you did not run.'

'No. She wanted me to leave. I promised her that I would.'

'Then why?'

I thought for a time. 'I have a friend,' I said. 'He too is in the feud. While they hunt me, they shall not hunt him.'

He spat on the ground. 'I doubt that. They will think you dead now.' He looked at me closely and I saw a coldness settling into his eyes. 'I will have the truth from you or I will not have you stay here.'

I rested my dead hand upon the sword at my side. I felt for the markings of the runes, for the patterned whorls of the iron. I knew it was there, but I could feel none of it.

'I did not want to leave,' I said. 'I could not leave. There must be a world beyond this island, but I cannot seem to believe it.

I would be taking a ship to nothing. To be with the dead. And it is not my time to die.'

He nodded to himself. 'You speak the truth, I think.' He placed his hands on his thighs and sat upright, like a chieftain on the high seat. 'Now,' he said, 'you will sing.'

I was afraid, then – more afraid than I had been in the storm, or when Gunnar and I had hunted the ghost, or at any time that I had stood with blade and shield in battle. I thought of the stories I had heard, of the skalds who saved themselves with song. Egill Skallagrímsson, the greatest of my people, had ransomed his head from a king with a poem. This cave was no kingly court, but Thoris was ruler of it just the same. He had no headsman to execute me if I failed, but he did not need one. The ice and snow would be his executioners, if he chose to cast me out.

I sat upright in my blanket, took water for a throat raw from coughing, daubed my face with a wet rag to still my restless mind.

It had been so long since last I had sung that I was certain I had lost my gift. That the words would not come. That the poet in me had died out in the storm. Perhaps the White Lady, too, obeys the word of the law. Perhaps it is that an outlaw cannot sing.

But after only a moment, I felt the touch of the White Lady on my shoulder and knew that she was with me still. The words came, as they always had, and I could feel the warmth building in my heart and my throat, could feel the poet's longing, and knew, at that moment, that I could not have remained silent even if I had tried.

And so I lifted my head and closed my eyes. And I sang.

★

He had let his head tip forward and that iron-grey hair had fallen about his face. He had been still, silent for the length of the song, and it was not a silence that had spoken to me.

My voice had cracked many times, my rhythm had been uneven, my breathing weak. Yet even so, somehow I did not think that I had ever sung so well.

At last he reached out a hand, placed the tips of his fingers to my shoulder. He let it rest there for a time.

'Well performed,' he said, his voice soft. 'I thank you.' He swallowed. 'You can stay.'

'It has been some time since you heard a poet sing, I think.'

'Gudrun. My wife. She used to sing. But not like that. Who was he, this Cúchulainn that you spoke of?'

'The great Irish hero. You have not heard of him before?'

'No. I have never heard an Irishman sing.'

'I know many songs of him. How he lived and fought. How he died.'

'You will sing of him more?'

'Yes,' I said. 'But first, you must do something for me.' I lifted my left hand and showed him my fingers.

He hesitated. 'We should wait,' he said. 'You are still weak.'

I shook my head. 'There is no time,' I said. 'Let it be now.'

His mouth worked, but he did not speak. I think he was afraid – afraid that he would kill me, even as he sought to save me. That he would have nothing but the memory of song to keep him company.

He took a knife from his belt. My knife, the sharpest blade that we had, for his axe and seax were long since dull and rusted. He tested the edge with his thumb, nodded.

'Give me your hand,' he said.

I lay flat on my stomach and laid my left hand down on

the stone, black fingers on grey stone. The other hand I kept curled up close beneath my body, as if to protect it from him.

He touched the knife to my thumb, to the bottom of the black skin. He might have been holding the blade to another man's hand, for all that I knew of it.

'There,' I said. 'I feel nothing.'

'No,' he said. 'We must be certain.' And he moved the blade down further, until it rested upon the white flesh and not the black. I felt the cold metal against my skin. Every nick and mark in the blade, I felt it perfectly.

'There,' I said.

'Do not move,' he said, and he placed both hands on the hilt of the knife, ready to press down.

'Wait,' I said.

I looked on that hand one more time. It had carried a shield, it had born crops from the harvest, it had cupped the face of the woman I loved as I kissed her. And with it, I had killed a man.

'Now?' he asked.

I took a filthy rag, balled it up ready to be bitten. I turned my head away.

'Yes,' I said. 'Now.'

And he began to cut.

I tried to think of myself as a prisoner, bound with irons. And that Thoris was a friend who had come to free me, each strike of the knife breaking the link on a chain.

I tried to believe that a spell had been laid upon me – that Thoris was a priest come to cleanse my body of the curse.

I tried to believe many things as I listened to the sound of the cutting, as I shook and trembled against the ground. And none of them could still the pain.

It was only after, as I cradled my mutilated hand close against my chest as though it were a child of mine, rocking backwards and forwards, the taste of bile on my lips, willing the pain to end – it was then that there was a great and terrible joy. The joy that I would live. And there is no agony that cannot be overcome with that joy.

I forced myself to look on it – five wet stumps daubed in blood. And I made myself smile, as I knew Thoris would want from me.

'Another nickname earned,' I whispered. 'Kjaran the Half-hand.'

'There are worse names to have.'

I lay down and thought of all the gods who had been maimed. I thought of my God Odin: he had given up one of his eyes for the gift of wisdom. What gift would be granted to me, in return for what I had sacrificed?

I felt Thoris's hand on my shoulder. Almost tender.

'Rest,' he said. 'You bore it well.'

'Tomorrow I will help you,' I said. 'I will not lie in this cave like an old man any more.'

'As you wish. But tomorrow.'

I lay down and let sleep take me.

I dreamed of miraculous healing, of my fingers sewn back and living once again. I dreamed of being tied down and being cut upon by all who I knew, of bleeding and screaming, but being unable to die.

Then I did not dream of Sigrid or of Gunnar.

I dreamed of revenge.

*

It was three days before I was strong enough to rise. I woke alone in the cave and it took me a long time to fight my way to my feet. But once I had stood, I felt no longing to lie back down. I leaned against the wall of the cave and breathed, and felt the strength flow through me.

When Thoris returned, he said nothing at first. Merely watched me with a warrior's eyes, looking for weakness. When he was satisfied, he said: 'We must go to work. We do not have much time before the winter comes.'

I looked beyond him, out of the cave and into that land of stone and snow. It seemed impossible that this could still be called summer. I could not imagine what a winter here would be like. Of how a man could hope to live in this place.

Yet soon I learned that we were to be what Icelanders had always been: farmers and herdsmen. For he had a small herd in one of the outer valleys. Year-old ewes, diseased and weak, worms dripping from their nostrils as they breathed. But he treated them as tenderly as if they were the finest of hillside cattle. The endlessly patient and exhausted love of a shepherd for his flock.

We had a little field of crops, too, in some rare patch of green land. They were blighted, half of them dead with frost, but gave a scattering of grain for us. We tended those crops and that herd in a desolate land, and I thought of those first settlers who had come to Iceland in the centuries before us. Perhaps this was how they had lived then, alone in the cold, fighting with the land to survive, with no kin to count upon if the harvest failed.

It was not enough – even I could see that. The meat and grain we would have might last us a few scanty months. But it was not enough to survive the winter.

When I told Thoris this, he nodded.

'I lost much time caring for you. We need more food than I thought.'

'What must we do, then?' I asked.

He did not answer, for the answer was too shameful to speak out loud. He merely looked to the west, towards the lands of other men.

We waited for the clear nights to pass, for the clouds to come, for the moon to grow thin. We hiked by day across the barren mountains, slept a few restless hours in dusk, and when the night was truly upon us we went out into the fields of men we did not know.

We were the ghosts that leave a man's sheep butchered in his fields, the trickster elves who steal wheat and corn from isolated shielings, the shadowy figures who send boys running across the heath back to their longhouses, screaming of monsters in the darkness.

I had never been on a Viking raid, but still I felt it in my blood. My mother's people had been hunters and raiders, my father one of those taken as a slave in those same raids. And so I told myself that we were not thieves, but hunters. They had cast us out of the law, would kill us if they caught us. We owed them no shame. And so, night after night, we raided the farmers for grain and meat.

Always careful not to raid in the same place twice. Always taking little enough that the farmers might tell themselves that they had miscounted their herd, had forgotten where they had placed that sack of grain. They did not want to believe in thieves.

Sometimes we saw other men out on such night work – alone, for the most part, but sometimes in pairs like us. We kept far away from each other. A fear of discovery in large numbers, of a rivalry turning violent, and an unnameable fear of other outlawed men. For though they were like us, we feared them. We carried our bad luck with us like a stench: growing used to our own, but disgusted by others with whom we were unfamiliar.

We went many times, and I grew to long for those black nights. To walk in tended fields amongst cattle, in lands that were bare of snow and ice, was a little like being a free man once more. But I knew it would not be for long. I knew that it could not last.

We were walking back one morning, each with a ewe trussed up across our backs, when I noticed the change. Some absence that made me uneasy, a sensation that I had experienced many times before, but never as an outlaw. It was not until we were at the foothills of the mountains that I understood what it was.

'No birdsong,' I said.

Thoris nodded. 'Yes, they have gone. It will be winter soon.'

I looked down on my ruined hand: five fingers taken by the cold, and it had been late summer. I could not imagine what winter would be like in those mountains. I could not think of how we might survive it.

I have heard that in other countries winter is not so cruel. There are many who die in those winters, but through the slow deaths: the rattling cough that becomes wet and choking over many weeks, the endless rain that pierces a house and brings a killing fever, rot spreading unseen through a storehouse and ruining a winter's provisions. But you will know that your death is coming, long before it reaches you.

In my country winter is a killer of men. It does not kill in weeks or months, but in moments. You step outside in winter and feel the wind as if it were fingers tightening around your throat, a cold blade laid against your wrists. You can feel it cutting, killing, and you retreat to the fire, wounded and beaten.

I knew a man who stepped outside to walk fifty paces to the outhouse. He left the fireside drunk and smiling, joking that the wind might sober him up. We waited for him to return, and he did not. We searched for him, called for him, until the cutting wind drove us back. Fifty paces to the outhouse and he was lost in the storm. And we found him months later when the snow had melted. Carrion-picked. Eyeless and lipless, smiling blindly at the sky.

The sun barely passes the horizon, is gone as soon as it comes. The sea fills with drift ice; even if you chose to take to the water, following the birds to the south, your ship would be torn to pieces. The entire island is sealed away from the world; none can come and none can go. And so we seal ourselves away, too. We sing and drink, and try not to think of the dwindling food and fuel in our stores, the cold death that knocks at the door with every gust of wind, asking to come inside.

We made no more raids on the fields. We butchered our cattle and salted the meat, harvested what grain we had. We dug a pit and buried much of what we had, and took the rest to the cave.

Before we placed the food in the cave, one could not stand fully upright in it. And once all of the food was in, I saw that we would have to crawl in. Live on our bellies like snakes and eat our way to the bottom of the cave again.

'How will we know when it is time?' I asked the outlaw.

'You shall know,' he said.

20

A day like any other. We were burying the last of our provisions. A stronger wind, a sharper wind than usual, but I thought nothing of it. I saw that Thoris seemed tense, uncertain, but I did not know why. He felt something that I did not, knew something that I could not.

The snow began to fall. What did that matter? It had fallen many times in the days before. But I saw that Thoris had stopped moving and was staring at the sky. I felt the wind again, that familiar, killing wind against my skin.

The snow fell, faster and faster, and I saw that it would not relent. That the gods would drown us on dry land if they could. We ran, then – we ran for our lives.

My half-hand pulled my cloak tight against my skin, armour against the blade of the wind. The other hand forward by instinct, for the snow was so thick that I felt the urge to part it, as if it were some heavy piece of cloth partitioning a longhouse.

Three times on the way back to the caves we found ourselves lost in the maze of snow. Lost on ground that we had trodden upon dozens of times, and there is no more fearful sensation than that of being lost on familiar ground. Yet each time we chose well, until we could see that black slit in the side of the mountain. We crawled into the cave and watched the snow fall.

All too soon, it was piled up to half the height of the cave. I made to go forward, to clear it away, but Thoris waved me back.

'Let it be,' he said. 'There is no use in fighting it.'

I watched it build, the cave growing darker with each passing moment. The mad desire to rush forward, to flee out in the snow consumed me, for what man can be willingly buried alive? It was as though we lay looking up at the sky in our own graves, buried one handful of earth at a time, watching the sky disappear.

At last the entrance was sealed, and there was only darkness.

We lay in silence for a time, listening to the cry of the wind, feeling the cold begin to seep and settle upon our skin.

Then a voice from the black.

'You had better sing,' Thoris said. 'But make your songs last. We have a long time to listen to them all.'

Let me tell you of a day in winter.

I woke in darkness, yet I knew that outside it was light. I felt it, as those animals do who live deep beneath the earth and can still feel the sun stirring. Beneath me, sacks of grain and salted meat; skins of water. Somewhere below was the stone floor of the cave. I feared to reach down and find it, for I knew that if I felt the cold stone it would mean that we had no food left. That touch would be like the hand of a god on my shoulder, telling me that it was time to die.

I crawled forward to the front of the cave, listening for the sound of snow and storm. There was none, and so I took up the wooden pick and began to hack at that white wall. Chipping away in the darkness, until a point of light broke through, like a dagger in my eyes. No heat from the light, and cold air came with it that left me shivering. Yet I basked in it as if it were a summer sun that shone upon me. That light and clean air were our treasures, taunting gifts from the gods, before the snow came and buried us again.

There were some days where we were given only a few moments of light before the storms returned, the white fire falling from the sky. There were times where the snowfall did not relent, when we lived in darkness and foulness for days at a time.

But this was not such a day. It was a still day, blue skies above. And I listened out for any sound at all from the mountains around us. Sometimes there was music in the mountains: the singing of the wind, the calving of ice, the chatter of rockfall. That day there was not a breath of wind, no sound at all to be heard. An utter, endless silence.

Behind me, I heard Thoris stirring. Then his voice.

'How does it look?' he asked.

'Beautiful,' I said. And it was.

I threw out fouled blankets, empty sacks, old bones. The hillside was covered in our filth, yet I knew that the next snowfall would bury it all as though it had never been there.

It was as beautiful a day as I could remember, but we would not leave the cave. I longed to walk upon that snow, to climb to the high places and look for some sight of distant lands, of home. But I knew that I could not. I had seen days such as this, clear and beautiful, be taken over by a blizzard in a matter of moments. Winter sought to lure us out for the killing: it was as wily as any murderer in a feud.

But I dared to go as far as I had been in months: to the edge of the cave, my back resting against the stone. From there I looked out on the valley.

It did not matter that the day was clear, that the sun was bright. I did not need light to know that landscape, for I had been staring at it for many months and knew every fold and turn by now. Like a prisoner in the old stories, whose only glimpse of the world is from a single barred window.

I tried to remember other places, the places that mattered to me. The mountains around Borg, the rolling landscape of the Salmon River Valley, the hillside of Hildarendi where my father lived. It should have been the simplest thing, to recall them. But I could not do it. They were fading from my mind – dust, and dreams. There was no place but this.

Thoris came out to sit beside me. He passed me a scrap of salted meat: the first thing I had eaten that day, for I had learned not to touch the food unless he permitted it. The custom was with us as it is with wolves, where none may eat except if the leader allows it.

We sat together and we did not speak. We watched the movement of the sun; it had been in the sky for so little time, and yet already it was fading.

He broke the silence. 'We shall have a fire,' he said.

'Are you certain?'

'Yes. Why not?'

I felt tears sting my eyes and turned my head so Thoris would not see them.

We gathered what little we had to burn, with all the patience at ritual of priests at a sacrifice. Every scrap of cloth, every fragment of wood, every piece of dung – all were so carefully placed. Nothing could be left to chance.

We waited for the sun to sink down and when it touched the horizon I struck sparks from the flint. A dozen points of light, each one visible for only a moment, yet I seemed to see all of them perfectly. I had such a terrible longing for that fire.

I watched the sparks that died and those that caught. I watched each place where the flames began – how they flickered and danced, grew and combined together – until the fire was burning strongly, the hiss and crackle of the flames like music to us. I held out that ruined hand of mine towards the fire and in the heat it felt whole once more.

The snow around us grew soft with the heat, melting and weeping like a woman at a funeral pyre. We grew busy, placing food over the fire, pots of snow to melt down for warm water. And I felt the longing that men and women always feel around a winter fire. A longing for memories and for stories.

I spoke. 'Let me tell you of the woman I love.'

'No,' Thoris said. 'I do not wish to hear that story.'

'Then I will tell you of my friend Gunnar. A great warrior.'

'No. I do not wish it.'

'Then tell me—'

'No,' he said, stirring the pot with his knife. 'I do not wish to speak.'

'Why?'

He said nothing for a long time. Then he said: 'There is no world but this place. There are no people other than we two. Do you understand?'

I wish that the fire had been stronger, so that I might have seen his face better, to know what it was that he meant. But perhaps I did understand.

'Sing for me,' he said. He had spoken those words many times before, but never as he spoke them on that day.

I had won my life with song, earned my keep with song. A cripple, unskilled in the arts of the outlaw, it was all I had to offer. He had always commanded and I had always obeyed.

But that day his voice was different. He did not demand that I sing. He asked me to.

I gave him the song I knew he wanted, that he loved above all others, the first that I had given him. I sang of the death of Cúchulainn, and in those words perhaps he saw a death that he desired. Not frozen and starving, alone in the mountains. But dying in battle against hopeless odds.

I did not think of my death as I sang. That might have been the only hope left to him, but not to me. For he had given up on dreaming of those beyond the valley, of lives unlived and paths untaken. But I had not.

If I were to think of those that I might envy, there would be a danger there. Of Olaf in his great hall, filled with warmth and good company. Of Björn and Vigdis spending the winter in comfort, in victory. Perhaps this was why Thoris did not want to think beyond the valley. Perhaps there was a madness waiting there, in jealousy. But not that day.

I did not think of my enemies, or of fortunate men that I might envy, I thought of Gunnar, and of Sigrid.

I gave Gunnar a hundred different lives in my mind, imagining every path that he might take. I saw him on the water, captain of a ship once more. I saw him working his fields and tending his crops. I saw him clasping hands with his enemies and swearing to a peace. I saw him at the *holmgang*, dispatching his enemies one by one in honourable duels. I saw him die bravely in open battle, the blood of his enemies upon his sword.

I dreamed a hundred different lives for him and tried to think of which one might be true.

There was only one destiny that I dreamed for Sigrid. That she waited for me. I dreamed of a small stretch of farmland in the Salmon River Valley, where we might spend the rest of our lives. Of love in the darkness. Other dreams tried to find me, but I would not let them.

I thought of the callouses of Gunnar's hand when he clasped mine. The fineness of Sigrid's hair running between my fingers. The way her eyes seemed to catch fire a moment before she smiled. How strong and proud Gunnar looked when he shifted one foot a little in front of the other and took up the warrior's stance. I was losing those memories – hoarding them like a miser, and every day there seemed to be fewer to count. But that night by the fire, the memories seemed to grow stronger, not weaker. For a time, sharing our songs and dreaming our dreams, we were the living once more.

The flames began to die. We huddled close around it in silence, our hands outstretched and almost touching the embers. Until it was as though our roles had been reversed, that fire and I: as if I were trying to give my heat to the fire, trying to keep it alive. And just as the final embers winked out and went cold, the snow began to fall once more. Those steady, heavy pieces of snow, handfuls cast down by a god. We crawled back into our tomb and waited to be buried. The living became the dead once more.

As we did every night, we wrapped our arms around each other, sharing the warmth that was our most precious gift. And I tried to find sleep and dreams, before the cold gripped too tightly.

I could have told you of many other days. Of the days when winter sought to kill us: the day it grew so cold that my lips froze to each other and ice coated the inside of our cave, where we fought to light a fire with shaking hands. Or the day we were buried so deep beneath the snow that the air suddenly turned foul, and we fought against the snow like duellists in the *holmgang*, hacking and gasping and retching, until the clean air broke through and we could breathe once more.

And there were worse days than those that I could speak of. The days of emptiness that outnumbered all of the rest. Lying still in the dark, wordless, shivering, feeling the winter madness scratching at my mind, trying not to scream.

But I wanted to tell you of that day.

A good day.

21

Every winter of my life I had known what it was to be trapped in a valley. The plains around Hildarendi when I was a boy, the Beautiful Valley, the Salmon River Valley. Yet even in the worst of winters I could find a sign of another life. A trail of smoke from a cooking fire. A distant shadow moving on a hillside. A voice raised in song, carried on the wind. But not in that valley of the outlaws.

There were no others within the valley, and none would come. Even if our enemies had been mad enough to pursue us in winter, every pass was sealed with ice and snow. They could not come in to the mountains and we could not get out. We were alone.

We each grew sick in turn. Kept awake by the rattling coughing of the other man, too tired to feel pity, wishing only that he would either grow well or die. For there is a madness that comes without sleep. And we were both mad before long.

We barely ate. Scraps of dried meat, bowls of cold oats and snowmelt. Our flesh thinned, our bones grew light, until we were each reduced to a pair of aching lungs, a sluggish beating heart. I wondered if there would come a time when we knew that there truly was no hope. When we would go to our knees in that tiny cave, reach for our knives with shaking hands. When we would agree to try and give one another a warrior's death, rather than waiting to starve like cowards or beasts.

The snow grew weaker. The light grew stronger. The season began to turn. Yet for us, nothing changed.

At last there was a day when we had nothing left to eat. Our hands touched the bare stone of the cave floor, our fingers ran over bones that were notched with tooth-marks and scoured of any fragment of meat.

We broke open the snow and found it softer, wetter than it had been before. I stepped out and stumbled on shaking legs like a newborn lamb, the only sound that of the wind when it stirred, the crunch of snow beneath our boots. When the wind was still, when we were still, there was nothing.

At the frozen river at the bottom of the valley, the ice broke quickly. I filled a bucket, lapping the water from it as a dog would, careful not to reach in and gather the water in my palms. Thoris had warned me not to, for he had seen men maimed that way: a single touch of water on the skin that froze when the wind turned. I had no wish to lose the fingers on my other hand.

We went to a place where we had buried our supplies, chipped at the ground, digging up grain, frozen meat, icy wood to try and burn. Moving as much as we could that day, for who knew when the storms would come again? There was still so little light, so little time.

That night, as we lay exhausted in the cave, Thoris pressed me for a song more insistently than he ever had before. But I found that I did not have the heart for it. For the first time in as long as I could remember, the words would not come; I could not sing.

'It will come,' Thoris said. 'The first winter is the hardest. You will learn. And it is passing now. It is ending.'

I heard his words, knew them to be true. Yet still I did not believe.

'I should have gone abroad,' I said. 'I should have taken my place on that ship. I was a fool to stay.'

There are words that a man speaks, in the cold and the dark, that he does not mean. Winter can take over a man like a fever, and falsehoods tumble from his tongue. So long as he gives no insult that must be answered with blood, he will be forgiven for it. But I meant those words. I did not speak lies, but the truth.

There in the dark, I saw Thoris shudder.

There was a day, like every other before it. Of shivering cold and hunger. Of squalor and boredom. A clearer day, so we walked through the snow towards one of our more distant caches of supplies. Sick, bent double with coughing, for we were both consumed by the same sickness.

It seemed impossible that summer could come again, we had been so long in the dark and the cold. I had not seen any other man or beast apart from Thoris for so long that the thought crept into my mind that there were no others left. That we alone in the world had survived that winter, that Ragnarök had come and gone and even the gods were lost. That we were the last men left in the world.

A sound came to me as I trudged through the snow. A soft, fragile sound, like the first note struck by an unpractised musician. I thought it a phantom of the mind at first, for in the sleepless darkness of the winter I had grown used to hearing voices and sounds that were not there. I heard it again and could not make sense of it. Again and again it came, soft still but insistent, for the musician was growing more confident, was remembering what it was to play.

I turned back to face Thoris to see if he heard it too. He had stopped walking, stood in the snow with his head tilted shut and his eyes closed. I knew that he heard it too. I knew then what it was.

I needed to see it. I would not believe unless I saw it. And though until that moment I had not known if I had the strength even to walk, suddenly I was stumbling and running through the snow, casting my head about. I clapped my hands, yelled curses, hoping to scare out the source of the sound.

There! A moment of brown motion, an angry cry, and I saw it. A little brown bird, rising from skeletal brush exhumed by the sun. It circled me, scolded me, twitched its wings and was off.

He was the first, but others would follow. The birds had returned and spring would follow them.

I sank to my knees in the snow and gave my thanks to any gods who might hear me. I looked to Thoris and found him grinning at me. A child I must have seemed to him, for he had known this moment would come. To be at the worst point of winter, where no hope is left, and to hear the birds sing.

We laughed together like madmen, howling and screaming with joy, wrestling in the snow like children at play. If a god had spoken to me at that moment and told me that I would die the next day, it would not have mattered to me. To live to hear birdsong again, it was enough.

When we were exhausted, sitting in the snow and drunk on the memory of that music, I said: 'We shall have another fire tonight.'

'We shall.' Thoris scratched at his mutilated ear. 'Do you

still wish that you had taken your place on that ship? Was it not worth the suffering, for this?'

I hesitated, considering the lie, but already it was too late. He saw the truth of it in my face. He stood and struck the snow from his clothes with rough, chopping blows of the hands.

'Come,' he said. 'We must go back to the cave.' He began to walk away, but he had not gone far when he turned back to speak once more. 'I will have a song tonight,' he said.

He did not speak it as a request: it was a command.

22

'Do you see him?' I said.
   'Yes.'
'What shall we do?'
'I cannot say.'

I lifted my hand to shield my eyes from the sun and looked again down the valley. The day was clear, the sun was high, and yet still I could not believe what it was that I saw. There was a man walking through the valley. One man alone, coming towards where we lay in the snow.

It was spring – my first spring as an outlaw, and we had been going to tend the sheep that morning. Our new herd, for we had stolen some pregnant ewes whilst the nights were still long enough. And as we went to tend them, we had seen movement at the edge of the valley.

We thought him one of the other outlaws at first, one of those shadows we saw on the high mountains from time to time, and kept well away from. A thief who had come to take from us the cattle we had stolen.

But this man was different. Even from a distance we could see that he was well clothed. He walked like a warrior, not the shambling, exhausted steps of the outlaw who is always hungry, always exhausted. And he carried something in his hands, something long and slender. A staff, perhaps, though he did not use it to help him walk.

'One of the men who hunts you?' I said.

'Fool,' he snapped. 'Who would come here alone?'

'Another outlaw, then.'

'Perhaps.'

He was going towards the herd; soon he would see them. Half a dozen sheep, all marked with a different man's brand. There would be no mistaking them for anything other than the work of a thief.

'If he takes the cattle, we die,' I said.

'It does not matter if he takes them, if he has seen where they graze. He cannot leave. We cannot let him go.'

We lay still, our bellies against the ground, and watched him walk towards his death.

He saw the herd, the first sign of life he must have seen in the mountains for days. I thought the sight might make him flee or scour the hillsides for the shepherds who watched over this thieves' flock. He paused for only a moment, his head cocked to the side, before he went towards the animals in the valley.

We waited until he passed our position, until he was deep within the dale. There was only one way in and out of this place; that is why we had chosen it to keep our herd. If he went deeper into the valley we would have him trapped, for it ended in impassable cliffs. If he tried to go back the way he had come we would have to close the distance quickly, to cut him off before he could escape.

Yet the moment we stood, he seemed to hear us. For he turned to face us and he did not run. He greeted us with a wave, as though he were hailing friends from another valley, and came towards us.

We stood, irresolute. We would have been ready for him to take flight, to draw a weapon. This courtesy was one we did not know how to answer.

'We should welcome him,' Thoris said. 'Let him relax. Then we can take him by surprise.'

'I will not murder a man like that. If he must die, he will die fighting.'

He cursed me. 'A fool's honour,' he said. 'You still speak as a free man. But we shall kill him your way.'

I had almost forgotten how free men looked: soft cheeks, clean tunic, silver rings on his arms. We must have seemed a desperate pair to his eyes, I half-handed, Thoris ragged from seven years in the mountains. More akin to wolves than men.

He carried a beautiful weapon, a sword too large to wear slung from his belt, and so he carried its scabbard in his hands like a staff, picking his way through the rocks with the sheathed point. Now he placed that point against the ground and rested his chin on the pommel. He smiled at us and I saw that half his teeth were gone, all on one side. The side of a shield, the flat edge of a sword, a wild horse's flailing hoof – something had marked him with a monster's smile.

'This is your herd?' he said.

'It is,' Thoris replied.

'I do not think so. They bear the marks of many different men.'

'They are ours now.'

He covered his mouth with his hand. 'So I see,' he said, his shoulders shaking.

'Who are you?' I asked.

'My name is Thorvaldur.'

'Why have you come here?'

'I am an outlaw, as you are.'

'Then go, and find another place.'

He raised an eyebrow. 'You would let me leave?' And he covered his mouth again.

I put my hand to the hilt of my sword. 'We cannot. But we will give you a warrior's death.'

'I thank you for speaking the truth.' He paused, then said: 'If I cannot leave, perhaps I may join you.'

'I have no need of another man eating my sheep and grain,' Thoris said and levelled a finger at me. 'One parasite is enough.'

'Oh, I may be of use to you,' said the stranger.

'How?' I said, and I remembered the words that Thoris had spoken to me in the storm. 'What can you do?'

'What can I do?'

'Why should we save you?'

He laughed out loud now, as though at some joke that only he had heard. 'I can tell you of God,' he said. 'Of the true God.'

'The White Christ?'

'He is called that by some.'

'We have gods enough of our own,' I said. 'We have no need of yours.'

'Fool,' Thoris said. 'The gods are no friends of ours.' He looked back on the stranger. 'But your God will be no different. We have no need of him.'

'Very well. May I have the names of those who will kill me?'

'I am Thoris Kin-slayer. And this is Kjaran the Luckless. Tell them to your God, when you see him.'

He cocked his head again. 'I have heard your story,' he said. 'You killed your brother.'

'Aye. That I did.'

'My God has a story of such a thing. You shall want to hear it.' He looked to me next. 'I do not know your crime. But perhaps I have a story for you as well. I would be happy to share them with you.' He tightened his grip on the sword. 'Or we may kill each other. It does not matter to me.'

I have heard many men make such a boast. Our gods honour none but the battle dead, and so we should hold no fear of death at the edge of a blade. Yet for all the boasts I had heard, I believed it from only two men: Gunnar, and the man who stood before us in that valley.

I had heard that Christians were unmanly, that their God was a coward. For that was what the White Christ meant: the Coward Christ. And yet here he was before us, ready to die.

'Wait,' Thoris said.

The silence grew. Perhaps he was thinking of the danger of a fight. We were two, but we were weak. He might only have to wound us to kill us: a fever or starvation would finish what he began. Perhaps Thoris merely thought of the odds, and that they were not in our favour.

But I do not think it was that.

'Your name is Thorvaldur, you say?'

'Yes.'

'Thorvaldur,' Thoris repeated, as though there were some spell in the word. Perhaps there was, for I could not have expected what he next said. 'You may come with us. I will hear stories of your God.'

At once, the stranger relaxed. He thrust the point of the sword into the snow and came forward to embrace us, as though we were his brothers.

We could have cut him down then; perhaps it would have been better if we had. But he knew that we would not. Already, we were under the strange spell he seemed to cast.

And so we were three. A farmer, a poet, a priest.

We took him back to the cave and lit a fire, our first in many days. It amused me to see Thoris light it. Even out here he wanted to impress his guest, as if he were an impoverished chieftain gifting his last silver ring to a visitor rather than confess his poverty. For it is better to starve than to be shamed.

We ate, shared a little of that mead that Thoris kept on the flask around his neck, and sat together in silence. I waited for Thorvaldur to speak, to share the words of his God, but he seemed to feel no haste. He waited for us to ask.

'How did you come to be outlawed?' I said.

Thoris's mouth twisted in scorn. I knew how he hated to speak of a world outside these mountains.

'I travelled with a bishop,' the Christian said.

'What is that?'

'A great man of God, from across the sea. We travelled together, visiting one chieftain after another. Then we went to the Althing, to speak the word of God.' He fell silent. It was the first time that I had seen him hesitate, seem doubtful.

'What happened?'

'They laughed at us. Called him unmanly.' He smiled at me. 'And so I killed two of them. It was a fair fight.'

'And yet you were outlawed.'

'They think to cow us Christians. Any other man would have been made to pay the blood-price for answering such an insult. But they thought to get rid of me.'

Thoris spoke at this. 'They have succeeded, it seems.'

Thorvaldur shrugged. 'For three years. And then I shall return.'

'Why not go abroad?' He pointed to me. 'This fool had the chance, but gave it up. Were you too proud to leave, too? Or too poor?'

'Neither. I came here to find men like you.'

'Why would you do such a thing?'

'The men out there. They are not ready to hear the word of God. Perhaps you are.'

'What do we matter to you?'

'Every soul matters to me. But that is a story for another time.' He spread his hands wide and said, 'Now, I will speak to you of my God.'

'Come, then,' Thoris said. 'Amuse us with your stories.'

'And if I do not amuse you? Will you kill me?'

Thoris shrugged. The question not worthy of an answer.

'At least I shall die well fed,' Thorvaldur said, and I could see the light of the fire shining on his teeth as he smiled. 'It is a long story. It will take much time.'

'We are wealthy in time, if in nothing else.'

'Very well,' Thorvaldur said, and he crossed his legs and straightened his back. 'Let me tell you how the world was made.'

And he began to speak, with words that were not his.

At first, little that he said seemed new to me. He spoke of the crafting of the world; we had a story much like it. He spoke of a sacred tree of knowledge, much like Yggdrasil, the tree from which Odin was hung in pursuit of knowledge. He told stories of a trickster god who took the form of a snake – Thorvaldur called him Satan, but I knew him for Loki. I began to grow bored as he spoke. From what little I had heard of the White Christ, he expected men to be willing to die for him. It did not seem like much of a faith to die for.

But then he spoke of a man and woman cast out from a paradise. Exiles – perhaps you could even call them outlaws. And I felt a coldness run up my spine, for that is where a story leaves its mark, when we know it to be true.

Thorvaldur spoke of two brothers. Of their rivalry and how,

in jealousy, one murdered another. A feud between brothers, a feud between a man and his God. And even in the darkness I saw Thoris tremble a little.

Thorvaldur paused. His voice changed, and he no longer spoke with a God's words but with his own.

'I think this story is familiar to you, is it not?' he said.

Movement in the dark. Hands reaching, finding. One shadow on top of another, and the light of the fire on the blade of a knife. And Thoris pressing his face close to that of Thorvaldur, while that man of God stared back at him impassively, a trickle of blood running from his throat.

'Do you mock me?' Thoris said.

'I told you that my God had such a story. I mean no mockery.'

'And what does your God say happened to him?'

'He was cursed to wander the earth. Cast out from his people.' Thorvaldur's eyes flickered over Thoris's ruined ear. 'And he was marked, so that every man knew him for what he was.'

'I know this story already. What use is it to me?'

'But you do not know how it ends.'

Thoris sat back, the blade still in his hand. 'Tell me.'

'He was branded for his whole life,' Thorvaldur said. 'Hated by the people of the world. He suffered, but God forgave him.'

'Why?'

'God forgives the evil that men do.'

'At what price?'

'There is no price but faith. For mine is a God of love.'

Silence followed. What answer was there to that?

Odin, Thor, Freyr – our gods are our chieftains, our kings. We honour them and they protect us. We anger them and they destroy us. We die well and they reward us. But how could a God love a man?

Thoris's lips curled – anger, perhaps even disgust. The knife still lay in his hand, gripped weakly.

'Enough of this,' I said. 'I will sing, if you want.'

'No,' Thoris said. 'I do not want your songs.' He pointed to Thorvaldur. 'Speak. Tell me your story. Tell me how it ends.'

23

What do the seasons matter in a place such as that outlaw's valley? What does summer count for in a land where nothing grows and there is no end to the ice and snow? Where the coming and going of the winter is marked by the birds and the sun, but by no other man or woman?

I dreamed sometimes that there was some second, secret world within those dead valleys. A gathering of the outlaws, perhaps even a shadow of the Althing. A place where, at the height of a frozen summer, we outcast men would meet in a frozen valley, beside a dead lake. There we could trade and share our stories, feel ourselves to be part of something greater.

Our people had come to this country a century before, forged a new people in an empty land. Could we retreat once more, found a country within a country?

But there was no such thing. This was not some second society, hidden away from the people of the coast. We were not pioneers, settlers of the ice. There were no women, no children. We were not men. We were ghosts.

We passed the seasons shivering in the cave, working in fragments of daylight. On some of the long nights, I still sang – more for Thorvaldur now, for he clapped and cheered each song as though we were in a chieftain's hall. Thoris half-listened, scratching at the floor of the cave with the blade of his knife. He was waiting for something else. For on the days that I did not sing, Thorvaldur continued the story of his God.

I listened as a child will to the ramblings of an angry old man: all attention, but with little interest. I had the gods of two people already – from the Icelanders and the Irish, Odin and the White Lady, the father and mother of my poetry. I needed nothing from him.

Or so I believed, at first.

There came a day in late summer when Thorvaldur and I sat by a small fire, preparing a rare hot meal. Thoris was away – tending the herd or collecting water, I cannot remember which. But I was alone with the Christian, for a time at least.

'Will you speak of your God again tonight?' I said. 'Or shall I sing?'

'It will be as our chieftain wishes it.'

'Then I think that we will have your stories. I would lay a wager, had I anything of my own to gamble with.'

'You do not care for my tales of Christ?'

'I do not mind them. Some of them make for good stories.'

'But they do not move you.'

'I have enough gods at my side already. I have no need for another.'

'Perhaps I may tell you other things. What is it that you wish to hear?'

I hesitated. 'There is a man that I would hear news of,' I said. 'A woman, too, though I doubt you will have heard of her.'

'Name them. Perhaps I do know them.'

'Gunnar Karlsson.'

He thought for a time – recalling a memory or stitching together a lie. But I would know it if he lied. I wonder if I would have cut his throat for the lie. But at last he nodded slowly. And when he spoke, I believed him.

'I saw him at the Althing,' he said. 'I did not speak to him myself. But there were others who spoke of him.'

I felt an aching in my chest. 'He was well?'

'Well enough. Though he seemed to quarrel with many men.'

'That is his way.'

He considered me for a moment. 'I saw him go to the poets,' he said. 'To hear them sing. Thinking of you, I suppose?'

'He always liked to hear the poets sing,' I said. 'I am but one of many.'

A smile played across his lips. 'There was a woman there that he spoke to.'

I closed my eyes. 'Describe her to me,' I said.

'Tall, pale-skinned. Too thin. But I think you know of whom I speak.'

One more year, I thought. *Wait for just one more year. Please.*

'So,' he said. 'This is a woman that you love.'

'Yes, it is. Tell me more of the Althing.'

'What is it that you wish to know?'

'Everything.'

He laughed and would have spoken again. But we heard the heavy tread of Thoris returning to the cave.

He stood in the entrance of the cave, his hands resting on the stone above his head. He leaned forward, peering in, and looking from one of us to the other.

'What is it that you speak of?' he said.

'Nothing of consequence.'

'That is a lie. You speak about me, don't you?'

'No,' Thorvaldur said. 'We speak of the Althing. Of old friends.'

Thoris spat upon the ground. 'I do not want to hear of this. The gossip of the farmers, the schemes of the chieftains. What does it matter to me? If you will speak of such things, you shall not do it in this cave.' He sat down beside us, took a spoon carved from bone and dipped it into the cooking pot. 'Tell me more of your God.'

Thorvaldur stood and offered his hand to me.

'We have not finished speaking,' he said, 'so we shall leave your cave. Warm yourself by the fire. We shall be back before too long.'

Thoris's mouth worked, but no words came, and he looked on us like a man scorned by his lover.

'Go, then. And freeze, for all that I care.'

How long had it been since I had walked for pleasure alone? At first I could not recall, I had been so long an outlaw or caught in a feud where every motion held a purpose.

It had been the night we had hunted the ghost, Gunnar and I. A winter sojourn taken for the pleasure of the hunt, the joy of good company, and nothing more than that. Perhaps that was why I had lost my taste for an idle wandering.

As Thorvaldur and I walked from the cave we went not as outlaws, but as though we were chieftains surveying our lands or lovers seeking the peace of a secluded dale. And though I shivered with the cold and my weak legs seemed to drag at every step, I was glad of it. To be away from Thoris, for a time at least.

'Was that wise, do you think?' I said.

'I shall not be silenced by that man.' He regarded me for a moment. 'But perhaps it was not wise. I have caused a break between the two of you, I think.'

'No. Whatever is broken, was broken before you came to us.'

'Is that so? Tell me of it.'

'What interest is such a thing to you?'

'I am merely curious. Speak or do not. Be it as you wish.'

We walked in silence for a time, our breaths coiling and frosting in the air before us, as I considered what to say.

'We have nothing,' I said. 'Yet we fight for all things. I wonder if it will be that way on the day when the gods die, when the wolf swallows the sun. When there are only two men left in the world, when they have nothing but each other. Will they huddle close together in companionship or will one man's hands tighten around the other's throat? Will they feel love or will it be hate? I think it will be hate. I do not know why he has not cast me out.'

'He needs you, of course,' Thorvaldur said.

'And I would not survive without him.'

'A feud, then?'

'A feud of two lonely men. Fought with words.'

'No blood.'

'Not yet. I think we would have killed one another if you had not come to us.'

He cocked his head. 'Oh really? Then you owe your life to me?'

'No. He owes his life to you.'

'You would win the fight?' he said, his eyes upon my ruined hand.

'I have something left to live for. He does not.'

'That might have been true, once. But not any more.' He grinned that terrible smile of his. 'My gift to him.'

'And what of your gift to me? What more news do you bring from the Althing?'

He shrugged. 'Little enough, in truth. I was there for a day, before the killings began and they made an outlaw of me.' He stumbled for a moment, his foot swallowed by a deeper patch of snow. I caught him by the elbow and he smiled his half-toothed smile at me in gratitude.

'What will you do?' he asked. 'What will you do when your sentence is finished and you are an outlaw no longer? Go back to your friend? Marry your woman?'

'Aye. And I will settle the feud.'

'With silver or with blood?'

'I cannot say. And what will you do, Thorvaldur?'

'Oh, I will try to preach again. I will speak to the chieftains once more and see if they will listen.'

'And kill them if they will not?'

'No. Not unless they force me to. But I am waiting for something else.'

'And what is that?'

'You remember from my stories? The land where the White Christ was born?'

'You call it Jerusalem.'

'So,' he said, 'you have been listening. At least a little.'

'I remember such things. What of this place?'

'There are infidels who rule there now. They serve a newer god than my Christ.'

'You must find that a shameful thing.'

'I do. But it shall not last. God will not allow it.' He looked out across the valley, but I knew that he saw it no longer. It was a vision of a distant land. A place of red earth, a sun beating down like a hammer upon an anvil. Hordes of spears waving like trees in a tempest. The glitter of blades, held high against the light. And blood upon the sand, a new sea pouring out over a bone-dry land.

'There will be a great war,' he said. 'The Christians will gather. We will forget our petty quarrels and take back that city. I only hope I live long enough to see it.'

'A feud, then?'

'Yes.' He grinned at me. 'You see? My God does have a place among your people. A feud over a piece of land. What is truer to the Icelanders than that?'

'True. Very true.'

'But still you are not persuaded.'

'No. But I like to hear you try.'

He rolled his shoulders, like a wrestler before a bout. 'Come,' he said. 'We must return.'

The fire had been left to go cold, only embers remaining. I thought at first that Thoris had gone, for there was no sign of him. But then there was a stirring deep within the cave, and as my eyes became accustomed to the darkness I saw Thoris sat hunched up on the blankets, a king upon a squalid throne.

'I want more stories of your God,' he said.

'And you shall have them,' Thorvaldur replied. He sat, dipped a finger in the cooling soup and licked it clean. 'But first, you must give something to me.'

'I give you shelter, food. I allow you to live. You ungrateful—'

'No, I am grateful.' He held his hand out to me, the palm toward the sky. 'But Kjaran sings.' He brought the hand to rest against his chest. 'I speak of God.' He held that same hand out towards Thoris. 'What can you do?'

'Be careful,' Thoris said. The words as soft as snowfall, sharp as a blade lifted from the whetstone. But Thorvaldur did not seem to care.

'You must tell me your story,' the Christian said. 'Tell me of how you became an outlaw.'

A hesitance from the darkness. 'You know that story already.'

'I know what other men say. That you killed your brother and stole his wife. But I want to hear you say it.'

He did not answer. Many were the times, during those endless-seeming winter nights, that I had thought of asking that. Once or twice I had spoken the first word of that question. But Thoris had looked on me and had seemed to know what it was that I was about to ask, the way a great swordsman will seem to know each movement of your blade and every piece of pretty footwork a moment before you act. You have not struck a single blow, yet already you are defeated. And I had felt that to speak the question would be to utter my last words.

'No,' Thoris said.

'Then you will have no more words of my God. And you shall not know how the story ends.'

Thoris bowed forward, as though curling up around some belly wound, the kind that kills a man inevitably, slowly. His fingers clenched and unclenched around the cloth of his cloak and I waited to see them wander towards a weapon, for the killing to begin. But they went still. And he began to speak.

'His name was Kjartan,' he said. 'My brother. They called him Kjartan the Strong, and he was. There was no man who could stand against him in battle.' He looked at me. 'Even your Gunnar, who you must always sing of. He could not have stood against my brother. And he married the daughter of a chieftain. Her name was Gudrun.

'I heard rumours of what went on in that place. Whispers,

gossip, and I thought nothing of it. He was my brother. I loved him.'

He dipped his horn cup in a pail of melted snow and drank deeply.

'I was in his longhouse,' he said, 'in summer. I had come to visit him, but he was out hunting seals with his men, so I sat down to wait. His wife gave me bread and ale, and we sat together by the fire for a time. We spoke. I do not remember what we spoke of. Then she turned to me and she asked if I would help her to die.'

He drank the water again and I thought of those men who are cursed with an endless thirst, first for water, then for blood.

'I told her to go to her father, to seek a divorce. It was her right. But my brother was a powerful man. He had earned the father's favour, and her father would not help her. So she went back to my brother. And none of her kin would help her.' He lifted his eyes to us. 'I do not wish to speak any more of this.'

'Speak on,' Thorvaldur said, his voice soft. 'You have come this far.'

Thoris nodded, like a man half asleep. He said: 'There were those amongst her kin who spoke of killing him. But they were hollow words. I knew that they would not do it. They did not have the courage. And my brother had many men who were loyal to him. Brutes like him always do. It is the good men who stand alone.' He placed his horn cup upon the ground and I saw his hand tremble a little. His right hand, his killing hand. 'But he would let me in to his longhouse at night. He trusted me. And why not?'

I risked a question. 'You could have challenged him to the *holmgang*,' I said.

I thought that he would shout at me – perhaps even that he would come for me, blade in hand. But he nodded and said:

'That would have been the honourable thing. But what if I had lost? He was a berserker. A better warrior than I. Then she would be alone, with no one to help her.'

I was afraid that he would weep. For I was sure that he would kill us if we saw him weep, to leave no witness to his shame. But he breathed deep and spoke again.

'I waited until all were asleep and I went towards his chamber. He was a wealthy man, with a room to himself. Too proud to share the hall with other men.' He laid a hand to the weapon on his belt. 'This knife in my hand.

'But when I opened the door, I found that someone had been there first.' He shuddered. 'I could feel the blood soaking through a hole in my boot, still warm against the skin. I could smell it in the air, like fresh-forged iron. And on the bed, my brother and his wife.

'I could see his throat open. Torn out, as if some wolf had been let loose in that room. Three wounds in his chest, though none that could have killed him. They were no practised killer's wounds. Whoever had done them had learned to murder in that moment.

'She was there beside him. The blood so heavy upon her that it was as though she had been flayed. I thought that I had come too late, that some dark magic had been brought into that room and torn them both to pieces.

'But she moved. Her eyes were so white against the blood. And I knew then what she had done. Her left hand had been bitten. Down to the bone. For she had to keep him silent or we would have heard her.

'We did not speak. I could not risk the words. I sat down beside her, felt the blood soak into my tunic. I took her hand in mine.' And he clasped both of his own hands together – imagining, perhaps, that once more she was with him. 'What would they have done to her?' he said, speaking only to himself. 'I do not know. Our laws make no account for a woman who kills. She would have been beyond the law, as we are now. And anything can be done to such a person.

'So I took her away from that place, and I let men talk. I let the story grow and become what it is now. And you know what remains of it.'

'What happened to her?' Thorvaldur said.

'She came with me. To this place.' He reached out to touch the walls of the cave, to touch some memory of her that might still live there. 'I asked her not to, to go to her kin or travel to some other place. To live as a servant, a slave, rather than be an outlaw's wife. Anything seemed better than that. But she would not go. She lasted three winters. She grew weaker and sicker with each one. But she would not leave.'

He looked beyond us, out towards the entrance to the cave, to the falling snow beyond.

'She is buried in this valley,' he said.

That was the end of the story. If had sung it in a song or told in a saga that would be the place that my voice would fall silent.

'There is something more,' Thorvaldur said. 'Something that you are not telling us.'

'I have told you everything.'

'No. There is more. And I think that you wish to speak it.'

Thoris's head rolled back, twisted away from us, the way a man in fever will contort himself, seeking somehow to escape his own body, the body that tortures him.

'I do not know what kind of a woman she was,' he said, the words drawn out like poison that is sucked from a wound and spat upon the ground. 'That she could do such a thing. What kind of a man I am, who would love his brother's killer.'

Thorvaldur nodded, satisfied. This, it seemed, was his ending. The Christian ending that he sought. 'I thank you for this,' he said.

There was no absolution from Thoris. No relief at telling the truth. Only the sullen air of a man who feels that he has been deceived.

'There,' he said. 'You have had your story. Now, give me yours.'

Thorvaldur began to speak once again. Of God, of forgiveness, of redemption. I did not listen. I looked out on the valley and listened to the call of the wind, and wondered where it was that she was buried.

24

I had always wondered how an outlaw might know the day of their return. Those who flee abroad or have the wealth to make fortresses of their homes will know the date well enough. But what of men who flee to the ice and make their homes in the dead valleys?

For most, it does not matter. They die long before their day of freedom – starving or frozen, or dead on the spears of the men who hunt them. But what of those who do survive their three years? In all the stories that I have heard, it is never spoken that an outlaw comes back a day late.

Perhaps there were outlaws who had counted or marked every day, keeping their time with the greatest precision. Or did they have another art? I have heard of men in distant lands who may read the date from the movement of the stars.

No man would want to linger in outlawry any longer than he had to, yet it would be death to return before the time. Had a man ever come back a day too early and died upon the sword of the first man he greeted, hearing his mistake as the darkness closed over him?

No, before I was an outlaw I did not know how those men

could know when they should return. And yet when my time came, I knew it without a doubt.

I felt the shifting of the seasons and knew that it was the late summer of my third year. I had thought that I would have to wait until snowfall to be certain of the time, to waste a month in the agony of waiting so that I could be certain. But I knew the day itself when it came.

It was no guesswork or a counting of the days. Nor was it blind luck, and I do not think it was the work of a god. It was memory alone that told me that I could go home.

There was so much that I forgot of those three years as an outlaw. There was so little to remember. Yet I remembered everything of the day I had been outlawed. The precise curve that the sun had taken through the sky. The pattern of the sunlight on the sea. The exact ripeness of the crops in the field, so that I could have picked out a stem of wheat from that day from a hundred of its fellows harvested a day later. For when a man or a woman longs for a day so completely, it will be known when it comes once more.

And so I woke in the cave on a late summer's day and I felt the unseen chains fall away from me. I was a free man once more.

I could go home.

The others did not speak as I made ready to depart. Thoris sat on the floor of the cave, his long arms wrapped around his knees, his head towards the ground, his ruined ear facing towards me. Thorvaldur watched me, a faint smile on his face.

I took a little food, a single skin of water, for I needed no more than that. I was a free man once more: I could call upon any farm in the land and the law of guest friendship would compel them to give me shelter for the night. I could sing for my food, cut corn and tend cattle, and receive bread and ale in return. They, still outlaws, had more need of it than I.

I wrapped the fur cloak around my shoulders, struggling to tie the clasp one-handed – three years of practice, yet still I had not mastered this. The knife went into my belt, my killer's weapon, its edge almost dull. Last of all, I settled the sword at my hip. Gunnar's sword, a weapon of heroes, that had not left its sheath for all the time I had been exiled. That blade was still sharp.

'It is time, then?' Thorvaldur said.

'It is.'

Thorvaldur nodded.

'We shall walk with you. For some of the way at least. Come, Thoris. We must see him out of the valley.'

I did not think that he would follow. He had barely spoken a word to me for months, for the sooner we drew to the day of my freedom, the less he wished to speak to me. He counted the days more than any of us, though their passage could bring him no reprieve. And sometimes I awoke in the night to find him watching me, his eyes cold.

But he rose without a word, and the three of us walked out together.

Down into the valley, the place that I knew as I would know a lover. The tall smooth rock that curves and hollows like the body of a woman. The place where the winter ice was thinnest on the river, where we had broken it open a hundred times for gulps of the piercing water. The rock wall that looked like a giant's face; the hidden hole in the moor that threatened to twist and snap an ankle.

We went to where the valley opened out, where the free

lands of Iceland lay stretched before us. Distant, the movement of the herds, the dancing of crops in the wind. A different world, that I could enter and they could not.

'This is as far as we may go,' Thoris said.

For a moment I did not dare look back on them. For I wondered if they meant to let me taste freedom for a moment before they cut my throat. We held no bond of kinship, of loyalty. I might earn great renown, bringing back the heads of those two outlaws. Perhaps they could not take the chance of letting a free man go, knowing that valley as I did.

But when I turned back to face them, they greeted me with silver, not with iron.

Thoris stepped forward and handed me a silver arm-ring, the double of the one I had traded away in Borg. In the three years we had spent together I had never seen him wear it. He must have kept it hidden away, one last treasure. A relic from his lost life. Perhaps a gift from a friend, as mine had been.

'Take it,' he said. 'You shall have more need of this than I.'

'I cannot take this from you.'

'What use have I for silver? I shall never spend it.'

In that cave he had been a tyrant and I had learned to hate him. I was free of him now, could nurture my hatred freely. And yet I felt no need for it.

'Why have you given this to me?' I asked.

'You sing well,' he said. He seemed to want to say more, but he could not find the words.

I turned from him and looked out on the frozen valley that I had called home. The prison which he could not leave.

'This will make a good song,' I said.

'Three years in this place and you think it will make a good song?'

'All men love to hear of outlaws.'

You will sing of me?'

'I shall.'

'What kind of a song?' he said, and I think there was fear in his voice. Perhaps he feared a flyting song, strange as that seemed. This man who would be forever exiled from his people, and yet he still feared to be mocked behind his back. Perhaps that was all he heard when he closed his eyes at night. Men laughing at him, a fool who had killed his brother for love.

'You have lived out here longer than any other outlaw. What is there to mock in that?'

He turned from me and began to walk away, slow and purposeless, like an old man who has forgotten himself.

'It was not a shameful thing,' I said, and he looked back to face me.

'What did you say?'

'There is no shame in what she did. The woman that you loved.'

He said: 'I thank you.' Then he was away, striding back up the slope of the hill, towards his cave.

Thorvaldur clasped his shoulder as he passed, whispered words that I could not hear. The Christian came forward and took my hand, smiled that terrible, half-toothed smile of his.

'Good fortune, Kjaran.' He looked back at Thoris. 'It was kind, what you said to him.'

'It was what he wished to hear,' I said. 'Just as what you speak to him, with those stories of your God.'

He shrugged, caught.

'Perhaps we shall meet in better times,' I said.

'I do not wish for better times. I am where I should be.'

'I cannot believe that.'

'You are jealous, I think. That he cares more for my words than your songs.'

'You came here to find desperate men. Desperate men who would need your God.'

He did not seem insulted by my words. He cocked his head, considered the thought.

'It does not seem so wrong to bring God first to those who need Him most. I thought to bring the word of God to the chieftains of this country. But I think that is not the way. The shaming I received, this exile – God is telling me that it is not the way.'

'And so you bring your God to men who will soon be dead. Men who will father no children. Your word will die with them.'

'Perhaps. But I say that it is time well spent. Two years spent saving a single soul, and I do not regret it.'

'You truly think that he will join your God?'

'He is close to it.'

'Yes. He wants to be forgiven.'

'And what of you?'

'I do not. I have nothing to forgive.'

'My God will love you.'

'I have a woman who loves me. What need have I of the love of a god?'

'That will change, in time. When it does, come back to me.'

'It will not change.'

'Then I hope we do not meet again,' he said.

There was a coldness to his eyes, where before there had been nothing but merriment. I wondered if this was what those men had seen in him, those men who had mocked him at the Althing, all those years ago. Had they seen that look in his eyes, before they died?

'Do not mistake me,' he said. 'I will make you a Christian, or give you a warrior's death. There can be nothing else between us.' He raised his hands, gesturing to the valley. 'There is a truce between us here. You sheltered me and I thank you for it. I like your company well enough and think you a good man. But I am a warrior in a feud. A feud of gods. And beyond this valley, you are my enemy.' He brought both hands to rest upon his heart. 'But I hope that you will be my friend, one day.'

'Be kind to Thoris,' I said.

'My God will be kind,' he replied. And then he was gone.

I watched them walk away, one behind the other. The slow, clumsy steps of Thoris and the careless stride of Thorvaldur. Like an old man close to death and the son who will succeed him.

I came back to the free lands as a traveller from another world. I stood tall and walked in daylight, wandering the high ground with no fear, the warmth of the sun against my skin. Let me be seen by every man and woman and I would not have cared. The law was once again my friend and I felt as though every man on the island walked at my side.

I had no horse, no silver that I would spare to buy one, no friend in that place who might lend me one. And so I walked from one farm to the next, out towards the west, striding towards the sea. As the sun sank low I would seek out the closest longhouse, follow the rising smoke like a sailor chasing a star. I knocked on those doors and asked for a place to sleep at night.

Most did not know my name, but they knew me for what I was. There was no mistaking the ragged clothes that I wore, the hollow body of a half-starved man. For the outlaw ages as a cursed man does, old before his time. Those three years in the mountains had stolen my youth.

There were some who looked on me with fear; they would let me in and give me bread, and let me sing a song or two, but they would not speak a word to me and sent me on my way the moment the sun rose. But most greeted me with kindness, gifting me old clothes to replace my outlaw rags, sharing unwatered ale with me. And at night they and their children gathered around the fire and listened to my stories. For all love to hear tales of the outlaws.

So I told them that a giant lived in the valley and a dragon slept beneath it. That we never saw the sun, that we fought monsters and sorcerers. And all of it was a lie, and all of it was true.

I asked them to tell me their stories. And I asked them to tell me stories of Gunnar the Killer.

Most had never heard the name. Some had heard of him and of the feud. A few even claimed to have been at the Althing when I had been outlawed. None could speak anything of use to me, for we were still a long way from the Salmon River Valley. Yet in their silence I found a comfort. If some disaster had struck, if blood had been spilt, surely they would have heard it.

One of them gave me a horse – half-blind and he twitched and shivered uncontrollably, but he still had a little life left in him. Enough, perhaps, to see me home.

I came to Borg on that horse and looked once more upon the mountains that had made me wish to stay, listened to the calling of the sea for the first time in three years. I looked for Ragnar's ship in the dock, but I could not find it. He was out at sea or was further north along the coast.

North, then. Through the deep valley, past cliff face and waterfall, rising up and up towards the Salmon River Valley. More carefully now, for I came close to the lands of men who might know me. I was an outlaw no longer, but that might matter little to Björn and his kin. They would risk outlawry themselves if it would see me dead. Only once I was with Gunnar would I be safe. The hills broke open and before me was the sea, the valley, my home. The great arcing curve of the bay, the great mountain of Helgafell behind me, the rolling land of the dales in front. I told myself that I would not leave it again, that nothing could compel me to do so. Not the lure of the Althing, the whisper of the sea. Not a sentence of outlawry or any curse or witchcraft. I would live and die in that place.

And suddenly, I was afraid.

Do not ask me how, but I could smell it, taste it, long before that could have been possible. And I was hurrying then, stirring that old, dying horse to one last great chase. And he was brave beneath me. He lifted his head and for the last time he seemed almost to break into flight.

We rode across the farmlands, past the grazing cattle, the remnants of the harvest. Until that smell, that taste returned, stronger than ever. The fire in my nostrils, the ash on my tongue. And I could see the smoke rising.

I did not want to believe, at first. I whispered to myself that it must have been some other place, some other feud in the valley. That Olaf the Peacock had angered some neighbouring chieftain and the great hall of Hjardarholt now lay in ashes. That Bolli's long dispute over grazing lands with Bjarni had finally been settled in blood and fire. There were so many feuds and disputes it did not have to be the one I knew all too well. Yet somewhere deep within, where men feel hate and love and all things true, already I knew what must have happened.

I came over the rise of the ground beside Gunnar's farm and looked down upon what remained.

It was the little things that I saw first. The fragments of

burning wood that danced in the wind like fireflies. The ground, marked with the passage of half a hundred footsteps, that carved a great circle around the farm. The little slivers of iron, chipped from sword struck against sword, that glittered on the earth under the light of the low sun.

Then I was ready to look upon the rest. The longhouse, black from fire and open to the sky. The wind shifting the great pile of ashes, so that it looked as if some great and monstrous creature were stirring unseen beneath them. And the blood upon the ground. So much it was as though a giant had been slain there.

But it had not. No giant had died there, no great beast slain. Only a man and his family.

I held my maimed hand out towards the gutted longhouse and felt a little heat rising from it. It had been burned the night before. I had returned a day too late.

REVENGE

No. Stop. Wait a moment and let me think.

Yes, you are right, I am tired. And yes, the ale has touched my mind a little. And yes, perhaps I do not wish to speak of this. This is a memory that I have interred as deep as though it were the body of a great king, whose tombs are like cities. But this is a memory like a ghost. Again and again I cut the ground for its grave and cover it with heavy earth. Still it rises, still it walks.

I will tell it to you. I am afraid if I do not speak it tonight, I will never have the courage to do so again. I would not live a coward.

But first, let me tell you a different story. Another story of Gunnar.

Many of them I have told you already. Of how we met in the home of Olaf the Peacock, how I charmed him with a song. Soon I will tell you the story of how it was that he died.

But now, let me remember this.

It was the Day of Movement in early summer, when wanderers like me must go on to their new homes. There was a rare sun that day, a heat falling from the sky that seemed to caress the skin. We sat side by side in front of the door, the earthen wall of the longhouse against our backs, and we basked in that sun, passing a cup of water between us.

'A good winter,' he said.

'Is there such a thing?'

'I had not thought it, but there is.' He paused. 'You sing well.'

'Well enough.'

'Better than that.'

'You have been kind to me.'

'Kind enough,' he said, echoing my tone, a little smile on his lips. 'Where will you go now?'

'To find some other place. Perhaps Olaf the Peacock will show me favour. He has a weakness for the songs of an Irishman.'

'You are only half an Irishman,' he said.

'Oh, I do not think there is an Irish singer in the whole of Laxdæla. He may settle for a half-breed like me.'

He ran his thumb around the rim of the horn cup, the nail catching on the nicks and whorls. 'What if you cannot find a place to take you in?' he said.

'There is always a place for a poet.'

'But what if you could not?' he persisted.

'I would die, I suppose. If I could not find a home for winter.'

He stared out across the fields, towards the distant sea. 'I would not want to rely on the kindness of others.'

'It is good to keep moving,' I said. But I felt that ache in the heart, where one must leave the place that one is meant to be, or leave the woman one is meant to love. When fate and desire do not meet, as they rarely do, and we must leave behind what matters most to us.

I stood and yawned under the heat of the sun. I turned to Gunnar, offered my hand and said, 'Good fortune, Gunnar. I shall see you at the Althing.'

He did not answer me. He simply stared into that cup as though he had been ensorcelled by it, and I thought at first that I had offended him. He blinked and looked up at me, and he said: 'Will you stay for the winter?'

'I did not think that you would ask.'

'Did you want me to ask?'

'Yes.' I thought for a time. 'For one year. I cannot do more than that.'

He reached out and took my hand in his for a moment, and there was a gentleness there that I did not understand. Then he remembered to clap his other hand to it, sharp and martial, and led me back to his home.

There, that is all. A little story, but it matters greatly to me.

Now, I shall tell you the rest. I will tell it quickly, for the sun will not sleep much longer. And when it rises, there is much for us to do.

25

Had the killers known? Had they waited for the day that I would return? To welcome me home with blood and still-warm ashes?

They could not have done. It was some god who had whispered to them, calling out to them on that night.

In those years of exile I might have spoken a word against Odin or Thor. I could have made a silent wish that Loki had twisted against me, as is his nature. Or had it been long before, when I was a boy – some curse or challenge thrown at one of them? How long had that god been waiting, to take revenge upon me? For the gods cannot forget. And our gods, the old gods, they do not know how to forgive.

I moved slowly, for there seemed to be no hurry. The stillness was complete, save for the dance of the smoke on the wind. I moved over the wet ground – for it had rained the night before – marked with many footprints. The circling, dragging steps of men in battle. The longhouse burned open, four black walls beneath an open sky.

I could see them there, lying on the ground, but it took me a long time to come forward to where he lay. I went first to the entrance of the longhouse, where the head of a dragon had once marked a doorway.

Two black shapes, curled on the ground, buried in one another. They did not seem like people, not at first. Fire plays strange tricks upon skin. Yet after a moment, I could see the curve of a foot, the white of teeth, and above all, there was no mistaking the way in which one held the other. Dalla and Freydis, curled up together in the ashes of their home. I could not see Kari, but I was certain that he was in there, too. I could not think why they had not run.

Then I came back, walking slowly, so slowly, to where Gunnar lay on the ground.

I sat beside him for a time and waited for him to rise. For cut skin to knit back, the blood to seep up from the ground and return to his body, for the terrible wounds to close. I waited for a miracle and it would not come.

I lifted his head from the ground and saw what they had done to his face. How they had marked him and left him unburied.

He was barefoot and shirtless. There was a broken axe at his side, and I touched the sword at my hip, useless in its sheath. What could he have done with that hero's weapon at his side? Not enough to save his life. But a better death would have been his. One that he could have been proud of.

I sat beside him and took his cold hand in mine. I rubbed the palm of my maimed hand against it, trying to instil some warmth in it. We sat together and I watched the fall of the sun from the sky.

I do not know how long I waited there. But in time a sound came to me. A sound so soft that I thought it a trick of the wind at first. It came again, from behind me: a sucking of the air. A little gasp of pain. Turning my head slowly, I laid Gunnar's hand back down and took up the sword.

Something moved within the ashes of the house. At first I thought it to be a spirit, a ghost, for it seemed that no man or woman could have lived through such a fire.

Then I was moving, retching and choking on the smoke that still rose, the smell of burned skin sharp in my nose. My eyes useless, my hands seeking, digging into the ashes of the home, pulling away pieces of burned timber, until my fingers found a different kind of warmth.

Half-buried, barely breathing. Kari, Gunnar's son.

The sun was falling from the sky and I did not have much time. Even over the wet slap of hooves against the ground and the crying of the wind I could still hear the rattle and gasp of the dying boy.

He had tried to crawl into that tunnel. The gap in the wall where, three years before, he had escaped into the night, looking for a lost horse. But he had not gone all the way through. He had grown too broad in the shoulders, too much a man to make use of a child's tunnel. And so he had lain there, trapped, as his family burned around him.

I had pulled him free and found that the fire had still reached him. Cloth burned away, the skin red and weeping. I lifted him in my arms, listened to the rattle and gasp of his breath, each one softer than the last. I threw him across my blown horse and pulled myself into the saddle, and set it to a gallop one last time. We rode for the coast.

Towards the sea we travelled. Towards a little longhouse that I had seen from afar, but never been too. For it was a luckless place, where a luckless man lived. Any who had wisdom would shun it.

The horse gave out on the edges of the farmland, going

to ground as noiselessly as a man who is speared through the heart. I gathered the boy up in my arms and ran as best I could.

The longhouse was small. No great chieftain's home, not even the place of a wealthy farmer. A home for a solitary man, a little scrap of land for one who had not earned the right to it any more.

I struck the door and tried to call out, but no sound came. I swallowed, spat and tried to call again, and this time my voice sounded.

I heard the shifting of a single pair of feet inside – no rush of a warband to the door. It swung open a fraction, and it was Ragnar who stood on the other side, looking at me with fearful eyes. Ragnar the Keel-farer, the Coward.

In his hand he held an axe in a slack, unpractised grip. He looked at me and I saw that he did not know me for who I was. I held up the boy in my arms a little higher, as though I were offering him as a gift.

'It is Gunnar's child,' I said.

I saw his skin go pale, his hands tremble. For he knew me, then.

'The others?' he said.

'They are dead.' I felt the boy stir a little in my arms. Perhaps even in the depths of sleep he could still hear my words. That his father, his mother, his sister – they were all dead. 'Can I come inside?'

I felt one hand on my shoulder, guiding me. I saw the other cradling the head of the boy in my arms, making sure that I did not strike it against a wall or the frame of a door.

In the light of the fire I saw that there were no others in that place. Everywhere there were mementos of his travels. Some piece of a stitched sail. Little relics of distant lands, coins and knives and worn pieces of whalebone. It was a captain's home, and even it seemed to long for the sea as much as Ragnar did.

'I know that you have no woman here. But I have nowhere else to go.'

'I have a wife now,' he said quietly.

'Oh? I am glad.'

He flinched at the word. 'Come,' he said, 'We must do what we can.'

The cooking fire burned high, though there was no one tending to it.

'Where is your wife?' I said.

'She is at the shieling.'

'Do you know anything of fire?'

He looked at the boy in my arms, reached out hesitantly to the red marks, the weeping skin.

'I have seen men burned before,' he said. 'We must give him cold water. Only a little. But we must keep his throat cold, and clear.'

He passed me a horn of water and I tilted it towards the boy's mouth. A few drops at a time, patient and constant, as falling water wears patterns into stone.

'Later, we must clean the skin,' Ragnar said. 'It will hurt him terribly, but it must be done. And that is all I know to do.'

'Will he live, do you think?'

He hesitated, his mouth working silently. Then shook his head. 'Burned men almost always die,' he said. 'I am sorry, Kjaran.'

I looked down on the boy and watched my tears falling upon his face. I felt no shame. It was as though I watched another man weeping.

'You must tell me what has happened.'

'Much has changed since you left us,' Ragnar said, and he seemed to diminish as he spoke.

'Tell me of the feud.'

He dipped the horn into a barrel of water and this time he held it out to me. I touched it to my lips, felt the sharpness of the cold water like a blade against my teeth. I drank it down in one draught and held it out to be refilled. Again and again I drank, Ragnar saying nothing. When at last I wanted no more, he spoke.

'They returned from the mountains. Björn and his kin. They said that they had caught you and killed you. And they bore Ketil with them, his leg maimed, as proof of what they said.'

'Ketil lives?'

'If you can call it that.'

'And you believed them.'

'Gunnar would not. But yes, the rest of us believed him.'

'And what then?'

'Nothing. Gunnar swore vengeance, but had not the followers to claim it. Neither side could move against the other.'

'Until today.'

'Until today.'

'There were no followers with him,' I said. 'Do you think they fled the fighting?'

'No,' he said quietly. 'They left before the fighting.'

A silence for a time, as the fire burned and my tears no longer fell.

'Tell me of this,' I said.

'There is little enough to tell. They left him, one by one. Some were bought, I think. With silver and promises of land. Others Gunnar drove away himself. Quarrelling with them, accusing them of betraying him, of betraying you. He was half-mad at the end, I think. And the last of them left when they saw this, for they saw no honour in dying at his side. So it went, until he stood alone in the feud.' He breathed deeply and let his head hang low. 'We have known this would come, sooner or later. One cannot stand alone for long.'

'You would not stand at his side. You were afraid?'

'He would have no company with me. He cursed me for letting you run to the mountains.' He lifted his head and I could see the sadness marked on his face. 'You must believe me.'

'I believe you.'

His eyes drifted to the boy in my arms. 'They burned them out?'

'Yes. The cowards. Ten against one, and they would not face him as a man.'

'He was a warrior out of the old times,' he said. 'They would not dare stand against him.' Ragnar reached out and took the boy's hand in his. 'Where did you find him?'

'The boy hid. It saved his life. It seems that all around Gunnar there were none but cowards.'

Ragnar flinched again.

'What of Olaf?' I said.

'He sought to keep the peace. His lands lay between those of Vigdis and Gunnar, and he would not stand for warbands roaming across his fields.' He rubbed his hands against each other. 'But I do not think that he will be sorry to hear of the end of the feud.'

'What end of the feud?' I said.

He dropped his head, spoke bare above a whisper. 'Even you must know that it cannot go on. You killed Erik and answered for it with outlawry. Gunnar killed Hakon and answered for it with his own life. The debt is settled.'

'What of his wife and children?'

'You must know that to be an accident. They would not kill a woman and child deliberately. It would be a shameful thing.'

'Perhaps. You are right.'

'You have suffered much. But the feud has to end. You do know that, don't you?'

I closed my eyes. 'Yes. I know.'

'Whatever I can do to help, I shall. But Kjaran, there is something more that you must know.'

'Tell me, then.'

'I do not know how to speak this.'

'What can you say that can hurt me now? I am beyond such things.'

He licked his lips. 'We thought you dead,' he said.

We. I would not have known, if it were not for that word. If he had said *I*, I would have lived in ignorance a little longer. But he said it, and I knew.

I heard the sound of the door as it swung open. And in a moment, she was there.

I could not look at her face, at first. To see the face that I had fought to remember in that maze of ice and snow, the sharp lines of her face, the light dancing in her eyes – I knew I had not the courage to look there. I looked instead upon her hands, remembered the way she had once touched my face with them, the touch light and soft as snow. I remembered the turn of her waist as it had felt under my hands, but now the key of the house was tied about her waist, as was her right. In the way she stood I could see the strength of a housewife who walks many miles in front of her loom each day – a serving maid no longer. No sign of a child on her body, yet somehow I felt that one was there. I knew it in a single look.

I bowed my head and stroked the hair of the dying boy on my lap.

I heard Sigrid sit. Then I heard Ragnar speak.

'They came back from the mountains. Björn and the others. They came back bearing a crippled man and stories of your death.'

'And you believed them.'

'Yes.'

'You believed the stories, too?' I said, looking at her for the first time.

Those strange eyes of hers met mine and there was no pain in them. Only a certain cold anger, the eyes of one in a feud.

'No,' she said. 'But what does that matter?'

'You may stay as long as is needful,' Ragnar said.

I gave a gesture of the head that could have been a nod, if they chose to take it as such.

'What will you do?' Ragnar asked.

'Will you care for the boy?' I said to Sigrid. 'I must go back to Gunnar's house.'

'What will you do there?' she asked.

But I had already stood, was already gone.

Above me, scattered clouds and a hollow moon. Below, the wet earth, scoured with rain. And soon enough, the smell of ash in my nostrils, the taste of it on my tongue.

It was dark by the time I returned to the farm. It was better work done at night, for the dead almost seem alive in the darkness. I was not digging graves, it seemed, but shelters. Beds carved into the earth, for them to rest and rise again.

The greatest men and women are given a boat filled with treasures to take them to another world, piled high with weapons and gold and slaves with their throats freshly cut, for their service does not end with death. What gifts could I find for that great warrior Gunnar, against whose sword none could stand? What gifts for his wife and child? A few carved chess pieces, a little wooden horse that had somehow escaped the fire, the chain of stones looped on to a silver wire. What had not burned had been taken, and these were all the treasures that I could give them for the afterlife.

Before I cast the first handful of earth down on to Gunnar, I looked on the sword at my hip.

'I cannot return this to you yet,' I said, 'for it is still bright and unbloodied. I will stain it for you first.' And I thought I saw his ruined face smiling up at me from his grave.

I could feel madness so close that I could touch it. Like a hand that is proffered in a dance by a smiling girl – one has only to reach out and take it. And I would, I promised myself, for that would be my reward. But not yet.

I laid the earth upon the dead and then I laid down myself upon it. No green fire dancing in the sky, not this early in the year. It was a short night, that late in summer. A few hours of darkness, and I did not sleep.

One more time I looked on what remained of the longhouse, the fields, the hills around it, the grave at my feet. I did not look on that place to fix it firm in my mind. I looked on it and I wanted to forget.

I looked down on the tracks, clear-marked in the wet ground, and not yet washed away or trampled and forgotten. The killing was there, simple enough to read. I saw where the men had circled the longhouse, where they had come forward to throw their torches and retreat just as quickly. I saw the single trail of footprints where Gunnar had gone to fight them alone. How he had reached a place, then turned in every direction, surrounded on all sides. And I saw another set of tracks, leading from the longhouse and back once more. I saw those footprints and I saw the story written there. I knew what had been done.

26

After a night without sleep, all things seem as dreams do. That morning I walked back through the valley as I might have walked through such a dream, through a world that no longer made sense to me. And so when I saw Sigrid sitting outside in the sun, outside a little longhouse such as I had one day hoped that I might own, it seemed to complete the vision. How many times had I dreamt of such a thing, in those years of exile?

It was only as I drew closer, and saw her stitching together two pieces of a sail for her husband's ship, that the dream was broken. She looked up, her hands curling into fists as she saw me.

'If we still lived in a time when women wielded swords,' I said, 'you would have been quite the warrior.'

'Do you think there was such a time? You poets like to sing of it, but I do not think I believe you.'

'I do not know. Perhaps.'

She looked me over, seeking some sign of where I had spent the night. Some mark of earth or of blood.

'Where did you go last night? How little courage you had,

to stay and speak to me. I would have thought I had earned that much.'

'I went to bury Gunnar and his kin,' I said, and I saw her eyes dim for a moment.

'That was well done,' she said.

I sat on the ground before her and made no answer.

'A battle?' she asked, looking at my maimed left hand.

'No,' I said. 'The cold.'

She paused for a moment. 'I often hoped that you suffered,' she said quietly. 'I do repent that now.'

'Which of the three winters past did you spend learning to hate me?'

'The very first,' she said.

'So soon? I see that our love was worth little enough to you. A little matter to pass a summer, I suppose. But it meant more than that to me.'

She tossed her head at that. 'What was it that you said Gunnar called you? Kjaran the Kind.'

I did not answer.

'I thought that once, too. Then I found a man who was truly kind.'

'And a coward.'

'I care not. Neither do you, I think.'

'I think much of Ragnar.'

'Do not think it some marriage of pity,' she said. 'He is a better man than you.' She cursed and threw her stitching to the ground. I waited.

She turned to me. 'You want to ask me why. So why not ask?'

'Did you think me dead?'

She thought for a moment. 'I did not know. I had always thought that I would know if you had been killed. When my father was killed I seemed to know it before they spoke it.

A touch of his ghost on my shoulder, a whisper in my ear, and then he was gone. But I never heard you speak to me.' She picked up the two squares of the sail and began to sew once again. 'And I had decided before they returned, before they spoke of your death.'

'When?'

'When they told me that you had not left with Ragnar. That you had chosen to stay.'

'You did not think that I stayed for you?'

'Did you?'

'No.'

Her mouth twisted. 'You see? I am not such a fool as you think. Tell me why you stayed.'

I could not answer for a long time. When I spoke, I said: 'I looked on the mountains and the sea and I thought it beautiful. I thought my country too beautiful to leave. So it was not for love of you. But for this island.' I looked down at my one good hand, turned palm upward to the sky. 'I suppose that sounds foolish to you.'

She said nothing for a time. Then: 'I have often wondered at the lies men tell themselves. I see that you tell them, too.'

'You think that I lie to you?'

'I do.'

'Tell me, then, why it was that I stayed. Since it seems you think you know better than I do.'

She closed her eyes and shook her head, and it seemed at first that she would not answer.

'For pride,' she said at last. 'You were too proud to run.'

To that, I found I had no answer.

She finished her stitching and rolled it up.

'Will you stay with us, this winter?' she said, and there was a challenge in her tone.

'Do you want me to?'

'I do.'

'Then I shall. For I have no place else to go.'

'And if you did, then you would.'

'Yes,' I said. But when I looked at her I could see the hurt that word gave. 'But I thank you for your kindness. I will stay with you.'

She leaned forward, letting her hair fall across her face, hiding it from me. 'What will you do now?'

'Wait for the boy to die.'

'And after that?'

'What do you want me to do?'

'I think that whatever I ask of you, you shall do the opposite. I will not say such things to you again.'

'After the boy has died...' My throat closed for a moment, but I willed it open once again. 'I will ask Ragnar to take me on his ship. I do not know what work there is for a one-handed sailor. But there must be something I can do.'

'You will not continue the feud?'

'No. They have won.'

'Does Gunnar not whisper to you of vengeance?'

'No. I do hear him, but that is not what he says to me.'

'And what do you hear him say?'

'He wishes for me to love you. And he wishes for me to live and to sing. I cannot do one of those things. But perhaps I may do the other.'

Her hand drifted towards my shoulder for a moment, before she drew it back again.

'You will do what you must,' she said. She hesitated, and then said: 'Will you sing for us? I would like to hear you sing.'

I thought of all the times that I had been asked that. Perhaps that was all that was left of me. A pair of aching lungs, a tongue and lips, a mind filled only with songs. And I answered as I always had.

'Yes,' I said. 'I can still sing.'

'I am glad to see that you live.'

'Is that the truth?'

'It is the truth,' she said. And perhaps I was a fool, but I believed her.

I stood and looked upon the valley, and listened to the calling of the sea. I went inside the longhouse and I waited for the boy to die.

I had hoped that Kari would not wake again. That he would slip from this world quietly, at peace. But I had never seen a man die by fire. I did not know what was to come. For he woke soon enough and he did not sleep again.

Each day, Sigrid and I scoured his weeping skin with sand, even as he screamed and begged for us to stop. We dripped milk and honey into his mouth, for his throat was too far closed to take any more than that. He did not sleep and so neither did we. Each night one of us would walk up to the shieling, for there we could sleep. Two of us stood as sentries on the watch, waiting for the night to pass so that we could sleep. Waiting for him to die.

I began to long for it, and it seemed as though I had never wanted anything so much before. At night when I could not sleep, when I listened to him cry out in pain, I prayed to the gods to let him die. I felt my hand drift to the knife at my side, and it would have been a kindness to do it, the greatest gift that I could have offered to any man. But Kari was all that was left in the world of Gunnar. I knew I could not destroy him. I would have taken that knife to my own throat before

I took it to his. And so we waited for the slow death to take him, and we fought it as hard as we could.

It was on a morning, as the summer began to turn towards winter, when I came back from the shieling, that the change came. I walked towards the longhouse, and there was a strange silence within. I listened at the door for a time, waiting for the choking cries to begin again. But there was nothing, and an ache of joy crept through me.

I thought to find Sigrid there, beside the body of the boy. But it was Ragnar who sat beside Kari, a fresh catch of salmon still dripping in his net. He spent much of his time working the rivers, sleeping at the shieling or in his ship. He took little part in nursing the boy – not out of cowardice, I think, but out of a particular courtesy. He knew that I did not want him there.

He started as I came in, like a man caught speaking conspiracy.

'Sigrid asked me to watch him for a moment,' he said, 'She will be back soon.' His eyes darted back to where the boy lay.

'Is he dead?' I said.

'No. He sleeps.'

'Then what concerns you?'

'It is no matter.'

'Tell me.'

He hesitated, then beckoned me forward. 'Listen to how he breathes.'

I came forward and I saw that the boy did sleep. A change there, for the pain always kept him awake. I put my ear to Kari's chest, and listened to the wheeze and rattle of his breath. I heard nothing different.

'Does he seem to breathe easier to you?' Ragnar said.

'I think that you imagine it.'

'Perhaps.' He sat beside him, reached out an uncertain hand. The slightest touch could hurt the boy, and so Ragnar merely extended one finger, and gave a gentle stroke to Kari's hair. The boy did not stir. 'I do not want him to die,' Ragnar said.

'I do. I want his pain to end.'

'Sigrid said that after winter you will go abroad. That you think to take a place on my ship.'

'If you will have me.'

'Of course.'

'I should have gone with you three years ago. It is too late now, but there is nothing else for me to do.'

'It is not too late.'

A sudden anger stole my sight for a moment, and when it returned I saw him with his hand to his mouth, his eyes open wide. I suppose I must have looked murderous.

'I am sorry,' I said. 'But it is a simple thing for a man like you to say that.'

'Yes.' He stood abruptly and made for the door, leaving his catch by the cooking pot. He paused at the doorway and said: 'I do not imagine it.'

'What?'

'I am sure of it.' His eyes drifted to Kari and then met my gaze with a rare confidence. 'The boy is healing.'

'I wish that were true,' I said.

I could not trust the word of a coward: it is all that we are taught, that brave men speak truth and cowards lie. But Ragnar never lied to me. In that, at least, he was brave.

The boy began to crawl back towards life, one breath at a

time. He bore the dressing of his skin with hisses of breath, not with screams. He slept entire days at a time without making a sound.

I could not allow myself to believe it for a long time. But I remember a night when we sat together, Ragnar, Sigrid and I. We sat together for hours without speaking, and we watched Kari sleep, and breathe, and it was as though we watched a miracle before us.

Ragnar looked at me and he smiled. 'The work of the gods,' he said.

'Perhaps,' I answered. And that was all that was said that night.

Our gods do not raise the dead. They welcome them, feast them, fight with them, but they do not bring them back. For if a man died well in battle and found his way to Valhalla, what cruel God would send him back to earth to suffer once more? And if that man died without honour, what favour would he have with the gods to give him life again? There is no charity from Thor or Odin. Only duty. I remembered then a story that Thorvaldur had told me – of a man they called Lazarus, touched by the White Christ and brought to life once more. But I put it from my mind just as swiftly.

He would be a monster to look upon, looking more like a wooden carving of a man than one of flesh and blood. But the boy would live.

He was wordless for so long, for in his pain he had retreated to some place beyond language. And even once the wounds on his skin had closed, it was a long time before he would speak to me. Sometimes I thought that I heard him whispering to Sigrid, but she would not repeat his words.

Once he was strong enough we walked him around the narrow longhouse, again and again, as a birthing woman is made to walk so that her child will come. Returning strength to legs that had forgotten how to walk, that had thought themselves unneeded and prepared themselves for death. And still he did not speak.

There was an evening in early winter, when I sat alone by the fire. Sigrid and Ragnar were gone, I cannot recall where. But as I sat, I watched the dancing of the fire. I thought of the coming summer and I tried to imagine the sound of the rolling waves, the sight of distant countries. I tried to imagine that future, and yet it would not come to me. I could see only the fire.

'Kjaran.'

The sound as soft as a whisper of the wind, but I heard it. I had waited many months to hear him speak.

I turned and saw his eyes glowing in the light of the fire.

'Yes. I am here.'

'Water,' he said, and I gave it to him. I went to pour it in his mouth, but he took the skin from me and, with trembling hands, poured it into his mouth.

'More?' I said.

'No.'

I hesitated for a moment and saw his eyes wander to my maimed hand, saw his warped lip curl in disgust at the sight. A strange thing, to see a cripple's horror at the sight of another cripple. But he did not know what he looked like.

'Did they do this to you?' he said.

'No. It was the winter.'

He put his hands to his face, felt the altered skin under his fingers. He turned from me and nuzzled his face against the furs and blankets beneath him.

After a moment I heard him speak once more.

'What shall we do?'

I did not answer at first. I listened to the rattle and wheeze as he drew breath into his scarred lungs. How many years would he have, before some winter fever would take him? For ours is a land where the weak do not live long. How much time would he have before he began to die slow, drowning on dry land? Before he died in his bed, with no blade in his hand?

'We stay here,' I said. 'We speak to no one else. It is better that we are thought dead. You most of all. The feud continues in you. They must kill you to finish it.'

He lifted his head and nodded.

'Kari,' I said, 'I need you to tell me something.'

'Yes?'

'I want you to tell me of the night of the raid. I want you to tell me how Gunnar died.'

'No,' he said.

'I must know.'

'Please.'

'I must know.'

'Later. I shall tell you later.'

'No. You must speak now.'

It took a long time. Again and again he looked at me in silence, a pleading in his eyes, waiting for me to un-ask my question, to free him from my demand. But I would not. I simply stared at him, my hand on the sword his father had given me, and I waited.

At last, he began to speak.

Sumardil?

You are so quiet in the darkness, I thought for a moment that you slept. So still, I might mistake you for the dead.

Sumardil. We have no strong drink left, yet still I have your name to speak, and it is sweet as mead upon my lips.

I am ready to speak that story now. I heard it first from his son, but now it is my story to tell. I am ready to tell you how Gunnar died.

We think of death in a feud as happening in a moment. The movement of a blade to open a throat, too fast to be seen. And what is the time it takes for the blood to pour from that cut? Count a dozen heartbeats and he will be dead before your lips say 'twelve'.

But it is a slow thing, to die in the feud. A death by inches, as one's favour slips away, as loyalties are tested and broken. Each day, there is one fewer man to count upon. Another sleepless night spent watching for enemies at the door. Crops that go unharvested, cattle that go missing. How many in a feud have died from hunger and sickness, and not from the blade? Too many to count. And it is after countless months spent sick, sleepless, alone, that finally the warband comes. By night, carrying fire, determined to end the feud before the rising of the sun.

Think of Gunnar, that night they came for him. For the first time in so long, he sleeps. With no companions left to him, he has not dared to rest, always watchful for the coming of the killers. But this night, the rain falls heavy and there is no moon in the sky. It is no night for a murder.

But the rain ceases while he sleeps. The clouds break open and the moon shines down. Men dress in black, the colour of killing, and steal from their houses, answering some sign or signal they have all agreed upon. They move across the dale – first one, then two, and soon a dozen or more, bearing weapons and torches. They know it is time, but Gunnar does not. He sleeps on.

What wakes him first? Is it the sound of footsteps across the roof? The clatter of arrows in a quiver as one is drawn? Or is it the crackle of fire as the first torch is laid to the longhouse? I cannot say. But in a moment of waking, he knows it is hopeless. He knows it is his time.

His axe is in his hand, the door is open a bare crack. He hopes that they will be foolish enough to rush the entrance, where he can fight them one at a time, but it is a vain hope. The fires are already lit, the house is burning. The men outside only have to wait. They know that Gunnar will come to them, as sure as a sailor knows the passage of the tides. It is as inevitable as that. Once the fires are lit, the men inside a burning house will come out to fight, and to die. For there is nothing else to be done.

Does he think of me, in that moment? I hope that he does. But what if in that moment he remembers that it was my words that began this? That I sent him out hunting a dead man? Perhaps he does think of me, and before he dies, he curses me.

He speaks to them; calmly, without rush or anger, as he might greet a traveller on the road, or as a farmer tending crops in the field. He asks them a question and he receives no answer.

He steps out from his home, his axe low at his side, his shield held close against his body. He feels the metal edge of the steel, cold against his bare chest. He feels the softness of the mud against his bootless feet, and by instinct he bends his knees and goes on to the balls of his toes, though his careful footwork will be of no use to him. In the light of the fire he sees them all quite clearly. Men who have always been his enemies, men he had once known as friends. He smiles at them all, so that they will remember that he was brave, that he met his death well.

This is no song, where one man may stand against one hundred. It is no tale where the warrior kills his sworn enemy as he dies. He does not even see Björn when he takes the first cut. For they are around him on every side and the blades dance against his skin.

He swings out blindly, is cut again. Men are all around him, so close that he smells the stink of their sweat, the foulness of their breath. But whenever he strikes out, fast as he is, his axe finds no flesh. It cuts through nothing but air, until it catches in the slats of a shield; the head breaks from the shaft when he tries to wrench it free.

He falls to the ground; the broken axe is wrenched from his hand. There has been no pain until that moment and suddenly there is nothing but pain. He waits for the killing blow: the blade into the side of the throat that rips forward, or that slides between the ribs or down through the shoulder and into the heart. But it does not come. The hands grip tighter, he sees Björn come forward, and he knows the slow death they mean to give to him. And at the last, he is truly afraid.

The knives begin their slow work upon him, and he tries not to scream for as long as he can.

That is how my friend died.

27

I let Kari speak and I asked no questions. He spoke haltingly, as though he were relearning the words as he spoke them. Several times, when his hesitancy stretched on, he seemed almost to drift to sleep, and when this happened I reached out my hand and gripped his wrist. I kept my fingers from the burned flesh, but it was no mother's touch I gave him. I let him know that he would have no rest until he had finished his story.

When he had done so, I watched his eyes close, his breathing go soft and steady. I thought of the story that he had not told me. The story that I knew well enough. The story of how his mother and sister must have died.

'Should I have died with him?'

I started at the voice.

'I thought you asleep,' I said. 'You should rest. You have earned it.'

'Tell me, Kjaran. Please.'

Should I have given him the truth? Perhaps. But I found that I could not do it.

'No,' I said. 'It is better that you live.'

'There is no shame in it?'

'Is there shame for me, that I was not there?'

'You were not his son.'

I had no answer to that. I sat beside him and we watched the fire. After a time I felt a hesitant touch against my hand. His fingers reaching out, as Gunnar used to do. I clasped his hand in mine and I thought of the friend I had lost.

'What will I do?' he said.

'We could leave Iceland. Find another country to live in.'

'We cannot run.'

'It is what Gunnar would have wanted.'

'That does not matter.' He shook his head, slowly, like a dozing drunkard or a man underwater. 'There is shame in letting him lie unavenged.'

'There is. But it is what Gunnar would have wanted.'

'What of my mother? My sister?'

'Björn would not kill them. He had more honour than that.'

'But I heard—'

'You do not know what you heard.'

He fell silent and I thought I had won. But I felt it, then. The way a wounded man does not know it at first, feels no pain. And a moment later, puts his hand to his chest and finds himself slain.

I thought of Dalla and I knew what she would have wanted. We could go from this place and find a new home. The shame of Gunnar's death, perhaps I could bear that. But to leave a father unavenged – what a thing it would be for him, to live his life with that weight upon him.

'I think you are right,' I said slowly.

He looked up at me and his eyes were alive once more.

'We shall kill them all?' he asked, hope in his voice.

'Yes.'

He smiled and for a moment he was a child once more, filled with the joy of the child at a dream. 'How shall we do that?'

'Be patient. The slave takes revenge at once—'

'But the coward never does,' he said, finishing the proverb for me.

On the first day of spring I rose before the dawn. I moved quietly in the darkness, but confidently too, like a blind man in a place he knows well. Through touch, I found the things I had placed the night before. A sack of salted fish. Several skins of water. A thick blanket, marked up with earth and grass. I left Gunnar's sword sheathed and lying by the fire. A parting gift for Kari. And when I was ready, I laid my hand to Ragnar's shoulder and woke him gently.

'Speak soft,' I whispered to him. 'Or do not speak at all.'

He nodded and waited.

'I shall be gone for some time,' I said.

'Where do you go?'

'It is better that you do not know.'

'Kjaran…'

'Do not speak. Listen. There is a chance I shall not return.'

'What shall we do?'

'Convince him to go abroad, if you can.'

'And what else?'

I looked across to Sigrid. She lay still, with her back to me, in a semblance of sleep. I think that she merely pretended not to wake, but I could not tell for certain.

'Raise your children well and be kind to her,' I said. And as I spoke those words, I think I saw her shudder.

Then I was gone, out across the dale. On foot with no horse beneath me: a single whicker in the darkness might give me away. I walked and ran, stumbling and rising once again, heedless of the bogs and stones that waited to trip me. Winter had only just ended and the nights were still long, but I had to find my place before the rising of the sun.

I saw what I was looking for: a shadow on a hillside, squat and ugly like some great monster lurking in the darkness. I circled to the right, my hands held before me, until I felt branches twine against my fingers, budding leaves under my palms. I lay down amidst the brush and the low trees. I wrapped myself in a blanket and with my good hand cast earth and twigs over it.

The sun rose, slow and reluctant, still half-asleep from winter, and it shone down on a building amongst the hills. Not a longhouse, but a little shieling, on the good grazing uplands. And I hoped that what I had heard was true.

For days, I watched and waited.

It looked abandoned at first – the untended roof sagging inwards, one wall bowed and holed as a longship shattered on a reef. It was too early in the season for a man to be staying there. Soon the few sheep who had survived the winter would be brought to the highlands to graze, but not yet. It was no place for a man to live.

At noon on the first day a slave came to the door bearing bread, and he left with empty hands soon after. Later, I saw a man come from within, a thick-bearded man with no rings of silver upon his arm. A servant or a slave, for he did not have the look of a landed man. He chopped wood and took it within the shieling, but he left before nightfall. The wood he chopped was not for himself.

A second day passed, and a third, and I lay on the ground, unmoving except at night. If they came in search of firewood, they would catch me and kill me. But I had the favour of the gods, or simple luck, and no man came to the forest. Slaves and servants came and went, but no man of note: not Björn or any of his kin, or another from the war band. And I never saw the man who lived within. I saw the smoke of his fire, smelt the meat that he cooked. Sometimes I thought I heard a sound from within, the sound of a man singing softly to himself. But he never left the shieling.

I marked the comings and goings, scratching into the earth to count the men who came and went. But I had to wait for many days to be certain that the man within was alone. I had to be certain that the man I wanted was inside.

It was the fourth day, when I could feel a fever begin to burn underneath my skin, that I saw him. Just for a moment at the doorway, leaning out, his face pale and filthy. It was Ketil: the man I had cut in the storm and left to die in the snow.

On the fifth day I scratched and unscratched my marks on the ground, until I knew for certain that Ketil was alone in the shieling, that none would come to disturb us. The night fell and the wind began to whisper, carrying voices to me from memory. The voices of Gunnar and his children. I stood from the brush. I walked to the shieling, with no attempt at stealth, and I pushed open the door.

There was a small fire burning: a handspan's worth of dung chippings and twigs, a fire built for a lonely man to sit beside. Ketil sat beside it, his crippled leg stretched forward, a rough-cut piece of wood beside him to help him walk. He lifted his head slowly as I entered, fixed me with a dull-eyed stare. His eyes widened at the sight of me for a moment, but then he nodded to himself and leaned back against the wall of the shieling.

There was an axe at his side, but he did not lay a hand to it. Not yet.

'You are not a ghost,' he said, flatly, after a moment's silence.

'You can be certain of that?'

'You would have died too far from here to roam this far. From what I know of ghosts, at least. You would have haunted those mountains forever.' He rubbed his thumb across cracked lips. 'And I lived through that storm. Why wouldn't you?'

'I am not a ghost.'

He wrinkled his nose. 'You smell like a dead man, though. I can smell your stink from here.'

'I have been hiding in the brush for days. You should cut it down, if you do not wish to be watched.'

'It did Gunnar little use,' he said. Slowly, he rubbed his dirty hands against each other. 'You have been waiting to catch me alone, then. Are you here to kill me, Kjaran? There is little honour in the murder of a cripple.'

I did not answer at first. I felt water dripping on me from the neglected roof, could feel the fingers of the wind finding their way to my skin through the broken walls.

'Why are you here?' I said. 'You have a farm on the lowlands. And I am sure that Bjorn or one of the others would take you in.' I glanced at his leg. Even beneath his clothes, I could see how withered it was, the strange angle that it hung at. 'You have earned that much.'

'I will not live on the charity of men such as that.' He spat on the ground beside him. 'I cannot stand the way that my wife looks upon me. Or my children. It is better that I am here.' He lifted his left hand, moved his fingers in mockery. 'I think you may understand that. We are no longer men.'

By instinct I drew my maimed hand behind me, and he laughed.

'If you had come back unhurt, I would have killed you, cripple that I am.' He hesitated and the smile faded from his

279

face. 'You did not answer, before. Have you come to kill me, Kjaran?'

'No.'

'Then what is it you want?'

I sat down beside him and I stretched one hand, my good hand, towards the fire.

'Do you remember the feast that Gunnar had?'

His hand, which had been rubbing and pawing at his wounded leg, ceased moving.

'I was not there,' he said.

'You were not at the table, but you were there. Watching from the shadows, with Björn and his kin.'

'Yes,' he said.

'You butchered the horse and put its head up on a scorn-pole.'

A pause, this time. Then: 'Yes.'

'But there was someone who led the horse to you. A man who was at the feast with Gunnar and me. A man who pretended to be a friend and who betrayed us. I want you to give me that name.'

He turned his face from me.

'Do you know what I despise most of all? About being a cripple, I mean.'

'Tell me.'

'It has made me a coward.'

Even after all I had seen and done, I still shivered at that word. To hear a man confess himself the worst of things. To feel that cowardice in the room was akin to being trapped with a leper or a man dying of the rotting fever.

'I was close to death, out there, after you left. As close as a man can come.'

'I was there as well. Afterwards, in the storm.'

'I do not want to go to that place again. Or beyond it. I do not like what I saw there. Yet all men do. And I shall go there soon. The next winter will finish me soon enough. As it should have done three years ago. As it should have killed you.'

He looked back at me and there was a strange hunger in his eyes – a kind of needful madness.

'Has it done the same to you?' he said.

'No,' I said. 'I am not afraid.'

The pain broke across his face, and shame as well. But he nodded, accepting.

'Why did you not kill me? Why not spare me this shame?'

'I knew it would slow the others. That they would not leave you. That was all. I would have killed you, if it were not for that.' I hesitated. 'What will you say to the others?' I asked.

'To Björn? And his kin? Perhaps I would speak of you to them, if ever they came here. But they do not. I will not speak of your return. I do not care who else dies in this feud. But you are a fool if you continue the killing.'

'And a coward if I do not.'

'And there is the trap. Our people came to this island to be free. Of kings, tyrants, men who would tell us what to do. Yet here we are. With less freedom than a slave.'

He picked up a stick and poked at the little fire.

'Put this aside, Kjaran,' he said. 'I am not a wealthy man. But I will give you silver – twice the blood-price for Gunnar and his family. Enough to settle the feud honourably. You can go to some other part of Iceland and begin your life again. Or I will give you the name. What is it that you want?'

'I must have the name.'

He waited for a time, his eyes fixed on mine. He gave me as much time as he could to change my mind.

28

I left the shieling and struck out across the dale. I did not go to the west, towards the sea and Ragnar, Kari and Sigrid. I went south, along the familiar path. And I broke the promise that I had made to myself, that I would never set eyes on the valley again.

I walked down through the mountain passage and at the first farm I came to on the other side I traded my last silver arm-ring – the one Thoris had gifted me – for a good horse. I rode until I was in sight of Borg, the mountains and the sea. It was time to turn east then, to travel along the path of exiles and outlaws.

I was afraid that I would not remember the way, but I need not have worried. Every point on that journey was marked in my memory. There was no shape of stone, no cliff face or river or curving line of earth that I did not remember.

The passage was easier this time. It was the beginning of summer and the snow was gone from the lowlands. Yet still, I came to the heights and here the snow remained upon the ground, for it is a place that knows no summer.

The coward's fear was building, every instinct I had warning me off that place. The horse beneath me felt my fear, in the way that beasts always do, wiser than men and cursed with silence. But as he danced and whickered beneath me, he reminded me to be brave. I touched my heels to his flanks and rode on.

It was before me once again. The valley where I had spent three years as an outlaw. A nameless place, for who would name a land where no man would wish to go to, where only the forgotten choose to live?

I could not see the herd of stolen sheep that should be wandering in the valley; perhaps Thorvaldur and Thoris had not gone raiding this early in the year. I tethered my horse at the bottom of the valley and it called out to me as I left it there. For he, too, could feel that this was a place where nothing should live and nothing could grow; the horse was afraid of being left there alone.

I began the slow climb up the side of the hill, pushing through snow slush and bog. I made my way towards the cave and I was afraid of what I would find there.

Perhaps they would cut me down: I was a free man and they still outlaws. But I had nowhere else to turn. And so I made my way up that hill and I remembered every step of the path, each little trap of earth and stone that waited to break my ankle, shatter my knee, leave me dying on the ground. Even the earth itself seems to long for the killing in such a place.

I smelt the cave before I saw it: the hot stink of close living that I had grown unaccustomed to. And I saw the shallow slit, in the side of the hill, above where some god or dragon slept. I let my hand drift to the knife at my hip as I drew close.

It was empty. I waited to see if some outlaw would stir from the blankets and filth, like a cursed man rising from a grave, but there was no one. I knelt beside the entrance, running my hand through the ash of a recent fire, the gnawed bones in a land where there were no flesh-eaters but men. In the air, the fresh stink of men in confinement. They had been here so I sat to wait, sitting atop that familiar warm stone at the back of the cavern where, deep below, a dragon still slumbered in the heart of the mountain.

I remembered lying in that cave, rotten with fever, my left hand dead to the touch. I remembered Thoris nursing me as he might have nursed a child. I remembered the coming of the Christian, the slow breaking of our friendship. I remembered swearing that I would never return to this place – another promise unkept. Then I heard the breaking of snow and there was no more time for memory.

A shadow at the entrance, the low sun at his back. I could not tell who it was at first. Once I would have known those men apart by smell alone, but I had lost that gift.

'Welcome, Kjaran.' It was the voice of the Christian that spoke.

'Thorvaldur,' I said.

A pause. 'I do not know that I am glad to see you again.'

'Where is Thoris?'

Thorvaldur made no reply at first. He slung his burden from his back: a skin full of water, fresh from the frozen river. He offered it to me first, as was my right as his guest. I let my hand wander from my knife to the water, but when I drank it it was sharp and piercing against my tongue. I winced, for I had grown unused to such things, and handed it back to the Christian. He chuckled a little and drank slowly, unmoved by the cold.

'Thoris died, in this past winter.'

'Did you kill him?' I said, speaking softly.

He laughed again. 'No, no. A fever took him. Quick and true.' He leaned forward and put his hands together. 'And now tell me, what brings you back here?'

I did not answer.

'You longed to see us once again? I had not thought that of you. Or have you earned outlawry once more through some rash action?' He rapped the fingers of one hand on the pommel of his sword. 'Or have you come to claim some reward, for the killing of an outlaw? I did not think you fool enough to come alone, if that be your intention.'

'You said that when we met again I could choose. Between your God and a death in battle.'

'That I did. Are you ready to choose?'

'Yes,' I said. 'I wish to choose both.'

He stared at me for a moment, his eyes hunting across my face. Perhaps he thought I mocked him, an insult that he would answer with blood. But when he saw that I meant what I said he crowed with laughter, eyes rolling like a berserker, clapping his hands against his thighs in delight.

'Oh, Kjaran,' he said, 'you do not know how long I have hoped to hear an answer such as that. The true answer. I have asked many that question, and none have spoken as you have.' He cocked his head to the side. 'Why do this?'

'There are men I must fight. Too many for me to face alone. Will you stand beside me? Will you fight and die with me against them, if I swear to your God?'

'Your feud?'

'Yes.'

His fingers tapped against his sword, dancing and moving, as if it were an instrument on which he played a silent tune.

'Are they Christians, the men you will fight?'

'No.'

He paused, considering. 'Then yes,' he said. 'But you must be made a Christian at once. There is no time to spare.'

'What must I do?'

He smiled at me, that half-toothed smile, a corpse's smile.

'Come with me,' he said.

Frozen water does not lie silent. It moans like a dying man. It barks like a mad dog. And when the wind runs across it, one can hear the sound of scratching fingers, of all the dead men that the water has swallowed, begging to be let out.

It was the start of summer and yet here the river was still frozen. I placed each foot carefully, hunting for where the ice seemed thickest, even as it groaned beneath me. I had seen a man swallowed by that kind of ice when I was a boy. A snap and he was gone beneath the water. By the time I got to him, slipping and sliding across the ice as I ran, the water had frozen over once more. I saw him beat against that ice once, twice, three times, but already I knew it was too late.

Thorvaldur strode out ahead of me, trusting the god to guide his steps, only pausing from time to time to look back and mock me with a smile.

'You are afraid to die? I thought better of you than that.'

'There is still much that I have left to do.'

He shrugged. 'Here, then,' he said. 'This will be far enough.' And he took a small axe from his belt; he handed it to me and told me to break the ice.

I have heard tell of how sometimes, in the worst of the feuds when an avenging warband has a man at their mercy, they will refuse to grant him an honourable death, a death in battle. They hand him a tool rather than a weapon, and they make the doomed man dig his own grave.

You may question why a man would do such a thing. Why he would not simply refuse and call on them to kill him cleanly. On this the stories are silent. Perhaps it is the threat of torture that compels him, or it may be that they promise to hand him a weapon if he does as they ask, to give him a chance to die well. Whatever it may be, it seems that the doomed man will always do as they ask. And whatever bargain is made for an honourable death, the killers refuse it. They put him into that grave and they bury him alive. They let him drown beneath the earth.

As I worked the ice, Thorvaldur sitting cross-legged on the frozen water and watching me in silence, I thought only of those stories. And yet I could not seem to stop.

I cut a circle in the ice – a fisherman's circle, though there was nothing to catch in this dead water. And Thorvaldur spoke the words in some tongue that I did not understand, his hands clasped together in prayer.

'A spell?' I said, when he had finished.

'There is no witchcraft here. Only words. And water. And God.' He pointed to the ice. 'Kneel with me.'

I felt his hand against my neck, the sound of more words, the cracking of the ice beneath my knees. Then the world swung upwards and I felt the water close around me. And from my mouth, the deadened sound of screaming underwater.

I was a sacrifice, a gift to his god from the water. And so I fought against him, my hands scrabbling at the edges of ice, trying to push myself free of the water. But he was stronger than I, his weight bearing down on me, pressing me into the black water. And I felt the mad longing to breathe that water.

The world returned and I traded water for the sky – lying gasping on the ice, my breath frosting before me. I tried to speak, but the cold stilled my voice; and Thorvaldur leaned over me, his hands on my shoulders. He laughed the way that wolves seem to laugh in the hunt, howling with joy, teeth bared and eyes wild.

'Oh, I am glad to have you with me. Do you feel it now? Do you feel the new god's hands upon you?'

'Yes,' I said. And I did.

Later, by the fire. It had been many hours since the ritual on the ice and I still could not seem to get warm. My heart beating sluggishly or threatening to pound its way from my chest, and I could feel myself growing weaker, moment by moment. I sat still and did not speak, and waited to see if I would live or die.

Thorvaldur was as restless as I was still. He poked the fire and looked at the sky, wishing the night away, praying for the coming of the dawn.

'How many are there,' he said, 'that we must kill?'

'Two brothers are the ones who matter. Björn and Snorri. Three kinsfolk with them. Bersi, Harald and Svein.'

'Only five?'

'There are others. There are always others to carry on the feud, are there not? But those five are the ones that matter.'

'Very well. And who else do we have at our side?'

'Only one. Kari Gunnarsson.'

'Gunnar's child? A boy?'

'Near enough a man. And he shall fight as one.'

'And what of the woman? Vigdis, you called her.'

'What of her?'

'Must she die, too?'

'Does your god permit the killing of women?'

'Sometimes he does.' He clasped his hands together and

leaned towards me. 'Tell me something, if I am to fight in this feud of yours.'

'Ask me.'

'Why is it that you do this? And do not lie to me. I shall know it if you do.'

'For revenge, of course.'

He studied me for a moment, then he wagged a finger as though I were a child to be scolded.

'No,' he said. 'That is not the answer. But no matter. You will give me the truth, in time.'

Without another word, he turned from me, rolled up in his blankets, and was asleep within moments.

I slept, too. Better than I had since the feud began. And I did not dream.

29

We moved by night, for Thorvaldur was an outlaw still, and it would be death to both of us if we were caught together. We moved over the land in darkness, sleeping in fens and riverbeds in the day, and the stories spread in our wake.

I would hear them later: the farmers who heard our footsteps in the night and thought us ghosts. The shepherd boys in their shielings, who caught glimpses of us silhouetted against the sky and mistook us for giants, their eyes playing tricks at the distance. Gods and monsters, making their way to the Salmon River Valley.

When I showed Thorvaldur the valley for the first time, we stood on the southern hills, risking the dawn light. His eyes traced over the rivers and the dales, the mountains and the sea. He nodded and said: 'A good land. But I would not die for it.'

'You do not have to die for this place.'

'I do not have to die at all. That is what you came here for, is it not?'

I made no answer.

He grunted. 'So,' he said, 'that is not your secret either. But I will find it, do not worry.'

'It is almost day. We must sleep now. They will be in the fields before long and we must not be seen.'

'Where is it that we go tomorrow?'

'To the house of a friend,' I said, though the words were like ashes in my mouth.

When we came to Ragnar's house I rapped my hands against the door – softly, with a thief's touch. Yet the door was open in a moment and it was Sigrid who stood behind it. I suppose she knew it would be me.

'I am glad to see you return,' she said, and I could see her eyes shining in the darkness. Her hand drifted towards me, hesitant, as though she thought me a spirit rather than a man, and would believe me only through touch. Then her gaze strayed past my shoulder to the man who stood behind me. 'Who do you bring with you?'

'An ally.'

She nodded and she was cold once more. 'I shall wake the others. Wait here.'

I listened to her footsteps, to soft voices within. And then I heard Thorvaldur's words in my ear.

'Who is she?'

'Sigrid,' I said, and I heard him chuckle.

'I know that name. Whispered at night, in sleep, many times over the long winter. And I recognise her. That tall, pale thing that you were pining for.'

'Thorvaldur...'

He grinned at me. 'I shall be quiet, do not worry.'

I saw her again, in the half-light of the fire, beckoning us in. Ragnar and Kari were both waiting for us around the fire.

'You should not have left without me,' Kari said.

'I know,' I answered. 'But it is done now. We have much to speak of.'

'That may be,' Sigrid said, 'but you do not have much time.' Her eyes did not leave Thorvaldur, as though I had brought a wild dog into her home.

'Why is that?'

'I have heard people talking. Of a stranger who roams the hills.'

'Do they think me a ghost? That would be fitting.'

'Some say so. But I am sure there are those who will guess at the truth. They are restless.'

Ragnar spoke, then. 'I have heard that Björn may be going abroad. He and his kin have spoken to captains. Friends of mine. They seek passage on a ship.'

'Why?'

'Raiding. Trade. He is a man of much wealth now. And burning a house is a shameful thing. Perhaps he fears the law being brought against him.' He looked at the palms of his hands. 'And perhaps he has heard the rumours. Perhaps he knows that you have returned.'

'We shall have to move quickly, then.'

'Good,' Thorvaldur said. 'I did not come here to wait.'

Kari seemed to look on the newcomer for the first time. 'Who are you?' he said.

'One who will fight.'

'Did you know my father?'

'Oh no. Only the stories that Kjaran has told me.'

'Then why are you here?'

'I like the killing. Don't you?'

'Thorvaldur,' I said.

He tilted his head to me. 'That is why you brought me here, is it not?'

'I have never killed a man,' Kari said.

Thorvaldur steepled his fingers together. 'But you want to?'

Kari dropped his head. 'Yes,' he said.

'That is enough,' Sigrid said quietly. 'Do not speak of killing in this house.'

Thorvaldur looked from the girl to me, grinning like an idiot. 'I have heard stories of you, too.'

'I have heard nothing of you.'

'Do you want to?'

'No.' And she turned to me. 'Who is this man?'

'He is called Thorvaldur.'

'This is a name I know. An outlaw.'

'Yes.'

Ragnar put his head into his hands, but he would not speak.

Sigrid said: 'This is too much that you ask of us. To shelter such a man.'

'You need do no such thing,' Thorvaldur said. 'I shall sleep in the barn, and if they find me, call me an intruder. No blame shall lie with you.' He looked to the boy. 'Will you come with me?' he said. 'We have much to speak of.'

I felt the touch of cold fingers against my skin – some warning from the gods, I once would have thought. But I ignored them. My new god did not speak in riddles or omens, did not lay hands upon His worshippers. I prayed and I heard Him speak. So I let Thorvaldur leave, and I let the boy go with him.

After a time, Ragnar sighed and dipped a horn bowl into the pot of stew above the fire. He handed it to me. 'Eat,' he said. 'You must be hungry.'

'I have brought trouble to you and I am sorry for it.'

Ragner shook his head. 'I owe you a great debt.' He licked his lips and said, 'I thought that you would kill me, when I saw you return.'

'I thought of it.'

'Why didn't you?'

I looked at Sigrid and she met my gaze without fear.

'It would have won me nothing,' I said. 'You believe that you owe me a debt for that?'

'I thought I was to die and I was not afraid. I thought that I... that I would not give those years with my wife for anything. Not even to die. I have never had courage. But I knew it then. And I thank you for that.'

There was nothing for me to say to that. I placed my bowl upon the ground, half-finished, for I no longer had the stomach to eat.

'What will you do tomorrow?' asked Sigrid.

'I will go to see an old friend. It is better that you know no more than that.'

I was tired then, the long weeks of night-walking bearing down upon me. With no further word I curled into my blankets and let myself drift half into sleep. Not fully – I waited to hear the door swing, to hear Kari return. But he did not. And when I awoke late in the night from restless dreams, the taste of blood in my mouth, the screaming of ghosts in my ears, I saw that he had not returned.

I thought little of it.

The next day was beautiful, yet I saw it would not last. Brilliant sun beating down upon us, but over the inland mountains the thick clouds were gathering, the promise of rain in the sky. But I could enjoy the sun for a time as I sat outside Ragnar's longhouse with my back against the wall. I was glad of that.

I heard Kari's voice, calling my name. And when I turned I saw him coming from the barn, dark whorls beneath his eyes.

'You slept little?' I said.

'I slept enough. You are going again?'

I nodded.

'Can I come with you this time?'

'No. Not yet.'

He kicked at a tussock on the ground. 'I will not be left behind a second time.'

'You shall. But there will not be a third. I promise you that.'

He looked back towards the barn and I did not know what that look could mean.

'He told me that you became a Christian,' he said. 'Is that true?'

'It is.'

'He says that I should become one, too.'

'Do not listen to everything that Thorvaldur has to say.'

He nodded absently. 'When does it begin?'

'The killing?'

'Yes.'

'Soon. We must be patient. We must wait for our chance.'

'I am afraid to wait.'

'Why?'

His fingers darted up to the burns on his face – a habit now. When he was in thought or he did not know what to say his hands would drift up to the strange, ageless, ruined skin. I had seen the children of chieftains play with carved dolls from across the sea. His face was akin to those: flat, still, not quite human.

'There is something else I must tell you,' he said. 'About the night that—'

'Tell me.'

'When father went out... to fight them... I heard him calling to me. To fight beside him. And I did not. I ran to the tunnel, to escape. But I could not get through.'

'And what then?'

'My mother and my sister. I could hear them crying out behind me, feel them pulling at my legs.' He looked up to me. 'Björn would have let them go, wouldn't he? Why did they not run?'

'I do not know,' I said. A lie, but a needful one.

He did not speak. He looked at me, awaiting a judgement.

'You ran from the battle?'

'Yes,' he whispered.

'So you think that you must die?'

He shook his head violently. 'No, no.' He wiped at his eyes. 'I do not want to die. But I cannot bear this shame. I have to...' He looked back at the barn once more. 'Perhaps then I will be forgiven.'

'We shall all be forgiven.'

'That is not what Thorvaldur says.' He turned back to me. 'Where is it that you go?'

'You remember the horse, don't you?'

Even in the dark, I saw his face go pale.

'I know who did it,' I said.

He was in my arms then, his head working into my chest, as though he thought to bury himself there. I held him as I might have held a child of my own, in another life, another world.

'Kill them for me,' he said, his voice thick.

Then he was gone from me, just as abruptly, striding back to the barn and wiping at his eyes.

Let them talk, I thought. Let him be a Christian if he wishes. I thought to keep Thorvaldur content, to feed him converts like a man sacrificing to his gods.

I was still thinking in the old ways, of the old gods. The White Christ took a different kind of offering. But I did not know that then.

30

I moved slowly across the land, an idle traveller. For years I had waited for this, yet the day had come and it seemed there was no rush. I stopped at rivers and dangled my ruined left hand in the cool water, as though hoping to find an elvish place that might knit my hand whole once more. Looking in the tussocks and the bogs for the bones of sheep or stones worn smooth, as a child searches the land for charms of good fortune.

As the sun peaked in the sky I made my way inland, near the good trapping ground on the upper banks of the river. I walked through a little patch of woodland, cutting at the brush with my knife to pass the time, collecting the twigs and wet leaves, feeling the damp matter between the palms of my hands before I drew them once more within my cloak. I did not know what I was waiting for, but there came a moment when I knew that it was time, and I knew that I was ready.

I made my way to the house of Kormac Bersisson. To the home of a traitor.

There was sound within. As I came close to the door of the

longhouse, walking soft upon the wet ground, I could hear men talking. Not many: two or three, unless they had one of those silent men with them, the kind that does not speak a word until there is blood to be spilled.

I backed away from the house, each foot placed carefully, though there was little need for such caution. Men in a feud listen for hoofbeats, for the whicker of horses. They do not expect soft footfalls of a lonely man on foot. And these men had no need to listen for a murderer's footsteps. The feud was over. They had won.

I waited for smoke to rise from the longhouse, for the fire within to burn high. Then I went to the door and pushed at it without knocking. It swung open – unbarred, an open house for friends and neighbours. I heard a curse within, for no doubt they thought me some sudden gust of wind. Then footsteps coming.

'Kormac,' I said, and the footsteps stopped.

'Who is there?' said the voice from within.

'An old friend,' I said, but I was sure to turn the corner before I spoke my name. I wanted to see them first, before I gave them such a warning as that.

There were two men there, sitting by the fire, looking on me as they might have looked upon a ghost. Kormac was there, older and fatter than when last I had seen him, and with him but one other man, whom I did not recognise at first. Bjarni – that was his name. Kormac's son. I had seen him at Gunnar's feast three years before. A boy then, but a man now.

Even in the flickering light of the longhouse fire I could see Kormac's face go pale at the sight of me, his eyes search me for a weapon. But I smiled at him and offered my good hand in greeting. He took it, more by instinct if not in friendship, and I sat down without waiting to be asked.

'Stoke the fire high,' I told him. 'Or am I not a good enough guest to burn the wood for?'

'Every guest has that right,' he said thickly. And he cast the wood upon the fire: a little fortune in brush and twig, his honour demanding nothing less.

The smoke grew thick and yet still I could see him well enough.

'Bjarni, you *remember* Kjaran.' An emphasis on that third word, a weight to give it another meaning.

'Yes,' he said, 'I remember.'

'You have been gone a long time, Kjaran. I did not know you at first.'

'Yes.'

'I had heard that you were dead.'

I smiled at him, to show that I was not afraid. Then I leaned over, stirred the ladle of the pot on the fire. 'Plenty of stew here for two men.'

He gave a half-laugh and attempted a smile. 'You know me. Hungry. Always wanting more.'

'Yes, I do know that of you.'

I watched the smile flicker and fade. I could see the shame biting at him, like some beast that lived within. But let it bite a little longer, I thought.

'I would have thought that you would be in the fields by now. It is near midday.'

'I took on more servants this year.'

'You have prospered since last I saw you.'

'Yes,' he said, and hung his head low.

'You are unwell.'

'Perhaps.' He hesitated. 'You should not have come back, Kjaran.'

The son moved, his feet gliding across the ground, a half-step towards me. I tilted my head slightly, to keep him in my vision.

'Why is that?'

He shrugged. 'You have few friends left in this valley.'

'That is why I came to you.'

A light in his eyes. He shifted on the bench and he tried to smile. 'A good thing. A good thing. You should tell me what you mean to do.'

'I do not think so.' I leaned forward and felt the heat of the fire biting at my neck, my chin. 'I know,' I said.

'What do you know?' he said. *How do you know?* – that is what he meant to say.

'You have not yet spoken of Gunnar,' I said.

He gave a little sigh, a soft breath of regret. 'No. I have not.'

'Send your son into the fields,' I said. 'He should not be here for these words.'

'I do not think I will,' he said.

'I had not thought you so shameless,' I said. 'But I should have expected nothing more from a man like you.'

'That may be so.' There was a little shame in his voice, I thought. But it was not enough. 'I do not think it is words alone that you mean to give me.'

All was still. All was ready. I concentrated on my breath – in and out, in and out, in and out. Never had that air tasted sweeter to me, when I did not know how many tastes of it remained.

Then a rapping at the door. The moment gone, a spell broken. A strange look on Kormac's face: fear and relief both. Who was it that had come to this place in the middle of the day?

I should have run then. Towards the back door, past the

barrels of whey and salted fish, out towards the light. The son would have his knife between my ribs if he were not lame or dumb, but it was a greater chance than if I were to remain. Yet I sat there, compelled to stillness by some strange force. A binding spell, though whether it was a curse spun by some witch or by my own heart I could not tell.

The door swung open and there came no band of men to end my life, no solitary enemy to cut my throat. A woman stood there – a woman I had not seen in many years.

Vigdis. The one who had begun the feud.

We stared at one another for a time, her cold black eyes not leaving mine.

'You come alone?' Kormac said to her.

'Of course,' she replied, and sat beside the fire.

'I did not know he was coming. You must believe me. I have not said—'

'It does not matter,' she said. 'Do not worry, Kormac.' She inclined her head to me. 'I did not think to see you again.'

'I knew that I would see you.'

'Did your god give you a vision? I have heard that of the skalds.'

'Something like that,' I said.

'Did your god give you a vision of Gunnar? Of the way he died?'

'No. But I know what was done there.'

'I am glad of it.'

'Does your child live?'

'He does.' She lifted her head. 'He is almost three now. Strong, like his father.'

'You have a son, then. Good.'

Her hands went still.

'Where do you stay at night, Kjaran? Tell me that. There is no harm in it.'

'I shall not tell you that. I have some friends yet.'

'But not here.' She lifted the cup to her lips, holding it in both hands like a child. 'You would like to kill me, I think,' she said.

'No.'

'No?'

'You spoke the words, but it was not you that did the killing. Others bear the shame of that.'

'But Björn?' She lifted a finger towards Kormac. 'And this man?'

I made no answer. She nodded, satisfied. 'It is as I thought,' she said.

'Will you tell me why?'

She cocked her head. 'I do not understand.'

'Why you have brought about this feud.'

'I have done no killing.'

'No. But there were so many times when peace might have been made. And every time you have spoken the words to break that peace. I wonder why that is.'

She considered this and I watched the firelight play across her skin: the shadow of the fire dancing over her cheeks, the elegant movement of her hands, the hollow of her throat. She truly was a beautiful woman. But not enough to die for. To kill for.

'No,' she said at last. 'I will not give you that. You will die ignorant.'

'I may die,' I said, 'but I shall know that, before I die.'

'I shall not see you again,' she said.

'Perhaps.'

'Perhaps,' she allowed. 'But I am not sorry,' she said. 'Remember that.' She stood, smoothing her skirts with her hands. She looked on Kormac and said: 'You know what must be done now.'

She was gone then, back into the light of the world, and we listened to the sound of hooves beating against the wet ground.

'I wish you had not come here,' Kormac said.

'You would kill a guest in your own house?'

'You are not a guest. You should not have come.'

'I should not be surprised. You have done some coward's killing already.'

'I had no part in what was done to Gunnar. That was Björn's sport.'

'That is not what I mean. I know what was done to Gunnar's wife. His daughter.'

His face went white with shame. 'You cannot know,' he said. 'None would tell you that.'

'And yet still I know it.'

He trembled for a moment, then stilled himself and looked at his son. 'What are you doing here, Kjaran?'

'I think you know why already.'

He looked on me, his mouth agape. And then, a little sigh of relief. 'You came here to die?'

I drew my hands beneath my cloak and I leaned my head forward towards the fire. The way I have heard that condemned men in distant lands kneel before an executioner.

'I have lived long enough,' I said.

And at the edge of my vision, I saw his son's hand go to the knife on his belt.

'Tell me one thing,' I said.

'What is that?'

I saw his son move closer still.

'Why did you turn against Gunnar?'

'You truly wish to know?'

'Yes.'

His eyes slid to his son. 'He thought himself better than the rest of us,' he said – slowly, grudgingly, but his words had the taste of truth. 'He thought that because he had a good hand with a sword and a taste for killing, that he was the greater man. All he had was that little plot of land, that herd of wormy sheep. No kin, no favour with his chieftain. And yet he thought he could do without the rest of us.'

I did not dare to close my eyes, but that was all that I wanted – to block away the world for a moment, to think myself dreaming. I do not know what it was that I had hoped for. That Kormac had been bought with silver or the promise of honour. Now that I had the petty truth, I wished that I had not heard him.

'You are right,' I said. 'He was a fool, to think that he could live without such things.'

The son was closer still. But I still had time to speak again.

'He was right in his own way,' I said. 'He was a better man than you.' And with that I lifted my hand, my good hand, from within my cloak.

Kormac was ready for me, stepping up and stepping back to escape a blade, his hand going to the weapon at his side. But he sought to escape a blade that was not there. I did not bring iron in my hand, but a heavy handful of leaves, still wet from the rain the night before. I cast them upon the fire and in a moment the longhouse was filled with smoke.

A hand grasped at my cloak, pulling me towards the point of a blade. But my cloak was unclasped and slipped from my back, and I was into the smoke, my hand over my mouth, my eyes closed. I listened.

The others were gasping, retching, stumbling. I sought Kormac through sound, through touch, as I have heard blind old men seek revenge at the end of their lives, their trembling hands searching in the dark for a throat, an eye, a beating heart to still. So it was that I went into the smoke, reaching forward with my maimed left hand until I felt it touch his chest. For it was my right hand that carried the knife.

Three times the blade went in and twice it came out again, for on the third stroke some trap of bone closed about it and held it there. I was away then, counting my steps back towards the door. I could hear his son moving in the smoke, circling the fire, crying out for his father. But he realised too late that I had made for the door.

I was into the blinding daylight, the smoke pursuing me like a vengeful spirit, my eyes streaming, sucking at the fresh air as a desert traveller drinks water. I looked back over my shoulder as I ran, for I thought that Bjarni would pursue me, that he would follow me out to fight and die beneath the open sky. But he did not. As I ran from the longhouse I heard the sound of a blade falling to the ground behind me, and a keening wail rose up, a son for his father, just as the softest snow began to fall.

31

What sign was it, this summer snowfall? For the clouds had come in from the sea, but they did not bear rain. The white was falling thick about me as I ran and scrambled from the killing house, back across the dale to Ragnar's homestead. What god spoke this way? The White Christ or the old gods I had left behind? Was it to cover my escape or to reveal my tracks, to leave no place for a killer to hide?

In that moment, I cared not. For the killer's joy burned like a fever, and how I had lived so long without it I did not know.

Now I understood the longing that Gunnar had felt, and I could not understand how he had tried to give it up, to trade the killing for a farmer's life. What a thing it was, to try and put up your sword, once you have known such a terrible joy. At that moment I loved him more than I ever had before. And I loved his son, for that was all that was left of my friend.

I took a long time to return to Ragnar's home. I circled around the high lands, waiting and watching for any sign of pursuit, for I could take no chance of being followed. Every so often I stopped to plunge my hands into the snow, leaving it red behind me, wiping away the killer's sign that I bore. It was only when I was certain that no pursuer would find me that I made my way towards the coast, back to Ragnar's longhouse.

I did not knock, but threw the door open and made my way inside. I could feel the smile upon my face, but I could not rid myself of it. As I entered, I found Ragnar and Sigrid speaking in close conference by the fire; Sigrid looked up at me and I could see the fear in her eyes.

'It is not my blood,' I said. 'I am not hurt.' For my hands were clean, but my clothes were still marked with gore.

She walked to me, put her hands to my face, held my gaze. I could not breathe for a moment, the ache in me was so strong. Yet I saw that I was mistaken. There was no tenderness in her touch, no affection. She meant only to be sure of my attention.

'Thorvaldur has gone,' she said. 'He has taken Kari with him.'

That cold touch upon my skin once again – the mocking warning of a god.

'Tell me what you mean,' I said, 'as quickly as you can.'

It was Ragnar who spoke now. 'I went out to the captains and sailors. To try to get some sense of the talk in the valley. What Björn and his kin might be doing. I... I wanted to help.' He hesitated. 'Vigdis has been riding all across the valley today. And it seems that Björn will go tonight, with the turning of the tide.'

For a moment I could not breathe. 'Where?' I asked.

'The north coast, near Kambsnes. He has a ship waiting for him there.'

'Surely no man will sail in this storm.'

'The wind is true and this storm will pass soon enough. It has to.' He swallowed. 'Thorvaldur said that it would be a coward's curse to wait. That they would ambush Björn as he made his way to the ship.'

'How many will go with Björn?'

'I do not know. His brother. A few more men as well, I would have thought.'

'Why did you not stop them?'

Sigrid spoke now. 'You invite a wolf into our home and ask if we shall stop him for you?'

Ragnar smiled sadly. 'I am sorry, Kjaran; I wish I could have stopped them.' He licked his lips. 'He called me a… coward.'

The word hung in the air – a killing word. A man or a woman needs magic to bring bloodshed. There are words that need no sorcery to make a killing inevitable: speak them and men will die. I saw Sigrid's lips go white with fury, her hands twitch as though they longed to close about a weapon.

'I will have to fight him, won't I?' said Ragnar. 'To challenge him to the *holmgang*.' He looked down at his sailor's hands. I wondered when was the last time he had held a weapon. 'I know what I am. But I cannot have it said.'

'No,' I said. Within me, I felt the killing joy change to something different. The cold, measured sense of revenge. 'If it comes to that, I will fight him for you. I think, perhaps, that is what he wants. How long ago did they leave?'

'An hour. They took horses.'

'I must have one too.'

'They took our two best. But take Snorri. He is old, half-lame. But he may get you there in time.'

A lie – a kind, hopeful lie, but a lie all the same. I took a spear from the corner of the room, felt the weight of it. An axe and shield lay there as well and I took them too. Kari had taken his father's sword with him.

They did not speak to me as I gathered my arms. They could not even look at me, nor I at them. At the edge of my vision, I saw her take his hand in hers and hold it close, and I shut my eyes against the sight. *They are glad to be rid of me*, I thought. *And I cannot blame them for it.*

Yet when at the door, I heard a voice calling to me.

'Kjaran, wait.'

I turned and looked on Sigrid. She glanced back at Ragnar, sat by the fire in the longhouse.

'Will you return?' she said to me.

'I do not think so.' I looked down at my hand, my good hand, and I saw that it did not tremble. 'I will see Gunnar again. And I shall save his son. And that will be enough.' As I spoke the words I thought of that burrowing embrace Kari had given me that morning. Had he known then? Had he sought to say farewell, but had not found the words?

'Are you afraid?'

'No.' I met her gaze. 'It is an easy thing to go to death, and to know it will bring joy to one that you love.'

She said nothing for a moment. Then: 'That is not true. For I did love you, once.'

'But not now.'

'No.'

'And never again.'

'I do not think so. But I did love you once. Truly, with all that I am. And perhaps that may mean something to you.'

'It does.'

I took in the flaxen colour of her hair. The whetstone edge of her jaw, those eyes with the touch of green at the centre. The way her hips had felt against my hands on that one night so long ago. I remembered it all then, and knew that I would not forget.

I was weary before I began. The killing lust had left me and I felt only the longing to rest – to lay down my head and close my eyes and let the killing be over for one day at least.

One last ride to the battle, I told myself. One more time and then it shall be done. Then there will be nothing but rest.

How would they have thought, those men who hunted men? What paths would they have taken? In places the snow had settled and I found horse tracks there. This was strange country to Thorvaldur, but he had Kari to guide him and none knew better the hidden places of this land than a boy. I struck north, past the beach where Gunnar and I had found the whale, and for a moment, amidst the storm-tossed surf, I thought I saw a figure there, raising a hand in greeting to me.

Wait, I told him. *I shall come to you soon.*

There was Laugar to the north; perhaps Björn and his men would stop at the hot spring before they set sail. And then they would go to the west, towards the mooring beyond Kambsnes. To climb the hill and look upon the Salmon River Valley one more time before they took to the sea.

I found the horses wandering free at the base of the hill. Cast to roam as they wanted, for their riders did not expect to need them again. There upon the ground, the marks of feet in the mud and slush: those of a man, those of a boy. Like a father and a son, walking together. And I scrambled up after them, binding my shield to my maimed hand as I ran, twining the strands of leather and cloth together.

Atop the hill now, a burning fire in my lungs, a hate in my heart. There, ahead, a figure lying upon the ground. So still that I might have mistook him for a twisted tree root in the shape of a man, a patterned rock playing tricks upon my eyes, a murdered man left unburied. But my eyes did not lie. Thorvaldur lay upon the ground, his hand upon a spear, his eyes on the valley beyond.

I came forward, one foot before the other, my shield before me, as soft as I could walk. A shift of weight and the shaft of the spear was resting on top of my shoulder, saving my strength for the throw. For all my caution, he heard me coming.

'Kjaran,' said Thorvaldur as he turned his head to face me. If he felt any concern at my levelled spear, his face did not reveal it. 'Kari said that you would come. That you would find us. I did not believe it.'

'Where is the boy?'

'Not a boy any more, but a man. For he will fight with us in the feud. That is what you wanted, is it not? That is why you gave him back his father's sword.'

'Where is he?'

'He is close. He is where he should be.'

'I shall kill you,' I said.

'Perhaps. But it will do you little good.' He pointed down. 'Look there.'

In the valley below I saw Kari standing tall. One hand resting atop the shield that was propped up beside him, the tip of the sword in his belt dragging against the earth, for he was not tall enough for it to hang true. He wore a black tunic: the colour of killing. There was no mistaking what he intended.

He saw me then, through the curtain of snow. He smiled at me and waved and was a boy once more.

I wanted to call to him. To tell him to run, to hide. To forgive me. But the words caught in my throat, for I saw, around a turn in the valley, beyond the sight of Kari below, a group of men approaching. I heard the wicker of their horses, the distant familiar chatter. I could not hear the words, but even at that distance I recognised some of their voices. The men who had hunted me through another storm. Björn, his brothers, and those who stood beside them.

I went to ground and lowered my head, feeling the wet grass against my forehead, like a cooling touch against a fever. When I looked up once more, I saw Thorvaldur with his hands held up, palms to the sky. He tilted his head and he smiled.

'The snow blesses us,' he whispered. 'A white blessing from the White Christ. Perhaps we may win this battle after all.' He extended a finger towards the warband. 'And look. There are only six.'

'We are outnumbered. He is a boy. I am maimed.'

'I am worth two of those men. Kari is worth two of those men. But are you?'

'We must get away from here.'

'It is too late for that.'

I knew that he was right. 'We could have waited.'

'What need is there to wait? You promised me killing, and your faith. You would give me only half a bargain?'

'I spit on your White Christ. I curse him. A coward's god.'

'And yet I am the brave man and you the coward if you will not fight today. You can curse my God, if you want to. But if you do, I shall not fight with you.' The mad smile went from his face as suddenly as it had sprung upon him. 'Pray to Him, Kjaran. Do it now, for we do not have much time. He will tell you what to do.'

I put my hands against each other. I closed my eyes and I prayed.

I could feel the closeness of death – like hands closing about my throat, a sharp coldness sliding between my ribs, touching against my heart. Death has a taste, I had learned: a dry taste, like iron upon your tongue. It has no smell at all: the sweat and stink of the world falls away, leaving nothing behind.

I prayed to the White Christ and his father to give me

strength in battle, the courage to destroy my enemies, to grant me vengeance for friends long dead. And it was but a moment before I felt the cold hand of God upon my shoulder.

My eyes opened. The world shone a little brighter. The taste of death grew dull, and I could smell the earth and the air once again. He would fight with me; I knew then it was as the priest had said. That this was a God of revenge.

I wanted to sing to Him then, and I thought to give a soft chant that the wind would swallow. I thought to give Him a new song, but I could not find the words. I tried to think of the old songs, ones that I had repeated a hundred times before, and though the words came close to my lips they would not leave them, like a river almost in flood that cannot break its banks.

My songs belonged to the Old Gods, and I had abandoned them. My new God was one worshipped in silence. I would never sing again.

Below, the warband turned the corner, and their talk and their laughter ceased. Björn and the others swung down from their saddles, came forward and faced the boy in silence. I do not think that they recognised Kari at first: they thought him dead, and his burned face gave them little to find familiar.

I saw Kari speak, but I could not hear the words. And I saw those men shudder almost as one, a ripple of shame passing through them. No doubt they had tried to forget what they had done.

Kari spoke again and Björn shook his head. The man pointed south, stabbing his finger towards the beach, towards safety.

Kari spoke one last time, louder this time, a single word. A word, at last, that I could hear. 'Coward,' he said.

Björn nodded, then. He pulled the shield from the saddle of his horse, drew the axe from his belt. Another man half-drew his weapon at the sight of this. But Björn snapped a curse at him, spoke loud enough for me to hear. 'Do not shame me!'

Gunnar's sword was out now – too big for Kari, but he held it well. Oh, but he was his father's son. The stance he held, the look in his eyes – even in that ruined face of his, there was still some ghost of the friend that I had lost.

Björn hesitated once more, looking on the boy who stood before him. Viewed from a distance, through the turning curtain of the snow, it was almost as though I was watching some battle from the old stories. Not a boy standing before a man, but a man standing before a giant.

The giant shrugged and spat upon the ground. And the iron began to sing.

I half-rose, my grip tightening around my spear, but Thorvaldur's hand was on my shoulder.

'Wait,' he said.

'For what?'

He did not answer. But I trusted him then. There is no trust akin to that of men who fight together. Whatever game he had been playing before, no matter how much he liked to make me dance for his pleasure – all that was gone now.

Björn was afraid of that sword, for he had seen what it could do. I could see him dodge back further than he needed to, to place his shield precisely in its way. His strikes were hesitant, in spite of all his advantages. Yet it was already clear how the fight would end. It was a beautiful sword, but it could not undo a foot of reach and fifty pounds of weight. Kari fought well, but he could not break the larger man's guard. And it was not long before Björn found his courage.

Wood was flying from Kari's splintering shield and I could see him gasping for breath as he backed away. He barely struck back, the occasional half-checked swipe with the sword, as he fought to hold the shield high as Björn beat against it. He had no art and little skill, but he did not need them: he only needed his weight, and time.

Soon, Kari could retreat no further and his shield groaned and cracked with every blow. Below, I saw the other men lose themselves, the hands half-rise, imploring. Longing for the death to come, to give them their release. Lost in the dance before them, they had no eyes for anything else.

'Now,' Thorvaldur said. But I knew it before he spoke and I was already gone.

Down the slope, leaping with great strides from tussock to tussock. Out of the corner of my eye I could see Kari had gone to ground, both hands holding up his shield, blood upon the fresh snow. But I could not look at him. I looked only upon the men that I had to kill.

I could feel some great sound bubbling up within me, scratching at my teeth, closing around my throat, desperate to be born, but I would not let it loose. Not until my spear was in flight, not until it had struck home in meat and bone, not until a man was screaming on the ground. Hearing that, I let the sound come from within me. It was not a curse or a war cry, not a song or a scream, but laughter. For a joy spoke through me, then: the berserker's joy, which knows only laughter.

The battle was not motion, it was stillness. Moments where the world ceased to move, where everything can be seen. In between those moments, a mist took my sight. I could not speak. I could not sing. But I could laugh. And I could kill.

In those still moments I saw everything so clearly. The white teeth of the man I had speared, the whorls of dirt on the hand he held up, the arcing shape of the blood as I brought my axe down across his mouth and left him a smiling corpse on the ground.

The next man seemed frozen in mid-swing, his axe moving towards my head as slowly as the motion of the sun. It was such a simple thing to place my shield in its way. He had no time to take up a shield of his own and held up his hand by instinct to bar my way. That shield of flesh was gone in two strokes of my axe. I touched his stomach with the blade – the barest touch it seemed to me, yet he knelt upon the ground at once and spilt his secrets into the snow.

His lips moved, but I could not hear what he said. I could hear nothing but the laughter.

I saw Thorvaldur, too. No shield in his hand, just that terrible sword of his clutched in both hands. He moved like a dancer and he left only death behind him.

And at the heights of my fury, I saw Björn. His leg laid open, yellow fat parted neatly before the bone. His shield cast down, one empty hand pressed to the ground, lifting him up. His other hand, the full hand, bringing his axe down again and again on the boy at his feet.

We grow close now, don't we? Close to the dawn, for the sun will crawl into the sky soon enough. And close to the end of my story. Our story, it would be more right to say.

Oh, I see you stir at that, Sumardil.

You will have it all, I promise. The end to all mysteries. All the truth that you could want – too much, perhaps. We shall see. I must linger but a moment longer, before we get to the end. I must speak a little more of Kari, Gunnar's son.

When I was a young man I never thought to have a child. With no land to call my own, it was too much to hope for. In truth, it did not matter to me so much. I wanted nothing more than to wander and be free. I thought that my words would be my children. A good song lives longer than a good son, after all.

When I found Sigrid and I thought we would be married, I felt for the first time that strange ache for a child. I understood it as I had not before. That longing to have more of the one that I loved brought into the world, to find a way to make your love cheat death. And I suppose in the end I did get my wish, though not as I imagined it.

Kari was our child, mine and Sigrid's, raised together. Not raised from his birth, but from his death. There was no child like him in the world.

I have loved a woman. I have loved a friend. Sometimes, I wonder if I have loved anyone so much as I loved that child.

Not even you, Sumardil.

32

The battle fury left me, and I could hear once more.

I could hear the calling of the wind and the rolling sea beyond the hills. Somewhere near me, a man lay sobbing. I could hear my own gasping breath, the beating of my heart like a fist pounding against a door.

But there was one sound that I longed for, but could not hear. The sound of a word or a breath or a scream – none of these came from the boy on the ground. And even at a distance, I could see the blood that stained the snow.

A wheezing, gasping chuckle, close to me. For Thorvaldur yet lived, hunched over and leaning upon his sword as an old man leans on a staff. I was bent over, too, for it seemed the battle had made old men of us both. And of Björn, it had made a child. I could see him dragging himself away, trailing blood behind him.

He was the only one left. His brothers, his friends – those five men lay dead at my feet, and I could not remember which of them I had killed myself.

The soft, wet sound of mud and snow beneath my feet, as I came forward to where Kari lay. He was on his back, arms thrown wide as though he meant to embrace the sky. One eye was gone, the other dark, like a bead of blackened glass.

The rip of grass, the drag of a body through wet mud. Björn, trying to crawl away from us. I should have felt an urgency: my revenge was so close at hand. I should have worried that other men might come, for the coast road was well travelled. But there seemed to be no hurry. There was no rush to do anything anymore. For as long as the feud had gone on I had felt time slipping away from me. And now there was too much time. Too long left to live.

Thorvaldur's hand was upon my shoulder and I saw his weary, half-toothed smile.

'Come on,' he said.

Björn had not gotten far. I could see the evil wound upon his leg, a great cut of the sword that had split thigh and knee open to grin at the sky. Kari must have done it, as he lay upon the ground. Exhausted, shield broken, body cut open. He could have laid down still, played the corpse and the coward and saved his life. But he had found the strength for one more swing of his father's sword.

Björn rolled on to his back as he heard us come near. Axe held close to his chest, as though he were afraid I would snatch it away from him, the way a child holds a toy it fears will be taken from it. He looked up at me, and knew me then.

'Are you a ghost?' he said.

'No.'

'My brother?'

'He is dead.'

His eyes dimmed and the hand on his axe slackened. He cursed me then, and I waited for him to grow tired.

When his oaths were finished, he said: 'You have done this for Gunnar. Because of what we—'

'No. It is not what you did to Gunnar.'

'Then...' He gasped with the pain and turned his head. 'Then why?'

I knelt down beside him, out of the reach of his axe.

'The footprints,' I said.

'What do you mean?'

'When I came upon Gunnar's farm, I saw the footprints. Two sets. One large, one small. They came out from the longhouse. Then they turned around and went back towards the fire.' I saw the shame there in his eyes. 'It was his wife and daughter, was it not? Dalla and Freydis.'

'Yes.'

'Tell me what you did.'

He looked up and down the trail – grey-faced, the sweat running thick on his face like a blown horse after the gallop. But he could see that there was no rescue coming. Only the falling of the snow and the two men who stood over him.

'We...' he began, then trailed off, gasping. 'They came out when we fired the house. I was going to let them go. I swear that. But...' He paused and he looked at me. I do not know what he hoped to find in my eyes, but he did not see it there.

'It was Vigdis. She told me... she said I would be a coward if I let them go. That my brothers would be ashamed of me.' He closed his eyes at the memory and he said no more.

I imagined it, then. A circle of men, a wall of shields. A burning house, the fire roaring high. A woman and her child beating against those shields, begging to live. And those men marching forward, one pace at a time, driving the woman back into the fire. Had they turned their heads from her, as they pressed her back towards the flame? Had they wept with shame behind their shields?

Had Gunnar died seeing that?

'It was a shameful thing we did.' He was whispering now. Shivering, his face gone pale as ocean-washed bone. His hands slack around the axe. 'I know Gunnar's last words. I know what he said. Promise that you will kill me well and I will tell them to you.'

I looked up to Thorvaldur. 'Your choice,' he said.

Nearby, I could hear the babbling of a stream. I knew then what to do.

'Put down the axe,' I said. He nodded, without thinking, and let me take the axe from him.

'Give me your arm.'

'What will you do?' he said, his teeth chattering with the cold.

I said nothing and I lifted him up so that he leant upon my shoulder. Thorvaldur came to his other side and together we helped him to the river – two brothers, helping an old father towards his bed.

We laid him down there and he reached out one hand to cup the water, to bring it to his lips. Yet when he had the water in hand, he seemed to forget what it was that he wanted. The fingers opened and the water spilt back to the river.

'Do you know how a man is made a Christian?' I said.

'No.'

'We are reborn in water. I will make you a Christian and you will tell me Gunnar's words.'

'You will let me live?'

'Tell me what Gunnar said.'

He looked down at the water. When he spoke, it was as though he were another man speaking.

'He called out your name. As if... as if you were some woman that he loved. That was all he said as he died. Your name, over and over again.'

I tried to hear Gunnar, then. He had spoken my name as he died – perhaps his spirit spoke it still, was whispering it to me.

I heard nothing. I thought of what I knew, of the words that a dying man must speak. I knew my friend then, for the first and last time.

'Put your head in the water,' I said.

He crawled to the river's edge. He looked at me once; doubting, afraid. Then he carefully placed his head into the running water.

One of my hands went to the back of his head. The other, my fingerless piece of flesh, hooked under his arm, and all my weight was upon his back. He knew what I intended then, and he fought me as best he could. But he had no strength left: he had bled it all into the snow.

It did not take long. When he was still once more, Thorvaldur spoke some words to me, but I could not seem to hear them. I found myself back beside Kari, the Christian trailing behind me. I sat and he sat beside me, but he knew not to speak first.

There was blood on Thorvaldur's teeth, dribbling from his mouth and on to his chin. But he smiled at me and I knew he was not badly hurt. The boss of a shield or the haft of an axe had struck him in the mouth, but it was no killing wound.

'What will happen to him?' I said.

'Kari?'

'Yes.'

'He died a warrior of Christ. His sins forgiven. He is in heaven now.'

'And what of his parents?'

'They died as pagans. He will never see them again.'

'A hard kind of justice, that our God offers.'

'It is a hard time we live in. A war for men's souls. A war we must win.'

I took the sword from where it lay on the ground beside Kari, and with my cloak I began to wipe the blood from it.

'Do you still wish to kill me?' said Thorvaldur.

'No. It was not you that killed the boy.' I sheathed the sword, the slap of metal against leather. 'I did. I should have taken him far from this place.'

'It is done, now. The spirits of the dead rest easy. You should be thankful.'

'I am not thankful.'

'It was a good fight. You fought well. I had not thought you to be a berserker, but I have heard that the poets often fight in such a way.' He grinned that awful, broken-toothed smile at me. 'A good fight,' he said once more.

My shield lay nearby and I took it up and placed it over the boy's face, so that I would not need to look on it any longer.

'He stood against Björn for as long as he could,' Thorvaldur said. 'He would not fall.' He spat blood upon the snow. 'It was a good death.'

I did not answer. I took the boy's hand in mine, as I had once held his father's.

When I looked up again, I found the Christian watching me, his head cocked to the side, a smile dancing on his lips.

'What amuses you?' I said.

'It was for the boy, wasn't it?'

'What do you mean?'

'All of this. The feud. You did this for him, didn't you? You would have run, but you fought for him.'

'Yes,' I said. 'It was for him.'

He clapped his hands together in delight, still grinning like a madman.

'That love you have for other men's secrets,' I said. 'It will get you killed, one day.'

'I doubt it not,' he said. 'But not today.'

'What will you do now?' I said.

'I go back to Norway. They will hunt me for this. They will hunt you, too.' He kissed the cross around his neck and held out a hand. 'Come with me. We will preach together, fight together.'

'No.'

'No?'

'I will never leave this island.'

He waited a moment longer to see if I would change my mind. He stood and he clasped my arm, and I watched him disappear into the snowfall, singing quietly to himself. A happy man.

I reached down and I touched my side beneath the cloak, felt the hot wetness there within. There was no pain to the wound – only a cold, absent feeling. The pain would come later, I was sure. Nausea passed through me and I thought I would retch. But the feeling went.

The sun was falling from the sky as I walked back into the valley. The snow heavier, and I left little drops of blood behind in it, like red berries falling from a poorly woven basket.

It was fully dark before long and the clouds covered the moon and the stars. Yet still I found that I knew the way. Had I been blinded and cast adrift in that valley, still I could have found my way to that place.

It was before me, then. A longhouse, like any other. Smoke rising from the chimney hole, the smell of cooking in the air. No sound from within, but I knew there to be life there. And death as well, perhaps.

I reached the door and I knocked upon it. A woman answered. She stared at me, and for the first time that I could recall I saw fear in her eyes. But only for a moment.

'Come in,' Vigdis said. 'It is cold.'

33

There was no trap inside. No kinsman waiting for me with blade in hand. In one corner of the room, bundled tight in blankets, I could see a child sleeping. Other than that, we were alone.

She gestured for me to sit and I did so. We sat across the fire and we did not speak at first. Perhaps, in that silence, we knew each other truly for the first time. There was a stillness to her, as though she were a piece of forged iron rather than flesh. A strength that she had been born with or that she had learned, and there was not a mark of fear on her face. Nor in her voice, when she spoke.

'They are dead, then.'

I nodded and watched her for any sign of sadness. There was none.

'And now you are here for me,' she said.

'Yes.'

'A shameful thing, to kill a woman.'

'Dalla was killed, was she not? And Freydis. Why should not you answer for that?'

'But it was I who killed them. Women may kill women.

Men may kill men. But we must not kill one another. It is a blasphemy.'

'You have killed men too, I think.'

'I did not wield the blade.'

'But you have killed them. And I will know why.'

'Yes,' she said. 'You shall. You have earned that much.'

She poured herself a cup of water, her hand almost steady; there was a slight tremor there, the way a swordsman's hand will quiver before the *holmgang*. In spite of myself, I could feel a touch of fear. I had looked upon great warriors before: Gunnar, Björn and others besides. I looked upon another now.

'Did you know my husband, Hrapp?' she said.

'Little. I saw him once or twice.'

'What did you think of him?'

'A cruel man. And stupid.'

'Yes, he was. But strong as well. All men feared him.'

'And you?'

'Yes. I feared him too.' She paused and looked into the fire. I wonder if she still saw him there. For the tremor in her hand went still – just the way a man's does, when the first blow is struck.

'He wanted no children. I do not know why. But he was not barren, and neither was I. I had many children.'

By instinct, I looked about the room for some evidence of what she said. But other than the child in the corner, there was none.

'We exposed them,' she said. 'No one ever knew.'

The unwanted bastard that shames a family, the slave's child that will only starve if it is left to live – these are the children that are abandoned in the darkness. Had my father not been freed from slavery, no doubt that is where I would have met my death: scant hours after my birth, crying in the night as the snow fell upon me. But it was something secret, something shameful. A coldness stole over me, to hear her speak of it so calmly.

'But I am grateful for it,' she said, one hand toying with the knotted braid of her hair. 'The first time, I thought that I would die from sadness. But I did not. And there is a strength to be found there. I think you understand that. You must, to have done all that you have done.'

'Why speak of Hrapp? You think that I shall pity you?'

She did not seem to hear me. 'I thought I would die a long time ago,' she said. 'There was a time when Hrapp was angrier than usual. I was certain he meant to kill me, after that.'

'You could have divorced him. Gone back to your family.'

'There was no leaving a man like Hrapp. Except in death. And I did not want to.'

'Why?'

'Because I loved him.'

I listened to the crackle of the fire, and I tried to understand. 'You thought that he would kill you.'

'To love is to die for what we love. Gunnar loved you, did he not? And he died for you. I learned to love Hrapp. For he taught me the truth of the world.'

'And what is that?'

She leaned forward, close to the flames, and I could see the light reflected in her dead eyes. 'Men like you came to this place, thinking to be free,' she said. 'But you will never be free. You will always be a slave to men like Hrapp.'

'And to women such as you?' I said. 'That is what you believe.'

'I do not fear to die,' she said. 'Perhaps I am even like you.'

'How so?'

'Perhaps I want to die,' she said. She looked to the wooden cross I wore on my neck. 'You wear the mark of Christ.'

'What do you know of him?'

'I know that he forgives.'

'Yes, he does, in the next life. But he is a god of revenge, more than anything else.'

'What will you do?'

I thought on this for a time. Wound-weary and with the heat of the fire there, I could have slept. I wanted to. But I knew that there was more left for me to do.

'I will not kill you,' I said. 'But I will take your child.'

Her mouth worked silently, the entreaties of a mute. And at last there was fear in her eyes.

'Please,' she said. She made to stop me then, but I held up the knife.

'Sit down. Or I shall kill him before you. Would you have that?'

'Please,' she said.

She went to her knees and she spoke more words, but I did not listen.

I went over to the blankets in the corner. A child of three, as old as the feud, sleeping by the heat of the fire. A boy with a smile playing across his lips. What was his dream? Was it of his mother? The father he had never known? Games in the fields and upon the ice? Many are the joys of the child, and how quickly the man forgets them. A mercy, to end a life so soon, when it knows only joy – that is what I thought. That is what I thought, as I picked you up in my arms.

'What is his name?' I said.

And she whispered, so soft that I could hardly hear it over the sound of the fire: 'Sumardil.'

You were still sleeping as I picked you from your blankets, but awoke for a moment when I took you. I looked into your eyes and you stared at me without fear or recognition, before you fell back into your dreams.

That was the first time that we looked upon one another, Sumardil. That was you, my child.

I was to take you to some quiet place and open your throat, for I would not have left you to wander lost and frightened on the snow. Your killing was a payment, a settling of a debt, not an act to be relished. And I thought I would die out there with you, that I would lie down on the cold ground beside you and let myself sleep. There seemed to be nothing else left for me to do.

Yet there seemed no need to hurry, if that night was all that I was to have left. And so I wandered in the cold, looking for a fine place to die. I was weeping, though it shames me to admit it, for the life that could have lived. I could feel your hot breath against my neck as I walked around and around those empty fields, up the rolling hills and back down towards the whisper of the sea.

I could not find the place, for that country held too many memories for me. A curve beside the river seemed as though it would do, but as I drew my knife I saw that we were too close to where Sigrid and I had made love. I wandered further, up towards the high ground, so you might see all of that beautiful valley one more time before I cut your throat. But now we were close to the stone and the tarn where Dalla and I had spoken together, and left no secrets untold. I could not do it there.

Again and again I thought I had found a place of killing, only to be halted by a memory. Like those great heroes of the old stories who have grown tired of life – their friends all dead, their women lost to them. And so they wander the battlefield, looking for the warrior brave enough to give them peace.

But none will stand against them, for their reputation is so fierce, and so it is that they cannot die. I was no great hero, but perhaps that was my gift, too.

At last, I found myself at Gunnar's longhouse, or what remained of it. As I sat on the blackened ground, leaning against one of the broken pillars, I thought to hear their bodies beneath the ground calling to me, begging for your blood to be spilt. But there was only silence from the dead.

You had not woken. You pressed your face close against my neck, huddled under my cloak, and you did not stir or cry out. I held you close and I thought to join you in sleep, a sleep we would not wake from. I thought to let the cold take us both to the next world.

Yet the sleep did not come to me. You did not wake. At some time in the night I found myself singing.

Soft, so as not to wake you, for I wished my words to find their way into your dreaming. My throat raw with weeping, dry and unpractised. Yet still I tried to sing, some of the old songs returning to me. Not the high, great songs of heroes and kings and gods, but the little songs I gave to children. Foolish rhymes, tales of tricksters and elves. I knew then that I did not want to die.

The night drew on and the sky began to lighten. I stood at last, my muscles aching from the trembling, stumbling on my numb legs. I no longer felt any pain from the wound in my side.

As we moved, you woke. You looked on me and there was no fear in you. You found yourself waking beneath the stars, in the arms of a stranger, and you were not afraid. You rubbed at your eyes and you said: 'I am hungry.'

I was hurrying then, running across the dale, laughing and singing to you so that you would not see my fear. I went back then, to the house you were born in.

I would give you back to your mother – that is what I told myself. And I would give myself up for judgement for the killings. They would outlaw me again and there would be none to give me passage this time. I would die upon this land and my death would end the feud at last.

At the longhouse once more, the door swinging open against my hand. And the fire reduced to embers in the hearth, the back door swinging open with every stroke of the wind.

I had returned too late. She was already gone.

34

Do you remember those days of waiting?

One day passed, then a second, a third, as we waited for Vigdis to return. She would come back in the company of what kin remained to her, seeking revenge. I would give it to her without a battle. All that I wished was for you and her to be reunited, that I might undo what I had done.

You asked me when she was coming back and I told you that I did not know. But you did not weep – I did, but you did not. There was such strength in you, it made me humble to see it.

Was it Vigdis who gave that to you? It must have been. Do you remember those days that you spent with her? You do not? Her holding your hands and pacing you around the long-house as she taught you how to walk, even as she plotted my murder. Her carving a wooden horse for you, tears springing to her eyes at your smile, before she spoke the words that goaded those men to burn my friends alive.

She destroyed all that I loved – almost all, at least. Yet with you she became what she was meant to be. And I took that from her.

Now I see your eyes asking what your words will not,

Sumardil. You want to know what became of her. And that, I cannot tell you.

She was lost in the storm or she cast herself from some cliff into the sea. Perhaps she fled to some other part of the island or a distant land far from these shores. None know, and you must believe what you will.

But there came a time when we both knew that she would not return. I asked you if you had any other kin in the valley and you named the men that I had killed.

I knew not what I should do. I only thought to wait a little longer, for some visitor to come to that longhouse. They would know where to take you. They would take you from me and then they would take my life. And in time, that man did come.

I woke in the night, my arms about you. For though you were brave in the day, you were afraid at night and you would not sleep outside of my embrace. I woke and I saw a man watching me from the doorway.

I thought him a ghost at first. It was only once the sleep had truly left me that I recognised him, a man I had not seen for many years. Olaf Hoskuldsson, the man they called The Peacock.

'Kjaran,' he said. He wore none of his finery, had none of his *thingmen* at his back. He looked not like the chieftain he was, but a simple traveller – an outlaw, even.

I held a finger to my lips. I looked down at you, but you did not wake. I broke away from you carefully, wrapping you tight in the blankets.

Olaf and I sat together by the embers of the fire and we spoke in whispers.

'They speak in the valley of a ghost in this place. A fire lit, but no man seen coming or going, except by night. I came to see if it were true.'

'It is true enough,' I said.

'We buried the dead many days ago. Björn and his kin.' He looked around the longhouse. 'Vigdis is gone?' he asked.

'Yes.'

He nodded. 'So only you and the boy remain.'

'That is so.'

'There is much I could have done to prevent this. I should have had them outlawed for the burning. I wish...' Olaf's voice trailed away.

'This is not your burden to bear. It is mine.'

'Perhaps. But I think that the gods will remember this. And there will come a time when I shall pay for what I did not do.'

'Another vision of yours?'

He tried to smile – I saw the firelight upon his teeth for a moment. But what I said to him next stole that smile from him.

'You must take in the boy,' I said.

He shook his head. 'I cannot take in Sumardil. There will be too much talk. You shall not survive, if it is known that you live.'

'I care not.'

'I do.' He hesitated. 'Why do you not return to Ragnar? And Sigrid?'

'They cannot protect me. And it is better that they think me gone,' I said.

He put a hand to my shoulder and he looked on me in silence for a long time. I remembered how I had looked upon Sigrid, when I had fixed her in my mind for the very last time. And then he was gone.

Gifts came, in the days that followed. Grain, salted fish, brought to us in the arms of a tongueless slave – a man of Olaf's household, who could not speak of what he saw. Perhaps it would not matter if he had, for there would be few who would believe him.

That was how we lived, that first year. And all the years afterwards, until you were old enough to work the fields yourself.

I struck a bargain with you, in those first days. That I would raise you and protect you, as best I could. That you might think of me as a father if you wished, but that I expected no love or kindness from you, though I offered both freely to you. But as a boy, you looked me in the eye and you accepted that bargain.

You remember that, don't you?

It is a hard life I have given you, but you have lived it well. You have grown into a man and I have grown old.

There is safety in solitude and so I have taught you to wander as a ghost on the haunted lands that are your birthright. The other men of the valley shun you and call you mad: the mad son of a ghost, wandering restlessly. And in that madness is your safety. You have grown up almost wordless, wild blue eyes like a wolf.

The Wolf, I call you, for there is no other beast that could live as you have lived. And so I think you must be half a wolf at least. Not as fast or as strong as other hunting beasts, nor as crafty. But you endure. You would die for your pack. You are like me, are you not?

You have never asked about your past. Does the wolf question its ancestry? Does it inherit revenge, as we do? It does not, and neither have you. I raised you to be free of the feuds. In this place, in our own way, we have been living as the first settlers thought we might. We live alone on the land, free from kings, free from the feud, sharing the love of a father and his son. Waiting for the rest of the Icelanders to join us. For the people to learn how to live as we have.

At night I tell you stories. Endless stories and songs, of heroes and gods and monsters. But I have never told you this story before, and you have never asked.

You wonder why I tell this story to you now. It is because there is something that I need from you. It is because there is something that you must do.

35

Go now and look outside the door. My old eyes may be playing tricks on me. But I think I see the sun creeping there: fingers of light crawling beneath the door, beckoning to us. Go, and see if I am right.

The sun has risen? Good, good. Let the fire die, then. No need to waste wood now. We shall finish just in time.

I have told you many stories, have I not? And you are kind, for you listen in patience and thank me for the telling. But perhaps you have bested me in this, as you seem to in all things. For the story that *you* have told me – that I think I cannot match. I would not believe it, from any other than you.

It is ten centuries now since the miracle of Christ, a miracle of death. Now, in our island, you tell me of another miracle.

For the word of the White Christ has been spreading. Men like Thorvaldur have come to preach the Word, and many of those who sail abroad – great men who seek favour in the courts of distant kings – return baptised, wearing crosses around their necks. All across the old lands, in Norway and Sweden, they kneel before the White Christ. It has only been here that men have clung to the old faith, cowards lurking beside a dying fire. We have become a people divided by the gods. And on this island, for the first time, you have brought me whispers of war.

Thorvaldur longed for such a war, between one god and another. But that is not our way. With men preparing for war, with distant kings contemplating an invasion of our island, you tell me that our people gathered at the Althing and decided what must be done.

A gathering in a field, a raising of the hands, arguments spoken and heard. You tell me that the Lawspeaker retreated to his tent, covered his face with his cloak and thought to himself for a full day and a night. At last the Lawspeaker made his decision. Thus are the old gods forsaken and the true God followed. In other lands the God has been brought at the point of a sword, the whim of a tyrant, with bribery in gold and threats to the soul. But not here. Not in our country. I have never been so proud of our people as I am now.

And yet I know we must leave.

You know that I love our God. I have taught you His stories, taught you His words. Yet I know He will destroy this place. This fragile land where there are no kings. This one God will teach us to love a single ruler. We will long for a man to kneel to, not just a God. We will have a king soon. We will be a country like any other. The dream of a free land will be gone, and I will not stay and watch it happen.

Where shall we go, you ask? Far from this place. But not to the old lands. We go to the new.

You have heard of Greenland. That joke of a name, to attract foolish settlers to an unlivable country. That is not the place for you. It will be destroyed in plague or famine, or it will become another land beneath a king. We must go farther than that, to a place untouched.

There is another land out to the west, beyond that sea we thought boundless. I have heard the stories that the sailors have brought back: storm-tossed, the sparks of Thor raining down around them, they have seen a new land to the west. Vinland, they call it. A land with forests that stretch on for days. A place where the sun is still high in winter. A country with land enough for every man.

I have sought to live as a landless man and saw how it made me a slave. So you must go to a place where a man's land has no value, where there is space enough for all. You must go there, to begin a new life, a new world. Perhaps there we shall get it right.

Yes, my child, you will go there. But there is one last thing you must do for me. I did not raise you to flee from what you owe, and you have a debt to settle before your journey.

Come out, with me. Come out into the sun. Bring your sword with you, that gift I gave to you when you became a man. Gunnar's sword. Kari's sword. The sword that killed your father.

We come out blinking into the sun, our eyes aching from the dark. And you do not see it at first. You look out towards the sea, back to the pale hills behind us, and you wonder what it is I have to show you. Look closer. Look there, upon the ground.

You see now there, don't you? An oxhide that I have laid upon the ground. The corners marked with hazel wands. It is not on an island, as it should be, but you know it for what it is. The ground of a *holmgang*. The place where men duel.

A wolf's smile upon your face, and you look around once more. You ask who it is who has wronged us, who it is you must fight. You are eager to duel, as you should be, and will let no insult go answered. But already I see the smile fading, for I think you begin to understand.

We are the last links of the feud, you and I. None of Gunnar's people remain except for me. Björn and their kin are all gone except for you. And so it falls to you. The duty of revenge. The greatest gift of all.

I killed your father and let his grave go unmarked. I killed what remained of your kin. I drove your mother into madness, and somewhere she lies unburied. I stole you from your people.

Be quiet, do not speak. You will tell me that you forgive me, but that is of no consequence. It is to our God that I make restitution. Against His forgiveness, what does yours matter to me?

Now, take up that sword. Take a shield and step on to the hide with me. And know that we will fight by the old law. The duel ends not with a drop of a man's blood, but with all of it.

You tell me that you love me. And I love you, but that changes nothing. I cannot come with you to the new lands, for no ship will take a cripple, an outlaw such as I. What is left to me, when you have gone to the new lands? I see myself alone by the fire, weeping like a fool, for unnumbered days. The remainder of my life, and I shall spend it alone. Would you condemn me to that? Would you accept that life if it were offered to you? I think you would not.

Step forward now, one last step. For now we both stand upon the hide and we cannot move away: you shall be a coward if you do, and I know that you cannot bear the shame of that. We must fight, and do not think to go gently against me. For I love you, but I shall fight in earnest. I will kill you or you shall kill me. For it is better to see you dead than see you live as a coward.

It is the fate of poets that we are to die on the hide in a *holmgang*, our blood upon the leather, speaking the name of the one we love most. Give me the death that I long for. Give me the chance to speak that name. I have lived long enough.

It will not be Sigrid's name. Or Gunnar's, or Kari's, or that of the White Christ. It will be your name, Sumardil, if I have strength for one last breath at the end. Listen for it. Listen for your name.

It is time. There are no words left.

Come. Let us begin.

Acknowledgements

This is a work of fiction, inspired by the world of the Icelandic Sagas. I have taken a fiction writer's many liberties in the writing of this book, but have sought to remain true to the spirit of those strange, tragic, starkly beautiful stories. For those interested in reading further, I recommended *Kormák's Saga, Njal's Saga,* and *Laxdæla Saga* as possible starting points; I hope you enjoy them as much as I have.

A book is the work of many hands, eyes, and hearts. Enormous thanks are due to Nic Cheetham, Sophic Robinson, Jessie Price, Ian Pinder and the rest of the team over at Head of Zeus for all the care and love they've lavished on the book, and to my early readers – Claire, Sara, Ness, Sholeh, Petia, Thom, Gill and Michael – for their enthusiasm, support and critique.

This book is dedicated to my agent, Caroline Wood. We writers like to think that we're in the business of making dreams come true, but she's made *my* dream a reality, against tremendous odds. It's been magical – thank you, Caroline.